From   ANTHONY JONES
A D Peters & Co Ltd
Writers' Agents
10 Buckingham Street
London WC2N 6BU

01 839 2556

THE MEN WITH THE GUNS

THE MEN WITH THE GUNS

G. F. Newman

SECKER & WARBURG
LONDON

First published in England 1982 by
Martin Secker & Warburg Limited
54 Poland Street, London W1V 3DF

Copyright © G. F. Newman 1982

British Library Cataloguing in Publication Data

Newman, G. F.
  The men with the guns.
  I. Title
  823'.914[F]   PR6064.E/

  ISBN 0–436–30535–6

Photoset and printed in Great Britain by
Redwood Burn Limited, Trowbridge, Wiltshire

Prolog

Tension had clamped his neck and shoulders like a vise and he couldn't get free of the pain. He considered taking another pill; he had been using a lot, but knew that no amount would remove the cause of the tension. It was fear.

Colonel Alan Parker stood at the top of the wide stairs and listened to the stillness of the house. He was alone, having lived that way for ten years, ever since his sister died; that had been Fort Worth; this was Fort Lauderdale. He was used to being on his own and ordinarily wasn't scared, but he had recently heard the rumor about the man tipped as becoming America's first ambassador to China in 25 years. This would frighten a lot of people.

There was no sound from the lower part of the house; then it was more a feeling rather than any particular noise which had disturbed Parker. He reached round and massaged the locked muscles of his neck, trying to ease the tension. He wondered about going downstairs, but couldn't move. This was crazy, he told himself, there was no one down there.

Despite wanting to believe that, he couldn't rid himself of the unease he felt.

Take a couple of pills, an inner voice urged, get some sleep. If there was an intruder it would be a burglar, the insurance would take care of it.

Colonel Parker didn't believe it was a burglar. His philosophy told him there was no such thing as coincidence, instead there was cause and effect; the threat he now believed he represented to that man going to China.

Take some pills, everything'll be fine . . .

No!

'Okay, I've called the police. They'll get here anytime.' His voice quaked.

Parker trembled and rubbed his hands across his face, trying to get control of himself. His palms were sweating and he felt chilled. Spring evenings in Florida could get cold enough for frost, but the house was warm. This really was crazy, he told himself, wiping his hands on his silk robe. Jesus, there was no one here, the house was proofed against burglars, the insurance company had made sure about that, living as he did in a neighborhood which attracted burglars. If someone had beaten his alarms then he could take care of it, he had handled more threatening situations both when running his oil company in Texas, and since going to work for Exxon, who had bought him out. Sure, he wasn't as young as he had been then, or as foolhardy as in his army days, but he could take care of a burglar.

But then the belief that if it were someone down there it would be no ordinary burglar shredded his resolve.

The shotguns. He remembered the pair of Luigi Franchi double twelve-gauge with the Purdy locks he had had tailored in London. He had shot grouse with them in Scotland back in August. The guns were in their cabinet in the study. There was no alternative; he would get one, load it, check the house, every room and closet, make sure there was no intruder. He would put an end to this nonsense.

Cautiously he started down the stairs. At the bottom the sound he heard caused him to go rigid, it was like someone breathing inside an ironlung. Finally he realized it was himself, but that knowledge accentuated rather than relieved his fear.

The study door was ajar, he ran across the wide hall and went in, throwing on the light; looking neither left nor right, he headed to the cabinet, opened it and seized one of the shotguns. His fingers trembled when he pushed the shells into the breach.

Prickles of apprehension ran along his spine as he sensed movement to his left. He whipped round, bringing up the shotgun, his finger against the first trigger. Drapes stirred in the gentle breeze and he noticed the door to the terrace was open. His breathing eased and his heartbeat began to slow. A lamp was overturned on the table and he decided its falling might have woken him; the breeze through the window could have upset it. This line of reasoning was making him calmer. He considered the open window. He had walked around the pool after dinner and had entered the house via the terrace door, and although believing he had shut it, he accepted that he might have been too preoccupied to notice not doing so.

He shut the door now and set the locks. Still he searched the house, taking the loaded shotgun. There was no one on the first floor. He switched out the lights and climbed the stairs, feeling more confident. He went through the spare bedrooms and the spare bathroom, but found no one.

Finally he returned to his bedroom, feeling both a sense of relief and foolish for reacting as he had. He leaned the shotgun against the bedroom wall and went into the bathroom for another pill to sleep and to blot out his fears. There was nothing he could do about the cause right then. He had thought about going to live in Europe, only was afraid it was being overrun by communists. At one time he figured the would-be ambassador to China had the answers. He remembered the men who had been brought to his ranch at Big Springs, their training; the brainwashing; he remembered the people who had called out to see them, all unshakable in their belief that what they were doing was right. Each with that same unmistakable look about them, a coldness in the eyes, faces which revealed no kind of emotion. Remembering such things disturbed Colonel Parker. Men would always remember that morning they drove away, and what had happened, and like Parker would sooner forget it, if for different reasons. Since that time he had made no move to discover additional information. Rather he had tried to forget. He wanted to believe the man who had set it up had forgotten, but his sister's death had never been satisfactorily explained, nor the death shortly after of the couple who had worked around the ranch. Why had the man waited this long for him? Maybe he should run, get far away from his sphere of influence. He would decide tomorrow.

Swallowing the valium, Parker pushed the bathroom cabinet shut, and his heart missed a beat. The mirror revealed a man in the doorway between the bathroom and the bedroom, the shotgun held in his gloved hands.

Parker swung round, unable to speak. His jaw made a spastic movement, a choking sound emanating from his throat.

The intruder beckoned Parker forward, and when close enough he pressed the muzzle of the shotgun against the older man's slack neck.

'I have money,' Parker managed to whisper.

The intruder nodded, his face remaining expressionless; without warning his top teeth dropped over his bottom lip in a joyless smile.

Parker's tension eased; the two thousand dollars in the house would buy him out of this.

The intruder watched Parker closely, waiting for the right moment.

Suddenly he dropped the butt of the shotgun, keeping the muzzle into the man's neck; when he estimated the angle was correct, he squeezed one trigger. The explosion was a muffled thump, the blast blew him against the washbasin before he crashed to the floor.

The intruder placed the shotgun in Parker's fingers, the barrels turned toward him like this had been his answer. He didn't leave the gun in that position, a suicide wouldn't be left holding it after such a recoil. The man knew ballistic science; figured where the gun might have finished, and placed it there. He checked his black leather jacket for blood. It was difficult to tell in artificial light. Reaching for some Kleenex, he wiped it across his coat; some flecks of blood had hit him, but most of the mess had blown away from him. He didn't flush the tissue. Blood had splattered the lavatory, had he flushed it a smart cop might have worked out that someone had been here after Parker's death.

The phone startled the man on reaching the bottom of the stairs, the bell perforated the darkness. The only possible danger this signaled was that a neighbor had heard the explosion and might call the cops if there was no reply. There were no lights burning at the house on the left of Parker's. The one on the right was farther away, perhaps a hundred yards with a lot of shrubbery in between. Lights showed there. The phone stopped. The man waited. If the call was from a worried neighbor, he reasoned, the phone would go again shortly. It did. If there was still no reply, the next call would be to the cops.

He didn't panic. So far his only one mistake was underestimating good-neighborliness in this part of the world. He had figured the kind of middle-class white socks who retired to Florida thought of no one but themselves and how they were cheating those previously endured winters. He had plenty of time before the cops arrived, the nearest station house was twelve minutes drive, unless a car happened to be cruising the area. He let himself out and locked the door with Parker's spare key. He moved calmly away, making sure to keep from sight of the lighted house. His car was parked a block and a half away. A five minute walk. He passed no one.

He was in his rented Dodge and headed out to the airport when he heard the police siren. He smiled his joyless smile, his top teeth hanging over his bottom lip. He was safe, his job successfully accomplished. He checked his watch, 11.05. He had time for a cup of coffee at the airport before making his plane.

BOOK ONE

Remember, that despite your
optimism inside you are wailing

One

'Ladies and gentlemen, we are now making our descent for New York's La Guardia airport, where we will be landing in a few moments. We must ask you at this time to extinguish all smoking material and fasten your seat belts.'

The passenger in the first-class no-smoking section stirred and thought about the hostess's words.

Small thoughts to avoid the kind of thoughts that were disturbing him more and more.

He hadn't unfastened his seat belt on the two and a half hour trip up from Florida. He had slept part of the way after a couple of scotches, having passed on Eastern's free non-vintage champagne. He needed to brush his teeth. He usually did after sleeping, whether after a nap in his office, on a plane, or eight hours in the sack.

Small thoughts.

He ran his tongue over his teeth, then began collecting his things on the seat next to him, trying to avoid thinking about the job he had just done. It made him feel like an asshole. A forty-two-year-old asshole described him, he decided. Being a professional asshole didn't excuse him.

The girl he had delivered to her parents this morning drifted across his mind's eye, her hurt, betrayed look; she had believed he wouldn't do it after what had happened in New Mexico. But what had happened between them had happened with other women. Her being only fifteen years old didn't worry him, he was more concerned over what he might have caught from her. The people she had been with on that commune were pretty dirty and her taking a shower at the motel they had stopped over at didn't guarantee much. He thought about Zell. He wouldn't like to pass anything on to her.

He considered the bleak, unenviable life in those crumbling adobes in the arid landscape of New Mexico, but believed he understood why a girl from such a comfortable background had chosen it; freedom, the need to get beyond those parental restraints and values which kids everywhere were rejecting. That was why he felt as he did, because of what he had taken her back to.

He thought about her move at the motel, how she had used her fifteen-year-old body to try and influence him. She had done so without enough experience of life. Had she been more experienced, able to read him better, she might have realized it would make no difference. He had as many weaknesses as the next guy, but one area where he was better than most was in the work he did.

His professionalism was something Zell saw as weakness; Zell was as professional in her work, but he let her have a free ride there.

On the drive in from Miami airport the girl had pleaded not to go back. Finally realizing he was unmoving, she had threatened to tell her old man that he had balled her.

That didn't worry him, nor did the fact that her old man was Ira Deitrick. He probably wouldn't have believed his kid anyway; nice girls didn't run away from home, and the skip-trace had been highly recommended.

He tried pushing the girl's future out of his thoughts. Rightly or wrongly he had completed the job he was hired for. Another satisfied customer; a little higher went his reputation among the legit Mafia hierarchy.

Since quitting the FBI four years ago and getting a private license he had done a number of jobs for the Mafia. One in particular had boosted his reputation, when he was hired by Joe Zevilli, godfather of the Detroit Mafia, to find Jimmy Hoffa's creative accountant who had spirited away some two million dollars of the Teamsters' pension fund. No one other than the Mob had been looking for the man, whom he had found more easily than expected; his instructions were to bring only the money back. He had had no problems handling those kind of orders then. The price was better than he had

4

made doing similar things for the FBI. It was a free choice, he wouldn't have taken the job had he figured he couldn't handle it. With every job undertaken he had the option to walk. He had yet to do so, but he was finding more and more that he was considering other aspects of the jobs he took on. He was a hundred years younger then, and now he wasn't sure he could live with himself after those jobs. The physical side of things wasn't a problem. He could shoot a gun still, and although his hundred seventy pounds was no longer exactly trim, he had stayed reasonably fit. The objection was moral. He didn't like what he was seeing happening to himself, which was why he had quit the Bureau.

'Can I take your stereo set?' the cabin attendant said, leaning over him.

He passed the ear plugs up. She was wearing perfume he didn't care for. He didn't care much for any kind, preferring the smell of women the way they were, even those coming out of the New York subway in August.

Eastern announced how fast they got the baggage to the collection point. Six minutes they said, but what happened was that the first piece of luggage to hit the carousel inevitably belonged to the last passenger to deplane.

Vanesco's only piece, a Bloomingdales canvas grip, a birthday present from Zell, was carry-on baggage, but large enough to hold all that he needed. Through frequent traveling he had learned a lot about paring down, one bag and no weight was the result.

Stepping up to a phone on the airport concourse, Vanesco called his answering service. The woman ran through his messages while he scribbled notes. She told him Clark E. Cunningham had called four times, and wanted Vanesco to get back to him the second he got in.

'Looks like I missed that shot, Judith,' he said.

'It's Carole, sir.'

'Okay, Carole. Just hold the messages.' He rang off, then pushed in another dime, but decided he wouldn't talk to Cunningham today. Instead he called Zell; a colleague said she had left for the day to collect her kid from school. Stepping across the concourse, he thought about Clark E. Cunningham. The fact he gave his middle initial each time he called said something about the kind of person he was. Cunningham was a successful Wall Street lawyer with an identity crisis. Vanesco wondered what he wanted so urgently. A lot of his work came through Cunningham's law firm.

'Manhattan?' The proposition came from a cab driver at the door of the terminal building. 'You wanna ride to Manhattan for five bucks?'

'Right now?' Vanesco asked. He didn't want to sit around while the driver hustled other fares.

'Taking right off, pal. Step this way.' He tried to take his grip, but Vanesco kept hold of it.

There was another fare already waiting in the cab. Vanesco exchanged looks with him, while the driver ran off after another passenger.

'How many's he planning to take?'

The man shrugged. 'I've been squatting five minutes.'

Just then the driver reappeared, his eyes seeking but not finding.

'When you planning to pull out?'

'Jes' lemme get one more. Right.'

Vanesco started out of the cab.

'Stay there – we're going right away. I seen one.'

'I haven't got all day, pal.' He flagged a cab that had pulled onto the stand.

'Hey c'mon. What's d'madder with you?'

Vanesco got into the second vehicle, a General Motors cab which was more comfortable and had no safely grille separating him from the driver. Most New York cabs, which had perspex grilles to protect drivers from stickup artists, made the passenger feel like a criminal trapped in a cops' car.

When the cab was headed out of the Queens Tunnel, Vanesco decided he wanted to go to 44 Hudson, in the village, instead of his apartment on West 23rd. That was the elementary school Zell's kid attended. Zell collected him every afternoon.

School was out when Vanesco got there, so he remained in the cab, his eyes sweeping the confusion of kids, parents and au pairs. Zell and Sam were crossing the schoolyard, deeply engrossed with each other. Sam was telling her something, and she listened like it was of paramount importance, which

6

Vanesco knew it was. At that moment he felt irrational jealousy for what they had going, and it prevented him getting out of the cab. Instead he watched them turn east off Hudson along Christopher Street.

It was crazy he should feel that way, but it was by no means the first time. When together Zell and Sam made a small private world, which he couldn't penetrate. It had little to do with his not being Sam's father, or that he was almost a generation older than Zell; at times he was competing sexually with the kid for the woman's attention, and losing out. There was probably no way he could win. Zell had invested her security in the boy, hoping he wouldn't let her down as his father had. Unfortunately Vanesco was identified with the father for no reason other than his being the man in Zell Kleinbard's life.

'This the address you wanted?' the driver asked.

'Yeah.' He decided not to pursue Zell here. 'Take me to West 23rd.'

'West 23rd. Whereabouts you want?'

Vanesco gave him the address. It was a brownstone apartment block between 10th and 11th with the dirtiest windows and the slowest elevator in Manhattan.

Vanesco lived on the seventh floor and had never discovered why the elevator only went to the sixth. He could handle the sixteen uncarpeted stairs to his apartment.

There was no mail worth getting in his box. Nobody wrote letters anymore; maybe no one had anything to say any longer. You couldn't put on paper the kind of noises that went over the nation's phones. Bills he got and advertisements.

Two notes had been pushed under his apartment door. One from Clark E. Cunningham. The other was from a community group, which assumed it was addressing a she, asking what she would do if she were raped, and proceeded to tell her. It happens, the note screamed, don't imagine you're immune. He wondered if women remained calm enough to follow the advice, or kept the notice to consult when it happened. It was a sad note, but a sign of the times. Being a rapist was easy in a city as anonymous as New York. People became rape victims out of a subconscious desire; instinc-

7

tively he had always believed that, but Zell had articulated it one day after they had been stopped on the 6th Avenue and asked to sign a petition censuring a New York senator for saying, as he had on ABC television, that rape was inevitable so women should lie back and enjoy it. Zell had shunned the petition and given the woman with the pen an argument. If you walked around in fear of being raped then you opened your aura which otherwise helped prevent such an assault. A neat theory, and one Vanesco didn't dismiss; he felt that way about having his apartment burglarized, he didn't fear it and it hadn't happened; he believed the same about cancer, that it could only live on people's fears.

A woman who had approached the petition line heard Zell's argument and said, 'I was raped. The mother' got fifteen years. Wait till you get raped, sister, see how goddam smart you are then.' She signed with an angry flourish and disappeared. Zell had neither the opportunity nor the inclination to tell her she had been raped.

Those thoughts were still preventing bigger thoughts. Why did Cunningham need to reach him so urgently? He could have called the lawyer to find out, but resisted. Instead he called a friend in the FBI's New York field office to see if he had got any leads on a crazy lady who, despite a court order restricting her, had jumped state with her two kids. There was no official FBI interest, Wisconsin agents were checking on the woman as a favor. The only hope the husband had of getting his kids again was by having a skip-trace call in some favors or know where to go to buy them; official law enforcement agencies no longer troubled with those cases. The FBI agent gave Vanesco an address the woman was staying at in Milwaukee. How long she would stay there was anyone's guess. Agents in the local field office wouldn't keep her under surveillance. Vanesco told him he'd square off with him in a day or so and hung up. The FBI had saved him a trip to Milwaukee. Maybe he'd have to go and get the kids. He didn't want to. He wasn't sure what the father's claim was. What the fuck did courts know about anything? For now he accepted that the mother was a crazy who shouldn't have her kids, but he couldn't help thinking about Zell in the same situation, what it might be like if Sam's father got a court order. Courts were corrupt, they were impressed by wealth and high powered attorneys. Anyone who could afford his services could afford a fancy attorney.

After showering and fixing a sandwich, Vanesco called Zell. She sounded pleased to hear from him. That gave him a lift.

'You back in town?'

'Ten minutes ago. How about we get together in a while, get something to eat?'

'Well I'll tell you, Jimmy, I've got a man here right now, I'm not sure how he'll feel about that. I'll ask him.'

There was disjointed conversation off the phone.

Zell came back on. 'I talked to the boss, and he said that sounds pretty good.'

That irrational jealousy slid obliquely into his consciousness. 'I'll see you in about an hour. Say hello to Sam.' He rang off, thinking that maybe she carried equality too far. Sam was five years old, but as neurotic as any adult.

Two

The apartment Zell and Sam rented was a two-roomed loft on Charles Street; with its small kitchen and bathroom it was still short of space, but cheap at eighty dollars a month. Too cheap for her landlord's liking; Abi Kali was one of the many scumlords who pressured tenants of rent-controlled apartments in the Village, trying to have them quit, in order to hike the rents. Kali was making some gross moves, sending around hoods who made threats or dropped garbage outside the door. Some apartment buildings had been set on fire. Zell had called the cops a couple of times, but nothing got done. Nothing ever got done. Zell had been there four years, the apartment represented her independence, and there was no way she was going to give that up.

It had taken Vanesco a while to come to terms with her independence, once realizing that he wanted to commit to something more than a carnal relationship. He wanted her to move into his apartment, but got instead her apartment key in exchange for his. They each kept their own territory, with no interchange of personal effects between apartments, and anything left in the other's home meant it had been forgotten. Vanesco saw no prospect of it being any different, so persuaded himself it was better this way; longevity wasn't guaranteed in his profession. Keeping emotional options open was something many people attempted, choosing to fuck their way around New York's singles bars, not understanding that finally they lost all their options.

Vanesco gave three short rings on the door buzzer before letting himself in. Another way of not intruding. Sam ran to greet him.

'Hiya, kid. How are you?'

'Hiya, kid,' the boy mimicked.

Gamely Sam put up his fists, and with a couple of feints, Vanesco grabbed him around the waist and boosted him into the air.

'You go for it every time, dummy.'

The boy giggled when Vanesco threw him across his shoulder and carried him across to Zell, who stood in the kitchen doorway. He brushed lips with her, then put his arm around her and kissed her, Sam caught between them.

'Good trip?'

He pulled a face.

He remembered the girl, and felt guilty now. Few women got him hard-on like Zell. Subconsciously he guessed he was getting off on the girl's old man.

'You find the kid?'

'Found her; delivered her; got paid.' He turned Sam over and swung him by his legs, increasing the arc as he laughed. 'Okay, kid, this time you go crashing down onna street. Outta window.' He threw him up and caught him.

'More. Do it some more,' Sam said.

'Hey, wait awhile. Lemme get my coat off.' He removed

his heavy coat and dropped it on the covered bed in the corner of the room.

'Swing me, again.'

'C'mon, Sam. Don't get so excited on top of your dinner, honey.'

'Oh my God, d'you mean to say he's been getting food. Food, boy! No wonder you're so goddamn fat.'

'I ain't fat, am I mom?'

'You sure aren't honey.' Zell wouldn't buy those kind of jokes against her kid.

'When I was your age I was locked inna closet and had crusts poked through a hole by a wicked ol' witch.'

'You didn't live with a witch.'

'Sure I did. That's why I'm so mean.'

He glanced at Zell, who stood watching. She was proud of Sam, and Vanesco figured she had cause to be. Sam was a bright, responsive kid whom he'd have gotten along with even better but for his neuroses. It was a problem that wouldn't go away by itself. Vanesco thought about that often, figuring that it was impossible for kids not to be neurotic nowadays, hearing the kind of things they heard: orbiting satellites monitoring people like Big Brother; nuclear brinkmanship that was going down; pressure points of world tension such as the Middle East. Kids were bright, they listened to what was being said around them, as a result often objected to what was being said directly to them. They had been as bright when he was a kid, only the previous generation weren't so aware; society hadn't gotten up so much steam. However, Sam's neuroses were made worse by Zell pandering to him.

'You want a drink, Jim?' She went into the kitchen where she had some Californian wine.

'Hey, who lives in New Mexico, Sam?'

He thought about it. 'Navaho Indian.'

'Good man. Who told you?'

'Mom.' He watched Vanesco go to his coat and get two packages.

Sam got the largest. Vanesco left him opening it, and went into the kitchen. He gave the second package to Zell, and put his arms around her while she opened it.

'It's terrific.' It was a turquoise and silver ring. 'Thank you, you're a real nice man.'

'You want me to be an asshole?'

'Hey, mom.' Sam stood in the doorway now wearing moccasins.

Zell pulled away as if afraid of physical contact in front of her son. Vanesco liked to think she'd have been the same with Sam's pa.

'They're too much, Sam. You even have them on the right feet.'

An enduring problem Sam had was getting his shoes on the wrong feet. Moccasins solved it.

'What do you say to the nice man, Sam?'

He said thank you. Vanesco thought about what she had said; how she purposely distanced him from her son. Maybe he imagined this, and it wasn't a conscious separation on Zell's part; but it was no more acceptable had it been a subconscious expression.

Soon after his excitement had waned, Sam was put to bed. He was one of America's underprivileged kids who was without access to television; he would grow up missing out on a whole subculture. Zell belonged to that minority who didn't own a tv. Vanesco did, and whenever Zell brought Sam over his first move was to switch on the tv. He figured he was missing something even if his mother didn't.

'Some lawyer was trying to reach you,' Zell said when she came out of the boy's room. 'His name was Cunningham. Clark *E*, can you believe.'

'He expected to find me here?' The information surprised Vanesco. He made no secret of his relationship with Zell, but didn't expect Cunningham to be casually aware of it.

His business was something he had always intended keeping out of her life, and figured he had until now. She asked him about jobs, and he gave an edited version: he was a skiptrace, operating in an area where the police had neither the inclination nor manpower to operate. He traced missing persons for money. There was nothing sinister about this.

'How the fuck did he get this number?' Vanesco said. Cunningham was beginning to irritate him, but he still resisted calling him.

'Some kind of problem?'

Zell put her arm around him. She took his glass and drank from it.

'I guess until I call him I'm not gonna know.'

'His secretary said it was extremely important.'

'It'll keep till the morning.' He gave her a smile.

'I missed you.'

'Did you?' That made him feel good. 'What about all your needy Welfare recipients?'

'Didn't even know you were out of town.' She opened the lower buttons on his shirt and slid her hand inside. 'Did you miss me?'

'Well I'll tell you, kid. I had the pick of a whole commune of hips...'

'Guys too?'

'You think I'm prejudiced? Inna dark you couldn't tell the difference.' He smiled.

His kidding like this expiated his guilt. Most people, even non-Catholics like himself, had been conditioned into believing that even a part-confession was necessary.

Clark E. Cunningham clung to his thoughts, maybe his laying Deitrick's kid had something to do with the calls.

'I thought we were going to eat dinner,' Vanesco said when his girlfriend took her tongue from his mouth.

Zell glanced at her son's bedroom door. 'Maybe we'd better.'

Vanesco considered then how Zell might reconcile their love-making had Sam stepped out of his bedroom and found them. When sleeping Zell would frequently start awake, the only sounds her ears were tuned to while she slept was Sam disturbing. She would rush to his room before he got to hers. Vanesco wasn't a heavy sleeper, he didn't wake at each change in the rhythm of Sam's breathing, but did when Zell got out of bed. In an age when too few parents gave their kids enough attention Vanesco still believed Zell over-responded. It was an emotional problem that one day she would have to deal with, but as yet didn't realize she had.

Making love to Zell was a comfortable, dignified process that neither any longer felt threatened by. It had leveled into this routine about a year ago when both had been instinc-

13

tively looking to exchange those subconscious keys which unlocked their sexual blocks; both had yet to fully unlock them. Their problem was that neither was able to fuck themselves, and until then they couldn't truly fuck anyone else. Thinking back Vanesco had realized it was to do with trust, when each knew the other had made an emotional commitment and was no longer trying to get off on the other. Zell mostly achieved orgasm when they made love, occasionally she experienced multiple orgasms, which was to do with her state, rather than any skill of his. He was no more than an average lover, but like cock sizes it was all relative. Sometimes he had a problem getting an erection, but not with Zell.

No sound emerged from Zell when she came, nor from Vanesco a minute or so later. At one time he had been a raucous lover, shouting and crying out at orgasm; he also wore pyjamas in bed now. He hadn't at the start of their relationship, but had slept naked, even on his own. At some stage after sex Zell always climbed into a nightdress. He guessed he should have protested, got her out of the repressed habit. Instead he had yielded, bought himself pyjamas. Who was he trying to fool anyway? His body wasn't exactly the firm muscled shell it had been on graduating City University.

He watched her slide out of bed and pull her nightdress on. Her hips had started to thicken, but otherwise she was slim.

'How d'you know I don't plan on doing that again?' he said.

'I thought you were asleep.' She stooped and kissed him. 'You can boost it up.'

She went to Sam's door and cracked it open.

He watched her go inside to make minor adjustments, tucking a stray arm back under the bedclothes. Although her attention was sincere it wasn't constant; Zell was devoted to the boy but wasn't prepared to go on Welfare to make it a full-time job. She worked for Welfare, giving much to the job; it was part of her determination to remain independent. As a result her affection for Sam was uneven, when she would overwhelm and confuse him, at times subconsciously challenge him to be her lover. Vanesco saw it manifest itself most frequently in allowing Sam to see her naked; seeing your ma naked was fine – he'd grown up believing all was one sex far too long, and then got initiated in the wrong way – but not for Zell's reasons. She would make subliminal sexual gestures toward him, stroke him excessively and have him do it back, and Sam went along with it because he was craving for attention. Once when Zell was putting him to bed they had wrestled and Sam had ended on top of her like he was fucking her, both were laughing. Sam hadn't understood but had laughed because his ma had laughed. Later Vanesco and Zell had rowed after he had pointed out what she was doing. Vanesco remained ambivalent toward Sam, feeling love for him, and at times resentment, yet sorry for him also because of the spasmodic torrents of affection he got, although in total it amounted to more than a lot of kids got. He saw him growing up with no less problems. Zell defended her position out of guilt, which was a common problem. Who wasn't without problems? Some simply handled them better than others.

'Is he okay?' he asked.

'He's a bit hot. I think he got excited about you being here.' She slid back into bed.

'I kinda affect people that way.' He pulled her close and kissed her.

She said. 'Yes, you do.'

He could feel himself growing horny again. After a moment he reached down and boosted up her nightdress.

Mornings Zell was always up long before her son. She got Vanesco up and showered before Sam rose for a different kind of breakfast to those he didn't know he was missing for not seeing tv.

Vanesco picked up a cab on Hudson Street. The Kleinbards figured they could handle the two-block walk to Sam's school, so he kissed them both goodbye, and rode across town to the Bowery.

Vanesco's office was on Division Street, a short section of pavement running east-west between Canal Street and East Broadway. Not the prettiest part of the city, but in some ways the most honest, Vanesco figured. The rummies who used up their allotments around the neighborhood had no kind of pretentions, and when they panhandled they said right off what they wanted, the price of a drink.

Vanesco didn't ride all the way to Division, but dropped the cab at Bowery and Canal and walked the two blocks to his office. It wasn't that he didn't want to be seen arriving by cab or needed the exercise, but a cautionary habit. He bought the NY Times and after glancing across the front page, folded the paper into his pocket. A lot of buildings were boarded up on the Bowery, a lot more than was good for any neighborhood. He thought it everyday. The city didn't give a shit that banks redlined that area. The only people buying property around here were Chinese, with panic-money that was pouring out of Taiwan ahead of the almost certain communist takeover. He didn't object to Chinese buying property, the guy he rented office space off was the reputed head of a tong in Manhattan's Lower East Side called the Green Gang, who weren't simply nice old orientals promoting trade with free China. He was glad someone was buying, but foresaw the day when the Bowery would be part of Chinatown.

'Spare somethin' for a bottle of Irish Rose, brother?'

The black guy had uncurled himself from a ball where he huddled against a shuttered bar. Vanesco stopped and looked at him, guessing he was thirty. He looked fifty.

'How much d'you need?'

The man rose. Getting someone to stop meant you'd made it, most people just hurried on by. Out-of-towners did it with a laugh, like they wanted to help but couldn't, New Yorkers with angry gestures; their anger was at the city because they were accosted this way.

'Well,' he coughed, 'I guess 'bout ninetyfi' cents.' He hadn't even got the bottle started, he had been too busy trying to hold out against the raw March morning.

Vanesco reached into his pocket. He had some change there, not much, and a fold of bills. He separated a single. The black guy couldn't believe his luck, his hand shook as he plucked it. Red eyes of other bindle stiffs came open, assessing their chances of scoring here. Some were too far away, and Vanesco was moving on.

'Thank you, brother!' the black called. It needed more; he had been helped into another day. 'I love you, man. I love you.'

Vanesco glanced back. 'You have a good day.'

It was easy making that guy feel good. Almost too easy to leave your conscience with the few bucks he gave away, or at the mail box with a check to some disaster fund. He had made seven thousand bucks for five days' work; he guessed that black guy hadn't made as much in five years. 'You really want to help those guys,' Zell had once told him after he had been panhandled, 'take one in, give him a job.' She gave change away too.

From the dingy entrance of his building, Vanesco collected his mail: an over-charge refund of eighty-four dollars from American Airlines; an offer from a company to remodel his office; the inevitable note from Clark E. He thought about Cunningham who might have gone up in his estimation had the note read: 'Fuck you, Vanesco, I called someone else.' It didn't.

There was no elevator and the stairs that extended beyond the second floor to his fourth floor office were narrow and uncarpeted. He could afford smarter offices, but this crummy one room, with two windows and a bathroom helped him maintain a low profile.

At nine-twenty his first priority wasn't to call the lawyer, but to shave, then change his shirt. In the bottom lefthand drawer of his desk were laundered shirts, in the bottom right-hand drawer were soiled shirts. Currently he had more soiled than laundered. In another drawer he kept a bottle of sour mash bourbon; pencils and scratch blocks in another; a couple were empty, and the last held a 9mm Browning taped to the underside. He kept no stationery, and no files. If anyone wrote him a letter he either threw it away or, if it needed a reply, replied on the back of it. He had abominated paperwork in the FBI, and had gotten no fonder of it since quitting. He had found his answer. He didn't take on at one time more clients than he could keep track of in his head, and insisted they paid in cash.

His first call was to Everett Griggs to tell him where his wife was with her kids in Milwaukee.

'You mean you found them? Just like that?'

'Just like that took four days and a lot of scuffling around, Mr Griggs,' said Vanesco. His fee was five hundred dollars a day plus expenses for that kind of work. He always collected a deposit; not many resisted paying the balance.

'Yes, of course. I appreciate that.'

'That's where they are right now. How long they'll stay put... You think about what you want doing and call me.'

The phone rang immediately he set it back on the rest.

It was Cunningham's secretary, the lawyer was right behind.

'You're a difficult man to reach,' Cunningham said. 'Could you stop by my office right away?'

'You got some kind of problem?'

'I'd sooner discuss that in my office.'

Vanesco told him he'd be there in fifteen minutes. When he hung up, he leaned back in his chair and thought about the attorney. The man sounded like he had a problem. He pulled the empty drawer from the desk and removed his gun from the bottom. The clip was full.

Dropping the heavy automatic into his pocket, he pulled on his outdoor coat and went to keep his appointment with Clark E. Cunningham.

Three

The offices of Dean, Englewood and Cunningham on Wall Street were palatial, and for Vanesco to compare his own crummy suite was like having a dirty thought.

'Go right in, Mr Vanesco,' said the Bloomingdale's secretary from behind the tidy desk in the large reception, 'Mr Cunningham is expecting you.'

Cunningham's door was one of six, all of which were tightly shut and offered no sound from behind the thick panels. It was that kind of law firm. Discreet.

Cunningham was on the phone talking to a client about a

forthcoming appearance before the Stock Exchange Commission. This was heavy money.

Sitting on one of the two couches across the room, Vanesco let his eyes sweep the office, which reflected Clark E. Cunningham's self-importance rather than provided utilitarian space. Then Vanesco acccepted that not everyone shared his own sparse needs; prestige and material benefit were what people all over America were working for. The Maurice Utrillo hanging on this office wall had, Vanesco was sure, little to do with Cunningham's appreciation of art, but was a valuable acquisition, and something for clients to admire, which supported their faith in him as well as his legal manipulations on their behalf. Vanesco had never been to the attorney's house out in Westchester, but guessed that was full of similar acquisitions.

After the call Cunningham rose from behind his desk, and extended his hand, signaling his intention as he came across to him. His insecurity with Vanesco came from the certain knowledge that wealth and standing in community neither impressed nor intimidated the skiptrace, and that made the man unpredictable. The only reason he gave him so much work was because his clients insisted. Jimmy Vanesco had become a legend among a section of the attorney's clients, he was the guy who had handled so and so's trouble. Such clients wanted the best; therefore the attorney was obliged to try and disguise his distaste for this unpredictable man.

'I'm pleased you could get over here so quickly.'

Vanesco didn't rise. 'Your message sounded urgent.'

'My client believes the job is.' He sat on the couch opposite. 'When did you get in?'

'Yesterday afternoon.'

The lawyer didn't say anything. Vanesco knew he wouldn't, but Clark E. figured the world shook when he farted.

'I had a call from Deitrick. He appreciated what you did.' He waited, his eyes measuring Vanesco, expecting him to fill in details. He didn't. 'How busy are you right now?'

'I've a coupla things.' There was a partner in a securities firm that the remaining partners were interested in finding on account of his taking off with their clients' money. There was

the lady in Milwaukee whose kids might have to be brought
back across the New York state line.

'Are those things important?'

'They are to someone.'

'Of course. What I'm asking is whether you can hold
everything you're currently on. I want you to do a job for me.
A big job. It could take you a while longer than usual. The
problem is time's running out.'

'You know my price.'

Cunningham flicked his well cared for hand as if brushing a
fly away. The price was less important. 'My client won't
quibble.'

Traffic along Wall Street was no less noisy than anywhere
else in Manhattan, but no sound penetrated the seventh floor
office as Vanesco considered the proposition. He guessed he
would take the job, despite himself and who the client might
be, his own unresolved insecurity as much as anything else
determined that.

'What's the job?'

'To find six men who are missing.'

'That's what I do. How long they been missing?' Vanesco
asked.

'Since 1963,' the attorney said. It might have been a couple
of days.

'That's a long while to pick up easy leads.'

'I didn't say it would be easy. In fact it might be extremely
difficult. That's why you've been offered the job. We can
give you some help. Some starts.' He went to his desk, where
he unlocked a drawer and withdrew a manila folder. He
didn't offer it to Vanesco.

Vanesco knew he was waiting for a commitment.

'For some reason tabs were kept on these men shortly after
their disappearance.'

'They didn't disappear then,' Vanesco pointed out.

'Semantics I won't debate with you. They disappeared
from their circles in the United States, and could be anywhere
in the world, not excluding the possibility of one or more
being behind the Iron Curtain. It's likely they're in Europe.
We've one fairly good lead on a man in Mexico.'

'Could get expensive,' Vanesco told him.

'This isn't a problem you need concern yourself about.'

Vanesco looked over at the tall lawyer, whose face was tense and dry like expensive parchment and looked as though as much care had gone into its manufacture. Despite wanting, and possibly needing to hire him, Cunningham was instinctively putting him in his place. This didn't piss Vanesco off too much.

The next question was an unusual one for Vanesco, and he wasn't sure why he asked it. 'Who am I working for?'

The attorney hesitated. He believed he could secure the man's services without telling him that, but his client was prepared to have his name disclosed. 'It's Harry Kohn.'

Vanesco nodded, showing no surprise. 'I'd better talk to him,' he said, uncertain what was taking him along this path.

'He can't give you any more information.' A tense edge had entered his voice.

It wasn't more information Vanesco expected from Kohn, but something to cause him to go after these guys like he wanted to find them. If Kohn was doing the hiring then he had the reason. Whether he would give it to him was a different story. Likely Kohn wouldn't give out anything without exacting a price. Harry Kohn was a Mafia boss.

Rising off the couch Vanesco plucked the folder from the attorney's hand. That was a commitment.

Reluctantly the attorney called his client. With the same reluctance Kohn agreed to see the skiptrace; slightly at odds with this was his agreeing to see him right away.

Riding a cab uptown on 2nd Avenue to Kohn's office, Vanesco questioned what might have occurred to bring these six guys so urgently back into anyone's level of consciousness. He could ask Kohn, but wouldn't, for they weren't the kind of questions he asked, which was why he got the jobs he did. But he was curious. Something must have either happened, or was happening. He accepted that Mafia memories were long, that they wouldn't let anyone get away with fucking them over; they might take years to settle the score, but then it wouldn't happen with the kind of urgency that was going down here, not without some external influence. What? The question hung in the back of Vanesco's thoughts, and worried him.

Harry Kohn didn't ease his uncertainty.

Large with good living, and not very tall, he gave no impression of having got soft on the life. The offices of his corporation were in a glass and steel tower on 3rd Avenue at 56th Street, and Kohn's office, like the attorney's, was full of expensive acquisitions. The corporation manufactured electronic components, and was, Vanesco had to admit, an advance on the olive oil import business.

'What can I tell you, Vanesco,' Kohn said, taking a cigar from the humidor and paring the end. 'I figured Cunningham gave you everything.'

The man behind the desk had huge, thickening jowls and wore too much antiperspirant, like he sweated more than his associates and believed that sweat was no longer acceptable. He sucked the flame into the cigar, then inspected the end, as he ran his tongue over his wet lips, which came together like a large overripe strawberry. 'You wanted to take a look at the guy writing the checks.'

'Something like that.'

'You figure you can find them, Vanesco?'

'A pretty tall order after all this time.'

Kohn looked at him and drew on his cigar. 'You come highly recommended. You don't ask half-assed questions is why. I like that.'

Vanesco assumed it was strictly Mafia business why this man wanted those guys found. He knew if he couldn't handle the moral implications then he shouldn't be doing the work he was putting out for; maybe it was time to quit, having started thinking like this. The only way he could operate successfully was by not caring about the people he found. The way he was thinking lately, logically he should first run a check on whoever offered him jobs, set codes of practice. He wondered how many of those he had worked for in the past few years would make first base, the government included.

He hadn't knowingly worked on Harry Kohn, but knew about him from his FBI record. Anyone figuring prominently anywhere had a file, but in the last couple of years he knew more about him from his publicity. He had many important clubhouse friends whom he frequently appeared on the $500-a-plate dinner circuit with; he had been photographed sailing

22

with the President off Key West, although Vanesco didn't figure he looked much like a sailor. He was the kind of man who would be all things to all men, provided there was personal gain. Vanesco's instinct was neither to like nor trust him, but that didn't preclude his working for him.

'What do I do about these guys when I find them?'

'I like that, Vanesco, a real positive attitude.' He leaned back in his chair. 'You find them, call Cunningham. Tell him where they are. That's all.' He waited, his dark, heavy lidded eyes measuring Vanesco, expecting more questions. He didn't get them. 'When can you get to work on this?'

Vanesco noticed the change in the man's attitude. It didn't mean a thing to him.

'I already started.'

Four

The start of any inquiry was the most difficult part, Vanesco found, especially on those he tended to get. With a regular investigation the start was the scene of the crime, from where things followed a logical pattern, clues, witnesses, modi operandi of known criminals. Tracing people who had disappeared as long ago as 1963, when their crimes were unknown to him, made it a different ball game.

For now Vanesco decided to assume they were criminals. Folks who took off like that often were, whatever justification some figured they had. A problem at the start of a skiptrace was that often there were too many clues, avenues to head up only to backtrack. Here the avenues were overgrown and Vanesco suspected he'd have to put in a lot of work hacking a path only to almost certainly come out empty handed. Mexico seemed a logical start, yet illogical, because if the party was still there then he wouldn't have been hired to run him to earth. Unless there was a reason for using him which somehow he hadn't seen.

The start was in Washington.

Fortunately Vanesco's departure from the FBI was for a reason which most agents wanted to quit over at some time: the selfdefeating bureaucracy which was the legacy of Hoover's lifetime. It conditioned agents into paying homage to the chief while mistrusting each other, to the point of informing on colleagues. Some did; some didn't; a few quit. Had Vanesco left under a cloud, then using the firm's resources as he frequently did would have been a nonstarter.

Before leaving New York he had called a friend in Washington and gave him the six names to run a check on.

John Bierwirth was glad to assist. It was only a matter of feeding the data into a computer. He would have the information for Vanesco by the time he arrived. It was a small favor, and he would do many more before he was halfway to paying back what he owed him.

Each time he visited the new FBI building on Penn Avenue Vanesco felt a chill; it was an awesome monument to one of the most awesome egos to stamp around the capital for over three decades. In his last years Eddie Hoover had hung in there like a dead lizard whose jaw was locked on its victim. No way was he going to let go the reins until the move from the old justice building to the multi-million dollar red-brick J. Edgar Hoover building was accomplished. It stood like an epitaph to a lifetime's hypocrisy; an expensive embarrassment to the administration.

'You have business here, sir,' a young agent said as Vanesco approached. He was on the wide perron, dressed in a regular business suit as if impervious to the cold spring air that squabbled with hats and coats along Penn Avenue.

'I planned to join a tour,' Vanesco said.

They had regular tours around the building, taking visitors from the facsimile of the dead director's old office, with its collection of self-sought awards, to the conclusion which was a shooting display on the firing range. Here visitors sat in a huge amphitheater, protected by a glass screen. Afterwards boyscouts would eagerly question avid agents.

The young agent seemed pleased, like the sole purpose of the building, and his existence was to accommodate tourists. 'Take the stairway to the left, sir. Go up to the third floor. The assembly point for tours is marked.'

Vanesco went to the second floor and called John Bierwirth, who came down to get him.

Like most who worked for the Bureau, Bierwirth was cleancut, homogenized, an older model than those agents moving briskly around the building in maroon jackets bearing the FBI emblem. He was tall, had all his hair, which was the prescribed shade of gray for a fifty-year-old agent who was now number two in the records department. He was lucky to be number two. Although his eyes had that disconnected look which came from daily devotions, he was conversely too much of an iconoclast ever to be number one. Hoover was gone but his ghost dominated the promotional structure.

'You didn't just grab six names arbitrarily for me to run a check on, Jimmy,' Bierwirth said after closing his office door. He was smiling but without humor.

Vanesco waited.

The FBI man took out a bunch of keys on a silver chain and unlocked a drawer in his desk. Removing a green file, he passed it to Vanesco. 'The printout from the computer. When I fed those names in that's what I got.'

The file contained a single sheet with the six names, each had a cross reference to the CIA. Vanesco looked puzzled.

'I guess you're not familiar with our new indexing, Jim. The files were pulled three days ago.'

What the skiptrace was still familiar with was the way in which the old firm worked. They didn't give out their life's blood without holding a copy.

'The file was started on each of these men back in '63. There was no FBI record before that. Our cross reference before the CIA request was to Hoover's special records.'

The expression on Vanesco's face remained unchanged. None of the doubt he was suddenly feeling was reflected there.

'You want to tell me what you're getting into?'

'I figured you were going to tell me. I've got no more than I gave you over the phone.' He had told him about the attorney, not about Harry Kohn's involvement.

'The director didn't put people in that special category for no reason. Nor did they get his attention for stealing store candy.' He paused. 'It's got to be political.'

'He was a whimsical old bastard. What Hoover saw as a political crime no one else would.' A regular felony committed by a relative of a politician was a political crime to Hoover, for it gave him a lever if he chose to keep the offense out of court.

'I'd buy that, Jim, but for two things. The CIA's sudden interest as of three days ago. And the fact that the cupboard was bare when I checked the Hoover file. The sheets on these guys were taken out in '64, a forged identifying flag was left behind.'

'You got no record?'

'All we've got are cross references.'

'Who at the CIA requested the information, John?'

'Would you believe the deputy director?' He reached into his drawer again for another file. 'I ran some checks on these guys, first with the passport office, then the IRS. Passports were issued to each of the subjects in October 1963. Photostats of their applications. Interesting, they were all typed on the same machine and submitted on the same date.'

Vanesco glanced over the xeroxed sheets as Bierwirth passed them to him, with photos attached. The passport applications were a major source of information, even though the photos were out of date.

'Careless maybe. If these guys weren't supposed to have any connection.'

'Did they file any tax returns?' Vanesco asked.

'Not in a long while.'

'Not since '63?'

'You've got it. They were all modest men, Jim. No big incomes, no big expenditures.'

'Any common factors?'

'They were all single, with no kind of family.'

When he looked over the xeroxed IRS sheets Vanesco saw why none of the men had filed for tax; they were dead.

It was an avenue he would have to back out of, but not

26

before he did some more checking. The details John Bierwirth had come up with for him didn't match those
Cunningham had offered in that slim file he had. Vanesco
wasn't being asked to track down dead men, rather six men
using dead men's identities. That was his belief, and he had to
establish that fact or else he'd be pursuing a pile of leads which
would take him nowhere.

Sewickley Heights was a small town about twelve miles
northwest of Pittsburgh, and was famous for nothing that
Vanesco could see. That was where Vanesco headed, to check
one of the names on the list. He was working from details
Bierwirth had given him, details which hadn't appeared in
Cunningham's file.

He started with the local cops. Being a small town they
usually got to know everyone, but didn't know of any Lance
Niles from around these parts. Vanesco guessed the cop was
thinking in terms of today, and he resisted giving him the information that he was dead. The man in the tan uniform
probably wasn't even a cop when Niles died.

'When d'you last hear from him?' an older cop asked.

Vanesco hesitated, then said. '1963.'

'Gee, that's a long time ago, fella. Could be your friend
ain't alive no more.'

'Could be.'

'Well,' the older cop said, 'you can check it out right along
the street. The local records office. Opens 9am tomorrow.'

Sewickley Heights wasn't somewhere Vanesco would
choose to spend a night. Instead he wanted to get his information and go. He couldn't find a hotel so drove to Sewickley
where there was a motel off US65. He could maybe have
found a better place, but guessed they'd all be much the same.

A sign on the forecourt announced 'Vacancies' and
Vanesco wondered, after he checked in, if they'd change it to
read 'A Guest'. It was one of those places.

Vanesco considered driving into Pittsburgh to eat, but
decided instead to use the restaurant attached to the motel. It
was a mistake. He was the only customer and probably had
been all week, yet still there was a smell of burnt cooking oil.
Everything there was plastic or manmade fibre, a fact of life

that most Americans had learned to live with. But it was never more apparent than in that restaurant; Vanesco crossed the orange nylon carpet and sat on a plastic chair at a Formica topped table and took up a plastic covered menu. It indicated what the food would be like. Vanesco sat for a couple of minutes before realizing there was no waitress service; the food at the counter was plastic wrapped under plastic hoods, carried away on plastic trays to be eaten off styrofoam plates with plastic cutlery. Vanesco took a couple of club sandwiches and a bottle of beer.

'S'that all you want, honey?' the woman on the check out said.

'This'll be fine.'

The sandwiches were tasteless, bland bread with a different textured filling. He moved it around in his mouth, then washed it down with some beer. He thought about rye and pumpernickel breads Zell bought from a deli in the Village, then got to thinking about favorite New York restaurants. None of which improved his stay in Sewickley. He guessed his antipathy toward middle-America about rivalled middle-America's loathing for New York city.

He went to his guaranteed sanitized cabin and read through the details he had on each of the six men. He was looking for obvious links, something that wouldn't be noticed unless the six men were looked at together, which ordinarily they probably wouldn't be. The most obvious fact was that all died without a known surviving relative. Someone had taken a lot of trouble to find these identities. He let his thoughts run at possible crimes that might have demanded such cover, and allowed for such meticulous preparation. He considered how these six men might have died, whether they had been killed for their own transgressions. He assumed not, or they might simply have been made to disappear. He questioned whether the record being left at the Internal Revenue Service was a mistake, if those files shouldn't have been pulled; whether the records of their death would have been pulled. So much work having been done, it was crazy to leave loose ends. Maybe errors of judgement had been made, this kind of investigation never being anticipated.

Vanesco had to wait for the records office to open. The

28

woman who arrived with the key had a watch which was ten minutes behind. He followed her inside and waited while she got her official composure.

'Are you a relative of the party you're wanting this information on?' she asked.

She evidently wanted to believe that he was, so Vanesco obliged her.

'I guess. That's what I want to find out.'

She looked at him, then said. 'No, I don't believe you are.'

For a minute Vanesco figured she had some power to divine truth. That wasn't the case. Instead she had a memory that needed a little space to tick over in.

'I don't believe Mr Niles had any relatives. He died intestate and the county took over his property, as I recall.'

She left her desk, telling him she wouldn't be a moment.

She was having more trouble with her watch, Vanesco figured, when she was gone about five minutes.

She returned with a satisfied smile. 'Yes, he died intestate. You'll have to go to the county records office in Aliquippa if you want further details.'

'Maybe you could tell me about his death. How, where he died. Where he's buried?'

She showed him a copy of the death certificate. Lance Jeffrey Niles died September 12, 1963 of a massive brain hemorrhage. He was thirty one.

'How'd it happen. An accident of some kind?'

'It's almost natural causes in these parts. His car was in collision with a truck. Right out at the end of town. Buried in the Presbyterian churchyard at the other end of town.'

Vanesco had the feeling she knew everything that went on in Sewickley Heights, and about everyone too.

'Does that help you?'

'Some.'

'Doesn't get you nearer knowing if you were kin.'

She knew as well as he that he wasn't.

The Presbyterian minister dug into his memory where they stood by Niles' tidy grave in the well-trimmed churchyard.

'He was a very private young man, I remember. He worshipped on an irregular basis.'

29

'Who tends his grave?'

'Friends of the church. They're all taken care of. He planned to marry a girl from Beaver Falls. I don't recall her name. I daresay someone might if you're going to be around, son.'

The skiptrace shook his head. 'This might seem like an odd question, but it was Lance Niles buried there?'

The pink faced minister looked at Vanesco.

'I've been asked stranger questions. I didn't nail the coffin down, but I went to Dixmont state hospital to identify the body.'

The same was told him in Springfield, Illinois, where one Clarence Paley had quietly lived and died, leaving nothing to denote his passing but a death certificate and gravestone in a cemetery in Grandview.

Vanesco guessed the story would be the same for each of the men on the list: dead, and oblivious to the fact that some kind of hood was parading their identity. He didn't see any point in traveling across America to check something he was certain of, especially not as one had died in Phoenix, another in Bakersfield, and a third in Livingston, Montana. He planned instead to go east, stopping in at Philadelphia, where he'd check out the fourth man's death.

William Rockwell Torbert, a second generation Irish-American, had died in a construction site accident; no known next of kin, his few personal effects had been given to the Catholic church.

When he boarded the plane for New York, Vanesco considered briefly again whether he ought to track the other three to the grave, but decided it wasn't important. The significant fact was that they had all died around the time new identities were required, had no traceable relatives and their ages approximated those of the six men he was trying to trace. He wondered if Cunningham or Harry Kohn had this information about the change of identities. Somehow Vanesco suspected neither did, but if that was the case it didn't make too much sense; but if they had the information, their not passing it on and so saving him these false starts made less sense. The thought that neither of them knew where they were at jumped into Vanesco's head, that one or both might be fronting for someone else. While that was the case with Cunningham, it didn't figure that Kohn would be in the same position.

The answers, if there were any, would maybe be found in Mexico with Peter Radulovic. Mexico was where he planned to head for. For that looked like his easiest avenue.

Five

Thunder rolled through the Sierra Madre, reverberating across mountains. Then the rain fell, instantly drenching the parched earth, those first sheets of water vanishing into cracks and fissures opened by the long, dry winter and the longer, drier summer before that. As the downpour continued the ground filled up and the surplus started to form riverlets, one joining another, forcing into gulleys, springing toward the rio de Sinaloa, which lay a mile due north. It rushed and burst around rocks, eddying, dragging stones, sand, sticks in its downward rush.

Lightning crackled, a silvery-yellow streak tearing through the predawn sky, snapping at the impeding mountaintops. Through the rain were glimpsed images of the mountain range, the strange light making them a candescent blue. Despite the years the man had lived there, and the storms he had experienced, both the spectacle of lightning and the sound of rolling thunder never ceased to impress him. Sleep would have been difficult, and would have been a waste; he could sleep every night; such storms were rare.

Although reluctant to stray from the window, the man knew he had to check on his burro. Rocinante probably little appreciated the grandeur of nature, though the animal would take it in its stride.

Pulling on his mackinaw, he stepped outside. The yard was awash, parts of it disappearing in gulleys running to the dirt track up the mountain. In the small corral the burro had a leanto shelter, which was designed to keep off the blazing sun that bore down on both man and beast from about noon onwards, it helped dissuade the flies that appeared from nowhere at the first scent of sweat. The roof was made out of sticks layered with mud and stones. It was better designed for drying Indian corn which was left there until used, rather than to keep out rain; water dripped steadily through, soon the mud would wash out, and the rain would bucket in. None of which would harm Rocinante, but the man thought a lot of his burro, so tried to ease her burden anyway he could.

'How you doing, honey?' he said, stepping under the leanto. The burro raised its head, not having heard the man's approach; then pricked its ears as more thunder rolled southward. 'Easy, honey. The storm get you up too?'

He found a spot behind the burro's ears and scratched it, causing Rocinante to snicker and turn his head into the man and rub against his chest.

The burro suddenly became alert.

A second or two later the rain stopped. Left was the sound of running water. The ten minutes of rainfall would help to fill the underground springs that would help carry them through the summer. Without this rain existence would have been more of a problem for the scratch farmers in the mountains, as well as for those lower down around the towns of Mocorito and Badiraguato. A lot wouldn't have made it, and would have headed into Culiacan, Torreon, Guadalajara or even Mexico City, looking for work. There was little work for those already in the cities, and the newly arrived only added to the squalor of the shanty towns. The city provided hope, and people in Mexico were still depopulating rural areas in order to reach for that hope, just as they had in America through the '50s and '60s. But the subsequent exodus from Mexican cities back to the countryside wasn't as certain, for the hopes of the people aren't fulfilled as they had been in American cities; migrant workers never made their fortune in places like Guadalajara, but begged and fought for space.

The man was glad the rain had come. The maize and bananas and coffee hill-farmers planted would have some chance, and the ajonjoli that was grown on the plains; it would mean fewer people leaving. Hearing of folks packing up and moving to the city distressed him, and when he heard of neighbors leaving he would try to dissuade them. Rarely was he able to. Their dark, uncertain eyes would hug the dry earth to avoid his eyes, and when they did look at him it was with darting glances, as though knowing if they looked into his pale blue eyes, they would recognize the truth. But the man was a gringo, he had come from America, with its rich cities and air-conditioned houses, where all the streets were paved and everyone had an automobile. They believed the gringo was there from choice and could return whenever he wished to that land. About everything they sought and heeded his advice, except when he advised against going to the cities, where they were convinced they could end their poverty.

The locals were wrong about his option to return to America. He no longer had one. He had burned all his boats, there was no going back, even had he wanted to. He was a prisoner in those few square miles of mountain, but no prison ever constructed could have held him faster than his conscience; from that there was no escape, any more than there was for the paysanos from their poverty.

On leaving the United States back in '63 he had gone first to Guadalajara, but hadn't stayed. He had believed that he could hide in the anonymity of a big city, both himself and his problem. But the knowledge had stayed locked inside his head, eating away at him, and no matter where he went he couldn't shake free. First he drank; then discovered cocaine. In Mexico money made the supply endless. But when he came out of a drunk, or down from a coke trip, nothing had changed, and at that point he hadn't understood that nothing would. He had moved on to Durango, but the only difference was the city and the bed he awoke in. He was rootless and friendless and lonely, but ordinarily all those things he was able to handle. Roots were put down when establishing property rights, but he had never believed them basic to man, who in his primal stage had been a wanderer, living on berries

33

and following the weather; then man had settled, planting the ground, discovered ownership, become more insecure rather than less.

When in the late '60s earthquakes devastated parts of Western Mexico he saw how frail property rights were, how futile the longing for security was. The first general call for help had drawn him out of the hole he was burying himself in. The quake around Culiacan had brought down buildings and power lines. The first figures of dead and injured were wildly inaccurate; overstating the case expedited aid, which flooded in, mostly from the United States, and quickly disappeared. Little of it reached the victims, but was sold instead on the black market by the army officers who were in charge of the rescue operation.

When the medical supplies, clothing and food had been disposed of, the profit counted against not too great a loss of life, there was a second, more devastating quake. The ground opened, in a series of mocking grins, streets disappeared, people with them. New appeals went out, but this time the world was slower to respond. While aid trickled in people died and disease spread, and the army shot wouldbe looters, a lot of whom weren't looters but people scrabbling after those few possessions it had taken a lifetime to put together.

The man had never been present at an earthquake before. He had been around Wisconsin floods in the '50s, where there were similar problems with the risk of disease. Panic was rife, and fear made people old overnight. The cause was something they couldn't understand, or come to terms with. He had been in Pericos, thirty miles north of Culiacan, when the second quake struck. The rescue workers had been worst hit. The church, which was being used as a casualty station, collapsed, killing the doctor and two medical assistants; the man had been in the building also, and escaped with minor contusions. People thought it a miracle when he crawled out alive; he might have thought otherwise, had he been able to think. When finally the ground stopped shaking and buildings stopped falling, there was left the noise of wailing despair; people scrambled through the debris calling for relatives, some got replies, most didn't.

Despite his limited medical knowledge there was nothing

34

the man wouldn't undertake. He threw himself into the rescue work as if immune from danger, and effectively he was, for he knew where his ultimate escape lay. Not for a moment did he consider the problem that had been eating away at him; no risk was too great, and when rescue workers hesitated about crawling among the wreckage, he went, taking what medical aid he had. First the morphine ran out, then the typhoid vaccine, then antibiotics, followed by medical dressings, while little else arrived. On the second day with the airless temperature in the 90s, the smell of rancid flesh hung in a pall over the town. A mass grave was dug for ninety-six bodies, and still there were people buried in the smouldering rubble. Scavenging dogs often found them before the rescuers, but rats had been there first. The first cases of typhoid were reported. The water in the town was condemned, adding to their problems. On the third day the urgency began to abate, and although not everyone had been accounted for, it was assumed they were dead.

Then a voice was heard in the ruins of a building rescuers had long since quit. Clearing some rubble they found a tiny shaft into the half cellar, but didn't dare risk moving anything else for fear of everything collapsing. Rats were seen scurrying around as the probing flashlight picked through the darkness. Then the voice was heard again, almost inhuman as it called upon God for mercy. It created an eerie atmosphere there on the dusty street while the sun beat down, and the flies dove in at the chilling sweat on tired, dirty bodies. This inexplicable fear caused people to hold back, resist climbing into that cellar. The man felt the same fear, but ignored it.

The floor beneath seemed to be moving in his flashlight as he wriggled head first into the shaft. Then he realized that what he was looking at were rats. He stopped his descent, uncertain about going on. But the cry to God for mercy reached across to him. He continued, recalling vaguely that only single, trapped rats were dangerous. What did it matter anyway, he questioned. Rats scurried and squeaked as he brushed past them, only to close behind him as he crawled toward the sound of that chilling voice. On the far side of the cellar the headspace increased to three or four feet where joists had fallen and jammed with tons of debris on top of them.

There he found the remains of an entire family, six in all, their bodies mutilated and smelling. In other circumstances he might have vomited. None of these people could have spoken; then he heard the voice behind him. He turned. The flashlight found an old woman sitting against the wall, her condition not much advanced on her family's. Her legs were pinned by fallen lumber. She didn't stir or blink as the flashlight explored her but went on asking for mercy in that same thin, mechanical voice. He didn't question her for he knew he would get no response, realizing she was dead and that only a nerve in her brain or something in her psyche kept her seeking the thing she needed above all else. There was nothing to be done for her medically. Instead he blessed her and gave her the last rites as best he could from memory. It was enough. The old woman's voice stopped and a loud hiss escaped from her lungs. She let go her hold on this world but kept her eyes staring, as though seeking a path into the next.

He sat unmoving, the weariness and heartache he had ignored over the past five days finally overtaking him, stretching resistance beyond endurance. Suddenly he noticed the rats scurrying away, and fleetingly thought of rats leaving a sinking ship. Then he heard a voice, or imagined he did, telling him he had given enough; possibly it was only the noise of the shifting debris. The shaft of light piercing the cellar vanished and there was a rumbling as the roof collapsed.

He remembered little of the days in that cellar, only his accumulating fear, which he slowly overcame, and the desperate sense of loneliness, more penetrating than he had ever known, the kind, he assumed, that caused people to commit suicide. Finally he came to terms with it.

His next impressions were antiseptic and clean linen in the makeshift infirmary in Mocorito, of people visiting him, children at first, bringing gifts of fruit or flowers, their light brown faces full of wonder, their eyes bug-wide in expectation. None of them spoke, nor did their parents when they came. He soon learned that they considered him special, believing he had received two miracles in return for his work in the disaster.

He realized then he had found a place where he could stop

36

running, people among whom he could live, who wouldn't care what he had been.

The sun nosed over the mountain rim, and he watched the line of light chase the darkness down the mountainside toward the sea. It took only seconds to cover the twenty or so miles, making the rainsoaked earth sparkle with silver light. He had seen this happen many times before, and would pause to watch it again and again.

'This morning, Rocinante, you get to lay in. Sure, you'd figured it out.' He rubbed the burro behind the ears again.

The donkey, he believed, like his dog and his bees, had the capacity to tune into his thoughts and anticipate him even before he had half-formed them. This morning there was no need to hike down to the river for water, nor would they for a while. The butts were full and the ground wouldn't need water in a month.

Removing his mackinaw and throwing it over the corral rail, he set about his chores before the sun grew too hot. He had both Rocinante, and Huascar, his dog, to feed, also his bees to check. The bees swarmed early and he had to ready empty hives for his earliest swarms. He had thirty-four hives in his apiary and lived from the sale of honey—he had money in a deposit box in a bank in Guadalajara, the best part of two hundred thousand dollars. It was bloodmoney and he no longer gave it a thought, much less used it. When he moved his bare feet sank into the mud the rain had made. He glanced back at Huascar, who stood in the doorway of the dwelling house, and briefly considered the wet yard before going back inside. Smart dog, he thought, and smiled.

Four hours later, by 9 am, the surface rain which hadn't either run to the sea or soaked away, had been sucked up by the sun, leaving the earth like it hadn't been barely rained upon. The sun grew fiercer the higher it got off the rim, but the man ignored it, working easily under his stained straw sombrero. He had stopped only for the thick dark coffee he drank throughout the day, eating his one meal of an evening. Pausing, he checked the progress the small figure who had been coming along the track for the past fifteen minutes, recognizing now José Iniguez, the Coke vendor's youngest son. The man stooped to his planting again, it would be

37

another five or six minutes before the boy reached him.

When he got there José was excited and breathless. 'Señor, señor!' he said. 'A man is looking for you. A gringo, señor. Norte Americano. He asked my father many questions.'

The man accepted the information without surprise even though throughout his time here no one from the United States had asked after him.

'You want some candy, José?' He made a fudge from crystallized honey, most of which he gave to local kids.

The boy followed him into the adobe.

'Did you tell the gringo I was here?'

'No, señor. He asked for Señor Radulovic.' He pronounced it like three separate names. 'Is he a bad hombre?' the boy asked, caught up with the excitement the man's arrival had generated in the village that comprised of six dwellings.

'I guess not,' Peter Radulovic said. 'Why do you ask, José?'

'My father says he has a gun, señor.'

Huascar nosed his way up to the table, and Radulovic offered the dog a piece of candy, and thought about the situation. There was nothing he could do physically about a man with a gun. He had once been such a man.

'If it's me this bad hombre wants, you'd better tell him I'm here, José. I'm not going anyplace.' He smiled, trying to reassure the nine-year-old.

Radulovic resigned himself to the visitor. He lifted his sombrero off the table and got up. He had a lot to do before the sun got too hot.

Six

The four-year-old Chevvy Vanesco had rented at Culiacan airport was in need of attention and had difficulty on the oil

38

road much less the winding tracks of the Sierra Madre. Vanesco had figured the old car would make him less obtrusive, but it made no difference once he reached Mocorito. An odd feeling of a conspiracy to protect Peter Radulovic, which had started back in Culiacan, a town full of pickups and big enough to get lost in, had been dismissed as paranoia – something he regularly experienced when tracing people. However, it wasn't paranoia which caused the feeling he got in Mocorito when he began asking questions.

Mocorito was an untidy, spread-out town of about four thousand people, and after the recent rain it looked a nice place to live; a day or two under the relentless sun and it would be arid and inhospitable, like the people when asked the wrong questions. Inquiries about Radulovic fell into this category. Although these ordinarily friendly people had admirable notions about protecting a friend, their reactions told the skiptrace he was in the right place; eyes that avoided his followed him along the dusty street as he went from the bank to Cantina. He tried offering people money, which most needed, yet refused. That made Vanesco intrigued by the man they were protecting, to question how he had rated such loyalty; additionally he had to consider the Mafia connection. Maybe Radulovic had been wetbacking for the Mob but was now freelancing. That didn't make sense, and it wasn't that kind of fear he had picked up from these people. Dope made more sense. He had heard someone refer to Radulovic as Dios de las Abegas. Vanesco had enough Spanish to get by in Mexico and his translation was God of the Bees, which made no sense at all.

The mountain road north out of Mocorito was a dusty rutted track like most of the roads in the town; the car bounced around on its weakened springs, its obvious familiarity with such tracks making the journey no less torturous. Vanesco's despair of the car making it to Cerro Blanco with the guts gone out of the engine sank to a new depth when any resemblance the track had to a road disappeared at a fork. The left hand branch disappeared, while the one which he had been directed to take looked like the dried up bed of a river. It was a rockstrewn track which a Willys jeep couldn't have negotiated, much less a whipped Impala. At that point he questioned if the barber in Mocorito had given him a bum steer or if he had misunderstood him. But for the fact of seeing tire tracks he wouldn't have ventured further. Every few yards there was a scrump as the transmission pan scraped across a rock and he was sure a hole in the pan would leave him stranded. A mile or so up this track he came to a dip and found the journey a little easier downhill, until he came to a river. Before him was obviously a ford. The water level was not his problem, but the fact that the path seemed strewn with boulders. The tire tracks that indicated something could get through persuaded him he could. But doubt followed after the track which ran along the river bank awhile, entered the stream to emerge on the other side, only to go on a short distance where it was stopped at a pool where a child played and two scrawny cows grazed.

'Cerro Blanco, por favor?' Vanesco called to the child, who looked up at him, and ran to the nearest house.

A short while later a man appeared from the same house, which was one of six, of rudimentary construction with pieces of corrugated sheet metal tacked to them. There were no other vehicles around, but bits and pieces of vehicles, mostly tires and broken seats. Amidst this obvious poverty stood a red and white Coke sign.

Vanesco repeated his question and got a long stare back. 'Cerro Blanco? Sí,' the man said finally, waving on up the track toward the mountain.

Although hot and sweating the thought of having to hit that water and get stuck made Vanesco sweat more. He revved the engine and went at it like a bull. It was a mistake as the car had to plow a lot of water aside. To his surprise he got through and pulled onto the opposite bank, by which time most of the people who lived in those houses had appeared.

It was an even bet, Vanesco thought, that whatever had been up this track it wasn't an American in a car. The look on the wall of brown faces was wonderment. Vanesco felt obliged to do a turn, and got out of the car to say hello. He figured he might even get directions from here.

Asking after Peter Radulovic brought the same reaction he had got in town. People averted their eyes. Finally the man whose house bore the Coke sign offered him a drink. Coke, inevitably.

Only the men had Coke, the children, fourteen in all, stood round in a semi-circle watching them, while the women went back to their chores. When Vanesco offered to buy the kids Cokes the dealer assumed he was asking if they were all his. He spat onto the dirt floor and announced that six were. Unbeknown to Vanesco the eldest of them had gone up the track to warn Peter Radulovic. It was only about an hour and three Cokes later when the boy reappeared and had a whispered conversation with his father that Vanesco was let go on his way, with directions. He was told the man he was looking for was at the end of the track. Having driven over the kind of ground he had today, Vanesco had assumed he could drive all the way there. But it disappeared altogether about two miles from the village and reluctantly he abandoned his car.

The sun was high and on that rocky, dusty path it bore down on him with an intensity he hadn't experienced in a long while. His breathing ran into trouble from both the climb and the elevation, which, according to his map, was seven thousand feet. He didn't know what he was headed into up here; could be the people below figured he would get lost and the problem he had brought for Señor Radulovic would go away. Somehow Vanesco didn't think it would.

He had been walking for about twenty minutes, handling the heat the best he could, wishing he had a hat, and shades to take away the stinging, bleached out glare off Cerro Blanco, when he reached a sharp bend on the track. Beyond an outcrop of rock he saw what he guessed he was headed for, an adobe clinging to the side of the mountain.

It was time to leave the path, Vanesco decided, even though he guessed there would be no surprising Radulovic now. The climb got harder, and he took an hour to get within striking distance of the dwelling. Long before he got there the dog stirred and barked, fiercely at first, then without interest, as if either finding the morning was too hot, or sensing there was no real danger.

The skiptrace removed his Browning from its holster and squatted in some rocks above the buildings and watched a while. The white and tan dog, that was something between a

41

spaniel and a French poodle, padded around issuing a worried growl before heading across the yard toward a cultivated slope, where a man in a white smock and a sombrero worked among beehives. The only other sign of life was the burro.

The dog barked when Vanesco moved through the cultivated strip toward the apiary, then quit for no apparent reason and lay on the ground. Slowly the man at the hive turned, his face from below his eyes was a mask of bees, where they hung from his chin like a thick beard. The sight disturbed Vanesco, he believed the man was in some kind of trouble, until realizing otherwise from his behavior; the bees were there because he let them be. At that point Vanesco felt foolish standing in the middle of the field holding the Browning. He lowered it, then finally put it away.

The beekeeper turned back to the hive, and Vanesco moved into the shade of some rocks and watched as he reached a bee from his mouth. Suddenly the bees left his face and followed his hand to the hive, the air was thick with them, the beekeeper could scarcely be seen. It was like a performance for his benefit and Vanesco watched intently, not noticing the dog had approached until it nudged his hand.

Vanesco reached out and stroked the dog. He had no fear of animals, believing most animals recognized that.

'That's Huascar,' the beekeeper said when he approached Vanesco. 'You should feel special. He doesn't take to strangers. Doesn't see many. You know who Huascar was? An Aztec prince. A big man in Mexico.'

He spoke quickly, as if not wanting to give Vanesco the opportunity to state who he was, why he was there.

'How d'you handle those bees? Didn't you get stung?'

Radulovic found a bee that had gotten trapped inside his shirt. He released it and watched it circle away toward the hive.

'I had the queen between my lips. They were about to swarm, I didn't want to lose them. The colony groups around the queen to protect her. There was no danger, they gorge themselves with honey just prior to swarming, it makes them amenable. There's no danger in them anyway.'

'You don't get stung?'

'The bee usually dies after using its sting. It knows this. It

42

has no wish to die. If you don't endanger it, then it won't panic and waste itself.'

There was a pause. Both men knew he was talking about this encounter.

Right then Vanesco didn't want the reason for his visit to intrude. He was talking to a professional, and no matter what line they pursued he admired professionals. He understood why this man was called god of bees.

'What about the queen. How can you put her between your lips without getting stung?'

'She'll only sting when her life force is threatened. Ordinarily she'll only recognize that threat from another queen.'

'You mean she can only sting another queen?'

'That's all she will sting,' Radulovic said.

'Amazing.'

'It amuses the folk around here when I do such things. Especially the children.'

'You bet.'

The pale blue eyes locked on Vanesco. 'They warned me you were coming.'

'Why'd you stay?' said Vanesco.

'You look hot. Shall we go inside.' He started across the field toward the house.

The dog climbed out of the dust and went after him, but then stopped and looked back, waiting for Vanesco.

The house was cool inside, a welcome relief from the sun that Vanesco had been in for over two hours. He watched the man reach into a small sack for a handful of coffee beans which he ground and threw into a pot and set on a butane stove.

'I grow the coffee. It's a thin crop on this terrain. The price makes it not worth selling. The farmers down the mountain can't afford guano. It would make the difference between economic survival and just staying alive.'

'You?' Vanesco said.

'My needs are pretty small. I trade for most things.'

'Who you got up here with you?'

The beekeeper shook his head. 'Huascar and Rocinante. I guess I dropped out.'

'Sounds pretty good to me.'

43

'Borrowed time.' He held Vanesco's look. 'Could be my credit's used up.' He swallowed some of the thick black coffee in silence. 'What's your name?' Radulovic asked as if starting a friendship.

'Does it matter?' He didn't want this getting too close, but told him anyway.

'You're not what I expected, Mr Vanesco.'

'Well you're not exactly what I figured on.' He reached down and caught Huascar's ears in his thick hands and pulled them, avoiding Radulovic's eyes. There was something about this man that caused Vanesco to respond other than how he was paid to, and he guessed the reason was most apparent in his eyes; they were soft, possibly made so by the life he had led or with some experience he had been through, they showed compassion. None of the other people he had run to ground for the Mafia had eyes like this. He remembered how most had been cold and dead, then terribly afraid, eyes of men who hadn't been prepared to die. But that wasn't the case with Peter Radulovic. His resignation caused Vanesco difficulty looking at him. Also the reason he was there would be clear to see in his own eyes.

'How long you had this fella?' he asked, catching the dog's ears.

'Going on nine years. I found him as a pup, he had a broken leg.'

'You fixed it?'

'He's gotta bad limp.'

'He gotta life.'

'Yeah.'

There was a long thoughtful silence. Vanesco could live with silence, had learned to let other people fill the gaps; that was how he had operated in the FBI. But across the wooden table from him was a man more capable of handling silence.

The only noise was the buzz of a lazy dogfly. Most other things at that time of day were sleeping.

'What the hell did you do?' Vanesco suddenly asked.

Radulovic lifted his eyes. His brain sifted memories, looking for one to anchor the question to.

'Didn't they tell you?'

'Somehow asking only tended to cloud the issue. I figured

44

it was Mafia business, that's usually bad business.'

Radulovic looked confused. He shook his head, trying to shake out memories that were best forgotten. 'Is that who you work for, Mr Vanesco?'

'I work for anyone who can meet my price. Who did you expect to come after you?'

Again the man shook his head. 'For a long time I've lived with the prospect of someone getting here. But not them.'

'You didn't tell me what you did.'

'No,' he said. 'I used to work for the CIA, a long time ago. That's who I figured would show up.'

Things started to fall into place. Vanesco understood about the cover the man had gotten, how records had been pulled at the FBI. But not why. He would have to know what they had done to understand that; also to understand both Kohn and Cunningham's involvement. Although the CIA employed some weird people to do equally weird things, he didn't believe they'd use a New York Mafia boss or his attorney. There had to be another party who was the catalyst.

'How come you stuck around until I got here?'

'When the choice is between running and not running, that's no choice. This way life is easy to reconcile; it's easier to live without ambition and without desire than it is to deal with those needs.' He paused. 'When I die I would sooner die among friends than among strangers in a city that offers nothing but anonymity. You did come to kill me?'

Vanesco didn't reply immediately. Instead he thought about how the question revealed Peter Radulovic, the trust and faith he had in his fellow man. The question wasn't rhetorical, he expected a straight answer.

'That wasn't what I was hired for. The deal is I find you, and call New York. The same when I find the other five guys.'

He watched Radulovic closely, anticipating that he couldn't avoid reacting. He had long since forgotten the technique of disconnecting face muscles and the nerves around his eyes. Vanesco offered him the names of the other five men.

'You know those guys, right.'

'I assume so. We were each given a new identity, unknown to the others.'

45

'You know where they are now?'

He didn't. 'We foresaw this situation. We had a plan for contacting each other and so minimize the danger of someone coming for us.'

'How d'you make contact?'

'The last I knew was through the personal columns in the Herald-Tribune. We took nouns from the first page of Websters.' A smile passed across his face. 'I had Abatis.'

'Does it still operate?'

'Who knows. I stopped caring a long time ago. I haven't seen the Herald-Tribune in a long while. The stuff it gets filled with doesn't touch my life here.' He offered Vanesco details of how contact was made. Then he said, 'The only one I met after leaving America was Abalone. He found me in Durango – he followed the trail of booze bottles. He figured we'd be better off together – he planned to take my share of the money.'

Vanesco waited, saying nothing.

'The price we got for the job we did. Abalone was living in Canada, by Lake Superior. He had a boat yard.'

The details were thin. Vanesco besieged him with questions, some he got answers to, others he didn't, but he didn't get the impression that the beekeeper was ever lying. The one question he wouldn't answer was what it was they had done. The memory of that made him an elective mute. It wasn't so much that he wouldn't tell, more that he couldn't.

The morning slid into afternoon and the more they talked the more Vanesco liked the man. Somehow this ceased being a detective questioning a suspect, rather he had a feeling of knowing this man a long time, and felt concern about the kind of existence he led.

'Don't you get a mite lonely up here?' he asked.

Radulovic thought about that. 'I'm not sure I know what loneliness is. I was always pretty much a loner. All I've done is quit easy access to people of my social and intellectual level. I chose this life. It was determined partly by my actions, just as my actions were determined by what I had been. When the idea of aloneness settles down, past, present and future flow together, neither one has any particular importance. It's like the death of someone close, it only affects you because of the relationship of the past. Without that there's no sorrow. I'm not even sure there is any death. This is all that is important, like right now, what we are, what we do.'

At that point Vanesco had the feeling that what he said or, more important, what he did would hold no meaning for Radulovic. Here was a man living on borrowed time and he had come to terms with the fact. Whether or not he was extended further credit didn't matter. Vanesco knew that was his decision, and as such he would have to get by with it.

He rose, watched by both Radulovic and Huascar, and went to the window. The sun was across the gulf and wouldn't be long disappearing behind the mountainous point of Baja.

'I guess you're not going to tell me why I came looking for you?'

Radulovic didn't answer. The skiptrace turned.

'How about the other five guys? Can you come up with anything on them?'

'I could try. You staying in Mocorito?'

'Got a room inna hotel. You figure they'll let me back in?'

The beekeeper smiled. 'I'll dig through those memories. Will you come back in the morning?'

Vanesco wasn't sure that he'd get back down the track, much less up it again, but said he would. All he had to do was get through the night with the questions that were now troubling him.

Seven

Vanesco's hotel room had been searched. He sensed it immediately, and on checking things out he knew he had been done by a professional. That increased his unease. Mocorito

47

wasn't a place he expected to find anyone who could search a hotel room in that way. There were a couple of cops in town, but had it been them they'd have busted in and taken things apart. Whoever it was had done it without assistance from the guy who ran the Insunza hotel, for although there was hostility in the sly looking face behind the desk, it had signaled nothing.

There wasn't a thing in the room that would have told anyone anything, and that, paradoxically, would have told the intruder a lot. Vanesco didn't check his bag. There would be nothing missing. He had another visitor, he noticed, as he pulled out of his clothes to wash off the dust. A lizard scrabbled out of the sink and slid into a crack where the basin was coming off the wall. He thought about his visitor who had been less conspicuous, what interested parties were involved here. The CIA had become the most obvious, and that begged several questions: why he had been hired to run these guys to earth, what they had done, why they were suddenly important. Also he wanted to know who he was really working for.

Thinking back over this trip, Vanesco recalled a feeling he had of being followed. It wasn't paranoia, he decided, yet had no more substance for the conclusion than an impression formed at Durango airport of a man in a tan leather jacket watching him; then later in Culiacan an awareness of a tan leather jacket, the face unseen, the presence unquestioned until now.

His thoughts moved onto to Peter Radulovic; what he was now, the way he lived, bore no relation to whatever he had once been. If Harry Kohn, or whoever it was behind him, figured Radulovic was a threat, then Vanesco decided he would have to set them straight. He would do that when he called New York and turned in his information. He would tell Kohn about the beekeeper, whose existence was totally innocuous. Vanesco knew a badass, was better than most at spotting someone who was dangerous; that wasn't Radulovic. Again the skiptrace came back to the question of what he had done, and wondered about his five former partners, if they would prove equally harmless. Maybe they were somehow making amends, reconciling their past existences, if not to Kohn, at least to themselves. What right did he have to intrude, dredge up the past? Vanesco was startled by his thoughts, and surprised at the effect Radulovic had had on him. Five hundred bucks a day plus expenses didn't give him the right, he told himself. Neither did the reasons of the guy hiring him nor the deeds of the person he was tracing. That was why in the past he hadn't questioned motives, his usually accurate assumption being that whoever was a badass, which was justification enough. But now there was Peter Radulovic. If Kohn had asked him to take care of those six guys, Vanesco realized how his decision about Radulovic would have come out, he would have gotten a free ride. But all he was required to do was call New York, give Radulovic's location; that should have been no problem. There would be some kind of follow up, and that was something he'd have no control over.

Raising the old-fashioned telephone, Vanesco asked the clerk to get him New York. He was told he would call him back.

Vanesco was in the dimly lit barroom when he got his call to New York. It was put through to the lobby where the booth was brown with cigarette tar and flyblown, and had a rank smell of stale animal fat and human sweat. The booth was hot, but he closed the door. Through the crackle he could detect Zell's surprise; usually he didn't call while he was away. Concern followed, and that made him feel good. She wanted to know if he was okay.

'I'm fine,' he told her. 'I just wanted to talk.'

'Gee, that's really nice, Jimmy. I'm missing you – I just put it aside, figuring I wouldn't hear till you got back.'

That was even better. 'I guess I'll be a day or two,' he said. He had plans to head directly to Canada. 'I wish I was getting in tonight.'

'So do I,' Zell said.

They talked awhile, Vanesco finally ringing off without telling her his problem. Conditioning rather than lack of trust stopped him. He had learned to deal with those needs which most people had to articulate their fears and doubts, a shutter instinctively operated inside him. It would take intense debriefing to change that.

49

After the conversation he felt lonely and would have preferred being with someone. He thought about going back up
the mountain to talk again with Radulovic, but knew there
was no way he'd make it in the dark. He decided instead to
eat.

Mocorito was too far south of the border for tourists and
west of nowhere, so there were few places to eat that he
would risk. The waitress in the only place he would risk
using gave him a lot of attention when she brought him
buritos and chili beans. She was plump and pretty and about
eighteen, and at twenty-eight would have thickened out of
recognition. When she brought him his second beer he
invited her to sit. The girl didn't even consider that she
shouldn't. Her ambition was to get to the US, where she had
four brothers. She had no money, but wanted to go in legally,
so she could work with children, and did Vanesco know
anyone who could help her. He smiled and shook his head.
He didn't want to lie his way into her pants. He couldn't get
her into the States, other than illegally. He figured she might
not return after she went to give the only other customer his
check, but was glad when she did.

'D'you know Peter Radulovic?' he asked.

That same attitude prevailed. She avoided his eyes.

'He's the beekeeper up at Cerro Blanco. I was there today,'
he announced like he was giving her some startling information.

'Are you police?'

He told her he wasn't.

'The people here wouldn't like it if cops came after Señor
Radulovic.' She knew not why they might come after him,
only that he was a good man. She told him how Radulovic
had worked to save people after the earthquakes, that the
people thought him a saint.

Vanesco understood then why people had reacted as they
had. This made him more curious to know what Radulovic
had done to make him so important. Whatever it was,
Vanesco figured he deserved a break. Ordinarily, he accepted
that a man couldn't escape his past, what it was, what he had
done, was immutable. The nature of his work supported the
philosophy. Only now he wasn't sure. Maybe if a man gave

enough of himself, made a sufficient commitment he could escape the consequences of his past. Those who tried running were the ones who couldn't escape, those people Vanesco caught up with and dealt with. Peter Radulovic had stopped running.

Vanesco had made his decision about the beekeeper: he wouldn't call New York. Maybe information about what Radulovic had done would change his mind, but he didn't think so.

Feeling a curious sense of relief on arriving at that decision, Vanesco thought maybe he should drive up and tell Radulovic right then, but the thought of that track even in daylight made him sweat.

Instead he found himself propositioning the waitress. What she saw in his offer he neither knew nor questioned, nor did he question why he went along this path; not as an alternative to loneliness. A one night stand in a hotel room wasn't the answer to loneliness anymore than masturbation was, it merely relieved a physiological need. What this amounted to was a bad habit.

The clerk was missing from the alcove when Vanesco came back to the hotel. That spared him embarrassment, and possibly the girl more.

In the bedroom she undressed directly, though she turned her back on him as she stepped out of her frock; her bra and pants she removed under the sheet. Vanesco was surprised, and would have made some pretense at affection. He would have been less surprised had she asked for money.

As they made love, he thought about Zell, not to compare them. The girl's lack of inhibition matched his lack of discretion, he realized afterwards. Who was she? This was a small Mexican town, he was a stranger, everyone would know. The issue wasn't moral but emotional. The people here resented him asking about Peter Radulovic; they might resent him more for this.

Vanesco wasn't asleep when the girl climbed out of bed and dressed, but was aware of the care she took not to disturb him; she lifted his pants carefully off the chair and went through his pockets. Vanesco didn't check how much she took, figuring she was smart enough not to take everything.

It was better this way, as he often felt that offering money in such circumstances was insulting, the assumption being that a service was being provided.

The two cops who burst into the room weren't concerned about disturbing Vanesco. The sun was way over the rim of the mountain and the morning was hot. The first cop lashed at Vanesco, the barrel of his gun cutting his face. He might have pistol whipped him but for the other cop getting in the way. Vanesco couldn't figure out whether he was trying to stop his partner or help him.

'You motherfucker!' he screamed, and scrambled out of bed, noticing now the angry, unreasoning faces crowding the doorway. His hand reached up the Browning, and when he blasted the wall over their heads, the cops froze, silence fell.

'What the fuck are you at?' Vanesco demanded. He was naked, his cheek smarting as blood dripped onto his chest. 'Get the fuck outta here. You! Vamoose!' The men in the doorway did so.

Vanesco didn't attempt to take the cops' guns.

'You killed Señor Radulovic.'

The news hit Vanesco hard. 'He's dead?' He sought one clear thought: the person who had searched his room came at him. 'How the fuck is he dead? I left him, he was fine yesterday.'

'He was found this morning when Roberto Valdez took him goats' milk. He had hung himself.'

Vanesco didn't believe that he had killed himself. 'He was fine when I left him,' he repeated.

'You coming here, sẽnor. You caused his death.'

'No way, pal,' he argued, trying to mitigate his part, to deal with his feeling of culpability.

When the policemen calmed down and put their guns away, Vanesco told his story as he dressed. He was there to find Radulovic for a New York attorney, as he had been left an inheritance – how that sat with his traveling with a 9mm Browning they didn't say. He didn't tell them his room was searched, or his feeling about being tailed, or the belief that Radulovic wouldn't have committed suicide. That would have complicated things, which were his to deal with.

No one could be in law enforcement without some close encounter with death. That fact of life Vanesco hadn't been spared in the FBI. Although in that Bureau he hadn't encountered suicide as frequently as regular patrolmen did, he had seen it often enough to know that wasn't how Radulovic had died.

Radulovic had supposedly hung himself from a beam in the roof, but allowing for the rope stretching, there wasn't the height to make such a death viable. Instead he would have choked slowly. An autopsy would show death by strangulation, and probably it would be recorded as suicide. There was nothing Vanesco could do about it right then.

'Was this how the room was when he was found?' Vanesco asked, casting his eyes about the dwelling.

'Nothing has been touched.' The cops were reasonable now.

As a trained observer, Vanesco noted details. The wooden chair that Radulovic had supposedly stood on to jump was conveniently tipped over, only had he stood on it he would have been stooped beneath the roof. It didn't make sense.

As details of the beekeeper's death along with those of his life crowded in on him so Vanesco began to feel a combination of rage, frustration, depression. He understood why the cops had burst in as they had. Somehow he was responsible for Radulovic's death, and whether he was murdered or committed suicide was immaterial. There was nothing he could do about it other than go forward, maybe discover why he had to die, and who killed him.

Maybe there was no way Radulovic could escape this, that it was impossible for him to escape the consequences of his past. However, that didn't make Vanesco feel better for his involvement. Instead he thought about how if he had tried to make it up there last night he might have prevented this. In reality he could probably only have prevented it happening last night. He thought of the waitress, whether she had any part; then about that possible tail in the tan leather jacket.

The police had no objection to him looking around, it was as if they preferred him do this job. Vanesco didn't expect to find anything, believing whoever had killed Radulovic would have been thorough. Instinct told him there would be nothing around connected to the man's past or to tell what he had done, or who he was, nor who his partners were. He searched just the same.

Huascar was missing, Vanesco realized. The dog would certainly have barked on their arrival. He asked the cops if they had seen him. There was only the burro in the corral.

He searched for the dog with a slight feeling of nausea, fearing that whoever had taken out Peter Radulovic might have killed his dog also.

He eventually found him, dead, but with no mark of violence where it lay among the beehives. At first Vanesco thought it was asleep, but there was partial rigor, which indicated it had been dead a while. There were no flies around the dog's body, Vanesco noticed, which was unusual. Then he noticed something more odd, there were no bees. He had walked among the hives without registering the fact. When he checked he found hive after hive empty. It was as if the dog and bees knew their keeper was dead and so had moved on.

Vanesco shivered in the hot sun. When he finally left the place it was with an odd feeling, one he knew would be a long time leaving him.

Eight

The plane into Thunder Bay circled for thirty minutes, waiting for the weather to clear. Western Ontario along with much of Minnesota had a snowstorm. In late March spring was usually showing itself, but now people were wondering what had gone wrong. Delayed spring planting would put livelihoods in jeopardy.

Circling above the storm in that Boeing and peering out at

the dense, swirling grayness, Vanesco's concern was whether they would actually get down. There was talk of diverting back across the US border. The problem that would cause was inconvenience. If put to it, he guessed, like most people who regularly took planes, he would rather go at risk than be inconvenienced.

Jimmy Vanesco did a lot of his thinking in airplanes, finding that a useful alternative to watching movies, or eating dull, overprocessed food. At that moment the other option was contemplating the plane smashing up on trying to land.

He thought about the reaction he had got in New York to his call about Peter Radulovic. Harry Kohn received word of the beekeeper's death passively, like it was of no interest. That had angered Vanesco. A man whom he had determined harmless had died because Kohn had hired his services, so the least Kohn could do, he figured, was show interest. He wanted to know why Kohn didn't care, and guessed it was pointless asking.

Reviewing the information he had given Kohn about his lead on Brad Coley, he questioned if that wasn't a mistake. It was information Kohn was paying for, but Vanesco figured it might somehow result in another death. Maybe Coley was equally harmless.

Right then Vanesco questioned if he shouldn't head back to New York as soon as his plane got down someplace, and quit this job. However, then he might never discover why the beekeeper had died. Finding out would do Radulovic no good, but Vanesco needed to know; he doubted that such knowledge would make anything right but it justified his going on.

The captain came over the address system to tell them the storm was easing, that they were landing. He told them not to worry as he had done this lots of times.

His piloting skill wasn't questioned, but there was a hush in the plane as the snow-covered ground loomed through the cloud. This was broken by the bump and lurch as the wheels churned along the runway and the aircraft slowed.

Having arrived from Mexico with only one transfer in Chicago, the cold here struck Vanesco forcefully. Spring had been shaking itself awake in New York; clothes that had been fine for Mocorito were something else in Thunder Bay. A woollen hat and parka were needed.

Along with boots more suitable for snow, the quilted coat and hat made him less conspicuous as he left Thunder Bay in his rented Dodge, taking highway 17 north around Lake Superior. He had a two-hundred-mile drive, with a stopoff for some sleep before he began in earnest to run down Brad Coley.

After his experience in Mexico Vanesco was conscious of the possibility of being followed, so checked at every stop he made. If he was followed, then Vanesco had to admit that whoever was better at the game than him, so there was nothing he could do.

Like most of Western Ontario, Randle Point had been taken by surprise with the late snowstorm. Just when they should have been getting ready for the tourists who started arriving around mid-April, they were sitting out the snow. Randle Point consisted of two dozen or so houses huddled for protection along the foreshore, with a general store that looked more like a ship's chandlers. It was there Vanesco made his first stop. He bought a map.

'What are the chances of hiring a boat around here?'

'Pretty good, I guess,' the young woman clerk said. She had an intelligent face, and looked like she had nothing other than this store to occupy her. 'There isn't too much going on right now. What kinda boat you looking for, ay?'

'Something pretty sturdy. A friend of mine was up here the summer before last. He rented a boat and skipper. The guy's name was Coley. I do believe it was. Brad Coley. Does that sound right to you?'

He watched the girl. There was no immediate reaction.

'Could be. I wouldn't know. He maybe runs a boat up here in the summer and takes off for the city when the snow comes. A lot do that.'

'The life's pretty tough up here?'

'You like snow, it's just fine, ay.'

'You don't like snow,' Vanesco said.

'There are other things about the life. Makes six months of snow unimportant.' A look in her eyes said she was remembering a previous way of life. Suddenly she became aware of him, and smiled. 'You got any notion what this guy with the boat looks like, ay? I might recognize him. You get to know your neighbors here. It's kinda nice.'

'He's about six feet, hundred and seventy pounds. Hell, I only saw him once in a bar in Thunder Bay,' he said, trying to make his story plausible. 'I think he had brown hair, dark brown eyes.' The details were from the file Cunningham had given him. He guessed some of it might have changed during the intervening years.

'You sure his name was Coley?'

'I ain't sure of anything, honey. Only that he was a pretty neat boatman.'

'Why not call your friend up, get the guy's name, ay?' It was an intelligent question.

'He's in Asia looking for oil.'

'Well, I can't help you. But don't let that put you off, he could be back in the woods some place.'

'It's no big deal. You wanna recommend another boatman?'

The man she recommended wasn't Brad Coley, but a gnarled, taciturn ferryman who looked older than he probably was. He lived in a house off on its own along the foreshore. When Vanesco asked he could hire him and his boat he was told he could in a way that ended conversation. The skiptrace asked him when he was available; was told anytime.

'When the weather clears, ay,' the boatman added.

That could be days, which suited Vanesco fine. He figured he could run Coley down faster on foot.

'You figure the snow'll clear soon?' Vanesco was trying to keep the conversation going.

'Maybe,' came the reply.

Vancesco figured this kind of reserve nearer to the nature of the people around here. The girl in the store was an outsider who had chosen this alternative, while the boatman had been born to the life. These were woods people who happened to live on the foreshore, and the fact that the whole area saw an annual influx of tourists made no difference to their insular outlook. He wasn't curious about Vanesco's accent, nor interested where he came from. Visitors came to hire his

57

boat, that was why he stayed on the foreshore.

'You know Brad Coley? He's got a yard this way.'

The boatman looked at him, and finally said, 'He won't give you no better deal, mister.'

'I'm hiring your boat. You wanna deposit?' He gave him fifty dollars. 'Where do I find Coley?'

The man shook his head. 'You could maybe find Cole Bradley, ay.'

Vanesco had known a lot of dumber name changes. He waited, but the man offered nothing more. 'Where is he?'

'Got an outfit over Terrace Bay, ay.'

There was a chance that Bradley wouldn't be the man he was looking for, but Vanesco felt he was moving forward.

'He ain't there. I heard he took a boat across to Lake Nipigon.'

The skiptrace headed out to Terrace Bay, which had a distinctly British look to it, like the folks here would have preferred to be in Britain. There were Union Jacks to be seen, and homes with names like Lakeview and Pantiles. Vanesco had no problem finding Cole Bradley, only he wasn't Brad Coley. This man was fat and six inches shorter than Coley's record said he was.

'Someone gave you a bum steer, fella, ay,' Bradley said. 'It happens, ay.'

'You get a lotta guys looking for Coley, ay?' Everyone up here seemed to suffix their sentences with ay, Vanesco noticed, and started doing it himself.

'It happens. I think the fella you want runs a coupla fishing boats outta Randle Point throughout the summer. Lives with his old woman in Nipigon in the winter.'

Vanesco wondered if the bum steer had been intentional, and if it was because one boatman didn't want to lose a customer or because he knew something.

'Is that what he calls himself? Brad Coley?'

'I guess, ay.'

It took Vanesco the whole of the next day to run down Brad Coley, and then it was his old woman and their five-year-old son whom he found. The woman was attractive, her age he guessed was late 20s. It was difficult to tell as her large round eyes were that swollen with tears.

With a distracted gesture she invited him in off the wind-blasted stoop.

'You from the RCMP, ay?' she said, assuming he was.

Vanesco watched her, wondering about her distress. He resisted asking questions about Coley.

'Jesus. He was always so careful about gassing up his boat. It's not sinking in. He was always so damn careful. I can't believe this. I'm waiting for someone to call and tell me it's a dumb joke. Tell me he's not dead, ay.'

She waited, hoping Vanesco was the bearer of that news. He shook his head, feeling that was indicated. Vanesco had the ability to walk into a situation like this, listen in a knowing manner, and finish knowing all there was to know.

Brad Coley had died earlier that day while gassing up his boat. The engine was hot after a trip and spilt gasoline had ignited. There was little of the boat left by the time the alarm was raised, and less of Coley. His body was cinder, and the prospect of having to go to Marathon to identify it distressed this woman. She was grateful for Vanesco's offer to go with her.

The numbness lifted briefly and she realized he wasn't a cop. He told her he had been hired to find Coley, but doubted she could deal with any more information.

She let out a cry on seeing Coley's charred remains, and turned, burying her face against Vanesco. Her cry affected him more than the incinerated body in the garage that served as the mortuary out back of the highway patrol post. Worse than the sight of swollen, blackened flesh was the smell, a cloying, sickmaking sweetness that caught in the throat.

The policeman who was with them in the small room looked embarrasssed, yet he was neither young nor inexperienced. He needed the identification for his report, but didn't push, and when his eyes met Vanesco's the skiptrace made it. Vanesco led the woman out and across the yard to her son, who had waited in the police post. The boy was either oblivious to his father's death, or uncaring, Vanesco couldn't tell which without knowing what kind of relationship they had. He had always believed caring for family just because of that relationship an odd social conditioning. Maybe the five-year-old boy instinctively felt the same.

'We going home now, Mom, ay?' He set his picture book aside.

There were some formalities. They didn't take long, but weren't something Vanesco could do. Basically form-filling that consigned Brad Coley to the hereafter via a post mortem examination.

As he waited Vanesco thought things through. His assumption was that he wasn't connected with this death as he hadn't found him, he hadn't led anyone to him. But possibly Coley had heard on the local grapevine that he was being sought, and as a result got careless.

The four-roomed cabin Coley had at Randle Point was starkly furnished, and parked alongside the utilitarian furniture were parts of boat engines, outboards, fishing tackle. Vanesco guessed every inch of this place reminded Brad Coley's common law wife of him. In her position he would have wanted to walk away from it.

Rum was the only booze in the cabin and Vanesco needed a drink as much as the woman, if for different reasons.

Moyra Yeston needed to talk, and Vanesco was prepared to listen. They drank the rum, and after eating soup, heated out of a can, the boy fell asleep and was put to bed. Vanesco felt tired but had no bed, so listened while Moyra Yeston, running on nervous energy, told of her life with Coley. She inevitably romanticized, but creeping through her disconnected words was an impression of a man the skiptrace didn't like. She said Coley was strong and independent; Vanesco read him as cold and withdrawn. Maybe this opinion was projection on his part rather than based on the words of this woman who loved him, and presumably knew him better than most over the six years they were together, who had borne him a child. Yet the feeling of remoteness and indifference toward his family continued to appear as she talked and drank and cried, and said how she still felt he was around. There was no laughter, no joy; where it existed between two people it always came out after one was gone. There was none, and that made Vanesco sad for her beyond the immediate feeling of grief. She was clinging to illusions.

Shortly after the bottle had died and she had talked herself out and cried herself out, she fell asleep. Vanesco picked her up and carried her to her bed, where he undressed her as far as her bra and pants, and covered her. The smart thing would have been to have gotten into bed alongside her, as she might have woken with a desperate feeling of loneliness, helplessness, needing someone to hold for comfort. More practically there was no spare bed in the cabin.

Instead he found some coffee and set a pot on the stove. While waiting for it to boil he idly checked the room. Afterwards he made a detailed search. The main room of the cabin told nothing of Brad Coley, revealing to Vanesco a man who had led a secretive life, purposely leaving no clues. This was the kind of existence a professional would choose, and not necessarily a professional who worked for the Mafia; that type, usually driven by ego, constructed worlds to their immortality. What Coley had done was strip his life bare.

The feeling recurred of things being involved on a bigger level than the brief Vanesco had been given. There were questions he had to ask back in New York, ones he'd want answers to.

He searched the boy's room, not expecting to find anything, nor in the woman's bedroom. But his professionalism dictated the search. Moyra Yeston disturbed while he was in her room, mumbled incoherently and threw off the bedclothes. Vanesco replaced them. Thinking about the life she must have had with Coley, a feeling of sadness slid across him. They could have had no present or future without the past, as everything had to be built on falsehood. People could pretend to be anything they wanted, that was okay and sometimes necessary to get through the day, but he knew relationships couldn't be built on lies.

The morning was bright and warm and began melting the recent snow. Vanesco woke tired from an uncomfortable couch, but felt better for moving around. He checked the cupboards. There was no food in so he walked to the store to get some breakfast. The few people around at that hour gave him curious looks, but said nothing. At the store a man was poking at a wood burning stove, looking to get some heat out of it. He greeted Vanesco.

'She soon heats up. You're about early, ay.'

'Got hungry,' Vanesco told him.

'We can sure do something about that. You staying around here, ay?'

'Over at the Coley place.' He watched the man.

'Jesus, ay. That was a real bad business him going like that. Real bad. You family?'

'A friend. You know him well?'

'I know there wasn't a thing he couldn't tell you about boats. S'why it was a surprise. Jesus. I'd a said he'd a known better, ay.'

'Accidents happen.'

'All the time. What can I get you, mister, ay?'

Vanesco ordered some eggs, milk, bread and cereal, and paid the man. 'You know him long?'

'You'd see him around. His old lady's taking it pretty bad, ay?'

'He have any kind of trouble around here?'

'He kept pretty much to himself. You wan' something else?'

Vanesco didn't, and figured he wouldn't get much more by way of information.

The woman was up when he got back. She was surprised to see him.

'I figured you'd split,' she said.

He smiled. 'I got some breakfast.'

'Yeah, we don't keep too much around during the winter.' She took the bag of food.

'He's not dead, you know,' she said suddenly while preparing food at the stove.

Vanesco waited.

'It's this odd feeling I have that Brad's still around.' She looked at him. 'You figure I'm crazy, ay. People do when I say things like that. I'm kinda psychic. I pick up real quick on vibrations. I'd know if he was dead. I'd just know.'

'Is that all you have, a feeling?' asked Vanesco.

'You *do* figure I'm crazy, ay?'

He shook his head. 'I think you're having a bad time. People grab at whatever hope, it happens. Sometimes it's better to let go, it hurts more in the beginning but less in the end.'

'I still got this feeling.'

That wasn't something Vanesco could dismiss by convincing himself that she was a dingbat, or plain upset. He sometimes had similar feelings, which mostly he chose to ignore, and which subsequently often proved to be right. So who was to say she wasn't right?

'Well,' he began, 'why'd he want to disappear?'

'Maybe because you're here, ay.'

Vanesco shook his head. 'That's no reason, sweetheart. I could be good news. I figure he didn't know I was up here.'

'I had a feeling about that too. Like Brad was always expecting someone to come looking for him. Especially after one of his trips.'

'Tell me about his trips?'

'What's to tell? He did a lot of shit. Randle Point doesn't rate its own getwell man.'

'He go across the border for his supply?'

'Mostly. He used to take his boat. He'd be away two or three days.'

That was a possible connection with the Mafia. 'If Coley didn't die in that boat, you know what that means.' He waited, she didn't respond. 'Means he took out some luckless guy and burned him. You figure he was capable?'

She thought about it. 'I think Brad would be capable.'

That uneasy feeling Vanesco had been getting about this case floated to the surface. Life might have been simpler for him if it was Coley who died in that boat—and it wasn't proven that he hadn't. This left the skiptrace with more questions unanswered, and a stronger conviction that the answers were in New York with Harry Kohn.

None of which Vanesco laid on the RCMP when he stopped in Marathon to see if there were any developments on Coley's death. An autopsy had established that the boatman had hung one on, there being a high alcohol content in the body. Vanesco wanted to ask if there were traces of heroin also, but that might have opened something up for the local cops that Vanesco didn't want them in on.

'You didn't leave your car back in the woods off Randle Point, ay?' the cop asked.

'It's right outside.'

'Sure. Someone left a US registered automobile up there

63

and ain't been back. We're running a check on the owner. I guess he could be out hunting. They sometimes get lost and show up a couple of days later, ay.'

Not this time. The thought flashed through Vanesco's head that the car owner was dead, burned out in Coley's boat. That meant Brad Coley was alive and running. Vanesco was certain.

Nine

'Mr Cunningham is in a meeting and can't be interrupted, sir.' Three times Vanesco had gotten a similar message, and was angry.

The same response from the smiling secretary when he went to the attorney's office didn't deter him.

'Go and tell Mr Cunningham that I figure to wait no matter how long his meeting goes on.'

The woman, who looked like she dressed out of Brooks Brothers, went to interrupt her boss. His meeting was terminated instantly.

'I'm sorry about that, Mr Vanesco,' he said, waving the skiptrace into a chair. 'There's been pressure all week. How can I help you?' He sat, avoiding Vanesco's eyes.

'You assume that's why I came? Not to give a progress report?' Vanesco was trying to make him defensive. A worried man was often careless.

'You're dealing directly with Mr Kohn. This approach indicates some problem.'

'You gonna help me overcome it, Mr Cunningham?'

'I can't . . .' he stopped and changed tack. 'Unless you tell me what it is.'

Vanesco looked at him until the lawyer turned away. 'Who I'm working for? And why are these six guys wanted?'

'You're working for Harry Kohn.'

'Horseshit!'

'Mr Kohn is the client,' Cunningham insisted. 'Why these men are being sought—I didn't ask, and you don't as a rule.'

'The first two guys I've so far come up with on that list have died. Coincidence? S'that how you figure the American Bar Association will react?'

'What the hell are you talking about, Vanesco? Are you crazy? One man committed suicide, the other died in an accident. Nothing extraordinary there.'

'Is that how you figure it sitting in your plush fucking office making smart fucking deals? You guys oughta get down onna street, find out what the fuck real people with real feelings are doing. There was a man down in Mexico who meant a lot of things to a lot of people who don't count squat. When I saw him he was about as far from suicide as you are. The guy in Canada knew too much about boats to die that way. Someone moving in behind me, is how I see it. I figure I'm owed some answers.'

'There aren't any I can give you.'

Vanesco rose. 'You're full of shit.'

'What do you plan on doing?' He was worried now.

'I plan on getting some answers.'

Harry Kohn was expecting Vanesco and took the same line as the attorney, said he didn't have the answers Vanesco was after.

Anger flashed in those round, bulging eyes in Kohn's fleshy face at Vanesco's demands.

'Unless I get some answers,' Vanesco said, 'you'd better find some other sucker to run the other guys down.'

'Who the fuck d'you think you are, Vanesco? Coming in here making them fucking demands. I ain't gonna crap myself at your threats. You get this straight, asshole, you don't threaten me. I'm Harry Kohn, I threaten people and when I do they're in trouble. That includes you. I hired you for a fucking job, which you ain't halfway done, pal. You'd better get it done. Right.'

Vanesco looked at him, understanding just how dangerous he was, but refused to be intimidated. 'I want some additional information.'

Kohn's anger flared again. 'There's none available. Not to you, me or anyone else.'

'Who am I working for? Cunningham?'

'Harry Kohn. That's who.'

Vanesco shook his head.

Throwing his chair back, Kohn sprang up, putting himself in a solid position, feet apart, his shoulders arched, head down. The sense of that menace Kohn gave off was something people usually heeded.

'You're going the right way to end up in the East River. You came highly recommended, I was told you didn't ask questions, that you were smart, did what you were paid for.'

'I don't like being used by some Mafia gimbo.' He watched the man's anger go higher, but didn't believe he would launch an attack.

'You cocksucker! I'll break your fucking arms.'

'I guess you could with a little help. You want me to find those other guys, you gotta come up with who's behind you. Why those guys are being knocked off.'

'You don't quit unless I say so,' Kohn said, stabbing the air between them.

'Blow it out your ass. I just quit.'

As he started out of the office, which smelt of aftershave and deodorant, Kohn grabbed him, and in the next instant found himself looking along the barrel of Vanesco's Browning.

'You owe me money, Vanesco,' was all he could say.

'It covered my exes. I don't make refunds.'

'You quit me, you mother, you'll regret it.'

The eyes of the man issuing that threat were those of someone who could have killed without concern, with no more emotion than fleeting anger. They were dark, violent eyes that showed the whites beneath the irises.

'You want me back on this, get me the information I want. Meanwhile I got other clients.' Vanesco put up his Browning.

Harry Kohn didn't try to stop the skiptrace. There was no way he could stop a guy who carried that kind of piece.

66

Whoever he sent after him now would have to be good, for Vanesco was good, and more, he would be expecting something. Two things were certain in Kohn's mind, one was that Vanesco wouldn't get away with a stunt like this, he believed himself too important to have a gumshoe dictate the terms; and two he wouldn't let the guy in back of him know. Not because he was scared of that man, rather because he respected him and knew one day he would possibly be one of the most powerful men in America. As to the information Vanesco wanted, Kohn couldn't tell him what it was those guys had done. Maybe the smart thing would have been to have given Vanesco a story about those guys being real badasses, then he wouldn't have given a shit about them getting burned. But Vanesco wasn't dumb, fooling him wouldn't be easy.

At his desk Kohn raised the phone and punched out a Brooklyn number from memory. The phone was answered directly. He didn't identify himself.

'Howard. Something's gotta be done about Vanesco.'

The voice at the other end sounded like a coarse file across soft metal. 'When?'

'Soon. Stop by after lunch. Make it early. I plan on going to Washington later today.' He gave the man no option. If he had something on he'd cancel it. Kohn always took priority.

Kohn hit the button on the stainless steel intercom.

'Jenny, get me a seat on a Washington plane around 5pm. Make sure I gotta suite at the Statler-Hilton.'

Harry Kohn didn't like Washington DC or its people. His associates there were politicians and although corrupt, most had the unhappy knack of making him appear inferior. In Washington DC a large part of the privileged section considered antecedence more important than clubhouse connection, this made Kohn feel uncomfortable. Politicians, like everyone else, cried for favors on the way up, and when at the top resented the indebtedness. He wondered if that was how it would get to be with Larry Wallechinsky, but decided not. The other side of Washington was black, which to Kohn meant dope and prostitution, though he no longer had any direct contact with that.

The Statler-Hilton wasn't the best hotel in town and catered a lot to fat conventions but Kohn liked it for its anonymity. This hotel was like New York in its attitude toward guests, if you could pay the going rate then you were the best there was. Kohn believed that's how it should be, rather than some asshole looking down at you because he no longer needed your help.

Politicians of today were something else, Kohn reflected as he called Wallechinsky's number. He preferred the old style politician who took the graft and made a commitment, this lot took the money then got skittish about some Senate or House investigatory committee, and were forever looking over their shoulders. The problem was those media cocksuckers were always trying to expose them, and if they weren't then some hero with a wire on was. Times were changing, priorities with them. No one wanted to be just rich anymore, but a household name also.

'Gimme Larry Wallechinsky,' Kohn said into the phone.

'I'm sorry, sir. Mr Wallechinsky is at a meting right now. Who shall I say's calling?'

Her tone changed when Kohn identified himself. There was a pause, then Wallechinsky came on.

'How are you, Harry?' Wallechinsky said.

'Fine. We should meet soon.'

'That'd be good.' He stopped. 'You in town?'

'Sure, I think we should have dinner tonight.'

'That's difficult. With the Senate Foreign Relations Committee sitting. How important is it?'

'Pretty important,' Kohn confirmed.

'What time's good for you, Harry?'

They arranged to have dinner at a club with a private dining room. When he replaced the phone, Kohn felt uneasy, as if Wallechinsky was brushing him aside. But he guessed the Senate Foreign Relations Committee was making the ambassador-elect nervous. Wallechinsky needed him more than anyone right now, and because of the services he was currently providing their relationship would continue as he progressed to higher office.

The private dining room at the Forties Club in Georgetown was discreet. Being seen with or boasting about the politicians you had in your pocket, like in the old days, made no sense.

68

Harry Kohn at fifty-two was neither an old Mustache Pete nor a new style Mafia boss, but figured he could handle whatever came his way. He could send in cops to eliminate the opposition or torpedoes, and whichever it was he personally always remained at a safe distance. Apart from talking to Howard out in Brooklyn, Kohn avoided contact with street-level hoods. They were dangerous; now he was a respectable businessman it was better to use people like Cunningham, and the skiptrace. He thought about Vanesco and started to get mad again. The guy had some balls. Kohn not only felt pissed off that he had walked out, but embarrassed about what he would have to tell Wallechinsky. The former deputy director of the CIA had been assured that what he had requested would be a simple matter; a mistake had been made in the choice of Vanesco. Maybe Wallechinsky would be prepared to put out the information that would get Vanesco back working, but Kohn felt sure he wouldn't, and as a result Howard would be let loose on the skiptrace.

The dining club where Kohn and Wallechinsky met was out of a vanished epoch, a world of gracious living. Waiters in black tails stole in and out of the red-plush dining rooms, purposely not hearing conversations or noticing the company. The dining club was neutral ground and any political persuasion could meet the opposition there without fear of misrepresentation. The only media people around were the tame kind who reported what their hosts wanted them to.

Despite this Lawrence Wallechinsky felt nervous in Kohn's company, not because of what Kohn was, rather because he was an immediate reminder to Wallechinsky of his own past. Currently appearing before the Senate Foreign Relations Committee, seeking confirmation in his appointment as US Ambassador to China, his past was the biggest likely impediment. The ambassadorship was important to Wallechinsky, who had close links with the Chinese leadership, and would provide a major stepping stone, without which his political career might not get started; certainly it wouldn't finish where he had planned, in the White House.

'You're looking in great shape, Harry,' Wallechinsky said across the table.

'I've taken up handball. Keeps you pretty fit.'

'That's what I need, more exercise. I should take up tennis again. I was good at college.'

'I figure it's gonna beat me, Larry. I'll be in there knocking that ball around, and zip. A past number.'

'Not looking as good as you do.'

The waiter returned to take their order. Wallechinsky chose onion soup and rack of lamb with rosemary to follow; Kohn went for prawns, a mid-rare steak, despite the club having one of Washington's best French chefs. They drank Charmes-Chambertin with their food, not because either knew about wine, though the ambassador designate was learning, rather because only people who could afford the best used the club.

'We have a problem?' Wallechinsky said as they settled into the main course. The waiter was gone, the door closed.

'Looks that way.' He told him about Vanesco.

'How dangerous is this man, Harry?' His tone remained level, despite anxiety.

'He's curious. That could make him dangerous. The cocksucker!' Anger exploded through his embarrassment. 'He wants to know who had me hire him and why those guys are wanted.'

'Is he going to keep asking?'

'What's there to know? He figures they broke the rules. He's smart. Normally he asks no questions but does what you hire him for.'

'What went wrong?'

Kohn raised his powerful shoulders. 'He figured the guys were harmless, that someone was moving in behind him. I didn't have no one do that. He's crazy.'

The man in the midnight blue tuxedo looked at his guest, but said nothing.

'How much of a problem is it having him quit?' asked Kohn.

'I want to know where the other four are, Harry.'

Kohn wiped beef juice off his chin, then blew his nose on the napkin. He hadn't finished his meal. 'I'll take care of it. No problem.'

'It remains to be seen what Vanesco's plans are. Either he's hired back, for whatever reason you give him, or make

70

certain he quits for good. What must happen before I take up my appointment, is I find the other four men.'

Wallechinsky spoke in an unemotional manner, as if reading a grocery list. There was no need for emotion, anger or fear; he trusted the man he was talking to. Had he the opportunity to re-enact his past he would have chosen not to be associated with Kohn, but that was a fact he couldn't change. Now all he could do was conduct himself as discreetly as possible with the likes of Harry Kohn. Although Kohn was now ostensibly head of a conglomerate, and a very glib political fund raiser, his antecedents were traceable and could do no one who was associated with him any good. Wallechinsky considered him a friend, but kept a sense of perspective: even friends could be a source of danger. There was no way he was prepared to have his past dredged up, he had worked too hard for any cost to be too high in burying it. The only thing standing between him and his future was his past, and the ambassador designate was rewriting that.

Ten

Since his appointment as ambassador designate to China anxiety had settled in the pit of Lawrence Wallechinsky's stomach like a knot of fatty, indigestible food. The reason was that six men, who as far as anyone knew, had long ago disappeared off the face of the earth, had risen like specters from his past, ready to destroy his future. Recently they had cost him more sleepless nights. Most other things had now been taken care of, the record rewritten, witnesses to the deeds obliterated, or rendered harmless. But those six men whom he had used when he had been number two in the CIA had been too alert to the dangers and had avoided being silenced;

he had believed that intervening years and the cover the six men had been given made them no less dangerous to go after. The real or imagined danger in looking for them was that it might have alerted them and caused any one of them to take offensive action.

When recently he had received word from the CIA about the activities of one of the six, Wallechinsky found he had no alternative than to pursue them, and deal with the threat.

The information Wallechinsky had been given that Clifton Scudder was working for the East Germans wasn't surprising, but what was disturbing was that Scudder's new brief was China, with particular reference to American détente, which Wallechinsky had been instrumental in achieving, prior to President Nixon's historic visit: the ambassadorship was not only his reward, but the logical move, for the Chinese trusted Wallechinsky, and he talked to them in a way no other diplomat could. Scudder's working for the East Germans wasn't in itself significant, however, the fact that he was now looking for his former partners was alarming. That prospect not only robbed Wallechinsky of sleep, but overfilled his stomach with acid also. Wallechinsky knew that if anyone was capable of reaching his former confederates it was Scudder, with all the resources of the East German secret police and no particular need of secrecy.

He also knew that it wasn't chance that this should have coincided with his appointment. He had worked too hard and too long to have it fall to pieces. The situation frustrated him. He recognized the danger and saw little opportunity of dealing with it explicitly. His projected career was suddenly in jeopardy.

Lawrence Wallechinsky was forty-nine years old and approaching that watershed which a fiftieth birthday represented in American politics if you hadn't gotten your feet set in the right direction. China-watching from the number two position in the State Department had laid out his course. Quietly working behind the scenes as he had, letting the Secretary of State and the President steal the limelight, had conversely been self-motivated, for although it wasn't him getting media exposure, he had made sure it was him the Chinese leadership related to, insisted on talking to. There were huge trade deals to be made, which Wallechinsky would initiate, deals of immediate material benefit to the Chinese that would generally benefit Americans morally and particularly benefit some Americans financially, and finally benefit him politically when he would allow himself to be drawn into the center of the stage. But right then he was aware that he would achieve none of this if he wasn't confirmed in his appointment.

Thinking about his association with those six men, Wallechinsky realized the mistakes he had made. The biggest was in letting them walk like they had and take up identities over which he had no control. What he should have done was made sure of killing each of them personally, rather than leaving it to the people who were around in those days to do that without asking questions. All kind of people who had witnessed the operation or the after events had died, some in less than satisfactory circumstances. One hundred and forty-nine to date, with no serious or connecting investigation being started. In theory those six members of the CIA had been dead from the moment they had been selected for the job and taken to Colonel Parker's ranch in Texas. They had ceased being traceable at that point, but instead of being eliminated they had each been given a quarter of a million dollars and a passport; safe passage they had arranged themselves. He re-examined his motive for permitting this course: it had been to test his personal power over the people who had approached him, to indicate that he was in control, and did what he had on his own terms, regardless of their enormous wealth and the huge collective power base they had represented. He had been a deputy director of the CIA, and possibly the most active person in political murder outside of the communist bloc. Wallechinsky had foreseen just such a contingency as this, but had committed to that course regardless. Now he had to deal with the consequences of that mistake.

His thoughts moved on to Vanesco. He considered the possible mistake he was making in leaving Kohn to find these men, but knew he didn't dare get involved personally in any way that could be traced.

Wallechinsky moved agitatedly across the living room of his house on 30th Place in Washington North-West, his ex-

73

pensive, imported shoes making a faint squeak on the washed silk Chinese rug. He poured himself a drink. A social habit rather than need. His old man had been an alcoholic and he had grown up with an abhorrence of what booze did to people; it made them weak and vulnerable. On numerous occasions he had been to Washington parties where senior members of the executive had told him things in drink they wouldn't ordinarily have. Usually a bitch about someone's indiscretions; such information Wallechinsky filed. However the whole process served as a salutary lesson, and if he hadn't already been a cautious drinker he would certainly have become one.

He drank gin swamped with Indian tonic water. He considered his reason for drinking now. It was because the person he was waiting for was late. That in itself was possibly a cause for concern. Usually Michael Chu was obsessively punctual, which suggested to Wallechinsky that either something had happened or he was making something happen that might harm himself. If he were in a meeting and was delayed he would have telephoned. He was driving in from Virginia, and had he gotten delayed by traffic he'd have stopped off and called.

Maybe he was trusting Chu too much. The thought set off alarm bells. A lot of details had been committed to Chu – little of the past that wasn't on record, but most of the favors related to his past – and maybe he would start asking questions, demanding reasons, as Vanesco had. So far he hadn't asked a thing, which was the way Wallechinsky liked it. There was no reason for him not to continue this service, which was after all only in return for what he had done for Chu while with the CIA, boosting him up in the organization. Maybe that was the reason in itself why his one-time assistant wouldn't go on doing what he asked: he no longer had any need of his former boss – unless believing, like many did, that Wallechinsky had an infinitely greater future. But maybe the current danger far outweighed the possible benefits. Maybe his reason for not questioning the moves was that he already had the answers.

The prospect disturbed Wallechinsky. It would make Michael Chu especially dangerous.

Lawrence Wallechinsky stood in the shadowy room and looked out on the small, tidy front garden. Snowdrops were in bloom and narcissi were close behind. A bluebird was scratching on the lawn in the gloom. Wallechinsky enjoyed this time of day with its gray half-light, when things lost definition and became difficult to identify. The black and white areas both of life and politics held little interest for him. He preferred nether worlds, which was why he had been attracted to the CIA from university.

It had been a general assumption that there was a big future for Wallechinsky in psychology, and he had been approached by a number of universities to join the faculty, including Columbia. He had remained undecided until approached by Carl Adnopoz, who had been in his class at Harvard. Adnopoz was working for the Company, and had been assigned to effect an introduction between Wallechinsky and Dulles, then head of the CIA. After that first meeting Dulles and Wallechinsky had frequent contact, the result being his going to work for the psychology department at Yale, where he discreetly recruited talent for the CIA. In addition he became a full time member of the Company, with associate director status, so that when he quit the academic world he wouldn't be joining the CIA at the bottom. He resigned from Columbia in '57 after a self-designed scandal which exposed his recruiting activities. It was a low key affair which neither the faculty nor the news media gave prominence to, unlike the furore such a revelation would currently have caused. But it served its purpose: the new CIA man was installed without anyone noticing.

Advancement hadn't been slow. Wallechinsky had identified the area in which his talents could best serve, one that had been under-exploited by the Company, and which held most potential: China. Wallechinsky made himself an expert on Sino-American affairs, but didn't limit himself to that area, for he correctly surmised that those seeds would be a long time germinating. He wanted to advance, and knew that the way wasn't at the expense of immediate superiors. Being a psychologist Wallechinsky understood the human mind and the effect of threats upon it. The way to secure control in a subordinate position was to render greater success to superiors without remaining an unidentifiable administrative cog, so that other power bases recognized the implicit force, the manipulative skill.

That talent had been appreciated by the West Coast group who had approached him in the early '60s, soon after the Bay of Pigs fiasco. They had known that that escapade hadn't been Wallechinsky's design; had it then possibly neither Cuba nor Castro would have survived. As the then number three at the CIA Wallechinsky had felt both embarrassed and endangered over the fiasco; embarrassed at being party to such apparent incompetence, endangered because as a result President Kennedy had threatened to bury the CIA. Despite Joe Kennedy's connection with the man behind the West Coast people, who effectively controlled the CIA, the President might have carried out his threat, but for the Company's sudden improved effectiveness, which came with Wallechinsky's move up to number two – so effective, in fact, that from then on central government knew little of what it was doing. Had that invasion of Cuba been a success, and President Kennedy played the prescribed role, history would have read differently. The recent course of American history had been set down in a series of meetings in Los Angeles during the early '60s and, as almost always happened throughout history, it was determined by a few powerful people. They had been prominent men, and most still were, supreme court judges, bankers, military chiefs of staff. The three people Wallechinsky had been in direct contact with were now dead, including the apparent head of the organization calling itself the New Republican Movement. They had been a threat, not because they might one day have blown the whistle – people in such positions rarely did, simply because they were never put under the kind of pressure which caused that response – their threat lay in the fact that they were a powerbase, for which survival would inevitably have dictated obliterating his powerbase.

Wallechinsky had no wish to be head of the CIA, for in that position he felt he would have been politically vulnerable. He had made known his wishes, so instead had gone to the State Department as number two. And there he neither expected nor wanted to occupy center stage, preferring instead his hands to be on the strings, shaping policy. That was where real power lay. The men behind the public face held the real power, just as those men behind the men with the guns were the real threat. Wallechinsky desired no other role for the present. The ambassadorship, when confirmed, was the route by which he would gain his ultimate goal.

The bluebird on the lawn found a spring worm, just when the worm figured it was safe to emerge with darkness falling. Wallechinsky saw an Oldsmobile go along the street and stop three houses from his. The driver got out and walked back. Wallechinsky didn't move, he couldn't be seen in the darkened room, but it was still light enough outside to identify Michael Chu as he climbed the steps to the stoop and rang the bell. He turned, checked the street.

Michael Chu was the ideal agent to have in the field, Wallechinsky reflected as he let him in. He was someone who never brought attention to himself, and despite being Chinese-American he was probably the least memorable person around. If ever bystanders witnessed Chu's deeds, they remembered only the result. He was average height, five-ten, and weighed one-five-four pounds, and was incredibly strong, which his appearance belied; he was easily taken for a bankteller or store clerk, and not even one who played handball. In the field he adopted whatever dress was appropriate, usually a leather jacket, Levi's and weejuns, like a phone company operator, which he often posed as. He carried identification accrediting him with working for Ma Bell. His face was slightly pulpy, like an average middle-class east coast American, with no distinguishing features, his hair was black and worn at a regular length. Bland accurately described Michael Chu.

This evening he wore a dark business suit.

'A good drive in?' Wallechinsky asked, bringing him into the living room.

He got him a ginger ale. Chu didn't touch liquor. He had a strict Buddhist upbringing, and although that forbade killing any form of life, he justified his field work by equating religion with control; whereas alcohol, like any stimulant, was abuse.

The man was obsessive in his beliefs, which was why Wallechinsky was attracted to him. His obsessions were employed to great effect. Wallechinsky was particularly skillful at identifying those traits, having developed this skill at Columbia. The company needed those obsessives, who would show unswerving loyalty, regardless of the job undertaken. The ambassador designate's skill at character assessment achieved form when he selected the six men he was now hunting down; they had been put to the supreme test; paradoxically, each because of their individual obsessive, psychotic personalities saw their task not as a supreme test of loyalty but as a self-righteous crusade. Having discovered them, Wallechinsky had finely honed their obsessions as they had undergone training at Parker's ranch. Of the original selection only two proved unsuitable and failed the conditioning process. Wallechinsky rarely made mistakes in character assessment.

No mistake was made in the assessment of Chu Tse-Sing the 3rd when he had become his assistant. Conversely it was because he was so efficient that Wallechinsky was beginning to have doubts. He had committed more to this man than he had ever committed to one person, and if Chu were to break or be turned, he could be a great danger to him. Wallechinsky's intention had been to take Chu with him as a member of his embassy staff, but so far he had proved too useful by remaining within the Company.

Each settled in the green chevron-covered couches on either side of the fireplace, where once logs had been burned to heat the room and now imitation coal was lit for effect only. There was no one to take care of open fires; his housekeeper finished at 4pm. He wasn't married, and any entertaining was done in restaurants.

'I only realized today, J. Edgar Hoover lived on this street,' Chu said.

'Almost directly opposite.'

'That's amazing.'

'Why?'

'I was a big fan as a kid. Along with every other kid in America, I guess.'

'He led a charmed life.' He smiled. Hoover was a crude, egotistical maniac, who survived by blatant manipulation.

Wallechinsky was infinitely more subtle, preferring the implicit rather than the explicit. Not only would he survive in the corridors of power, he would be welcomed there, unlike the late FBI chief. He hadn't been hostile toward Hoover when their paths had crossed, despite friction between the CIA and FBI. In fact, the old man's egotism had made him easy to manipulate, especially at the time of President Kennedy's death; he had funnelled information to the FBI suggesting that they, along with the Secret Service, had fucked up. At the time all of Hoover's energy had gone into defending his own position, covering up what he feared might be Bureau blunders.

'You're better than most of his operatives put together.'

The younger man hung his head as though embarrassed.

'What problems did you foresee?' asked Chu, changing the subject. He preferred not talking about his skill, it was a kind of superstition. 'Have any of our four remaining friends made a move?'

'Right now I'm more concerned with the man hired to find them. The New York skiptrace.'

He told them what had happened.

'You want him stopped altogether?'

Wallechinsky smiled. 'What serious danger this man is I don't know. I haven't assessed him. Possibly keeping him around would be an unnecessary risk. At the moment he believes he is working for the Mafia. Maybe it should stay that way.'

'What kind of guy is he?'

'Cautious. Intelligent. At one time thoroughly ruthless. Lately he seems to have developed a conscience, which has caused the problem. He began questioning what he was doing. He has a lady friend, a social worker. Possibly she's the influence. Perhaps she's his weak spot.' Wallechinsky gave this information with no change of emphasis.

'How urgently does this need looking at, sir?' Chu asked. His address was a response to business. More often he used Wallechinsky's given name.

'That would depend how active he becomes.'

'You figure he's "A man's gotta do what a man's gotta do" kind of gumshoe?' A smile sped across his face.

'He may feel driven into a corner.'

Chu nodded. 'Then it needs doing soon.'

Wallechinsky said nothing, but looked across at Michael Chu. He had just turned thirty-five, and the ambassador designate had a feeling he wouldn't see his thirty-sixth birthday. Despite their close relationship he felt no sense of regret, and when it happened he knew he would experience a feeling of relief, provided he determined how it would happen, as he was sure he would.

Eleven

The one person whom bindle stiffs and rummies camped along the Bowery didn't molest was the mailman as he pushed his handcart over the broken sidewalks. To people scuffling around close to skidrow, the mailman was good news, he brought Welfare checks – but only if you had an address, and most of those who lived on the streets had no hope of getting an address without first getting Welfare. The city had rules. But the mailman was an emotional link with hope as he nodded to familiar faces who packed themselves into the grimy crevices of crumbling buildings, sheltering from the wind.

His walk had gotten longer, the post office having merged two walks to make them economic now that so many companies had moved out and buildings closed up. He didn't mind, he enjoyed being on the street. The mailman made people happy. Everyone liked getting mail, even if the only letter they ever got was from the utilities.

Stepping into the dim entrance of the building of Division Street, he took out the slim package addressed to James Vanesco and checked the mail boxes. The opening was too small to easily accommodate the package, but nothing on it said don't bend. He squeezed it into the small opening in the gray, battered box, and as he did so the seal on the envelope caught and tore, and the package exploded.

The blast threw the mailman across the hall, the flash momentarily blinding him, particles of metal and paper tearing at his face. His hand stung, but the ends of his fingers were numb.

The mailman had gone to the hospital by the time Vaneso arrived, unaware of what had happened. The cops were there and, on rummaging through the debris, had identified who the package had been addressed to.

'It wasn't a big explosion,' the detective told Vanesco when they reached his office.

'Is the mailman okay?'

'Coulda been worse. You coulda gotten hurt bad you'd opened it. Depends how unlucky you are.' He looked round the office with evident distaste. 'You ain't got a secretary?'

'I can open my own letter bombs,' Vanesco said. The initial shock he felt was passing, and he resisted a sense of outrage.

'You got any idea who'd lay that on you?'

Vanesco shook his head. He knew, but felt it wasn't something he needed the cops poking in at.

'What kinda investigations you been on?' he asked, with no notion that a client's confidentiality should be respected.

'Nothing that'd get this. You wanna drink?' He got a bottle from the drawer and some paper cups. It was 10 am.

'You ain't making much money are you,' the cop in the fashionable suit and handmade tie said. He looked as though he paid a lot of attention to his appearance.

'Nope.' Vanesco was amused at the cop's assumption based on his office, but he didn't smile. He could easily have impressed this guy but saw no point.

'You ain't got so many clients you can't come up with one for this.'

'This was a client, you figure?'

The cop shrugged. 'Some wack with a grudge. This fucking city's full of them cunts.' He finished his drink like a man who was used to drinking all times of the day. 'Call us you get any ideas.'

That was the extent of the police investigation. Had Vanesco given the cops a hard lead they would have pursued it, otherwise there was too much crime in Metropolitan New York, far more than the cops could handle, even though a lot of it was their own creation: the graft, the pads, straight burglary – cops had the most opportunities. If Vanesco had the inclination he could have gotten some police action, but preferred to take care of it himself. He was sorry for the mailman, but the cops couldn't repair the man's hand, and the post-office insurance would compensate him.

After the police had left, Vanesco stood at the grimy window and looked down into Division Street and thought about the package. The smallness of the bomb made Vanesco more curious than something obviously planned to kill him would. The kind of people he had rubbed the wrong way would have tried taking him out with a .38, they wouldn't have fucked with letter bombs. This was some kind of warning, he decided, and Kohn was the most likely prospect. It seemed an odd way for Kohn to warn him off. Then he flashed on the idea that he might not be warning him off, but back in.

As his eyes ran over the street, sweeping up details; he noticed a man watching the building. The spectators drawn to the scene of the explosion had moved on, and the panhandlers were working them again, looking for eye-contact, but not with the man in the dark blue overcoat and gray hat, like they instinctively recognized that with him there was no opening. Vanesco watched him move off as the last of the police vehicles departed. He waited at the window for the time he estimated it would take the gray hat to step around the block, but he didn't reappear. Maybe he was just a working stiff on his way to the office.

It didn't surprise Vanesco when an hour later the man in the gray hat and dark blue overcoat walked into his office to hire him to find his wife. Vanesco gave no indication of having seen him earlier.

He gave his name as Michael Yeo, a soft drinks manufacturer; his wife had left him a week ago, walked out of their Westchester home with their two children and hadn't been back. He gave her description, her habits; described his

82

children; gave friends, relatives, places she might go. He spoke like he wanted them back and believed Vanesco had accepted the case.

Vanesco hadn't, and didn't believe he had a family.

The skiptrace told the man, who was part Chinese, that he'd be better off finding someone in Chinatown to do his gumshoeing.

The would-be client said that he had broken with the Chinese community. 'Why did you allow me to tell you all this if you don't want the case?'

'You seemed to want to tell someone.' Throughout the conversation Vanesco had noted no rise or fall in the man's voice. Either he had no emotions or he had learned to suppress them completely.

'I don't have that kind of problem,' Yeo said. 'I want my wife and children. I can pay your rate.'

'It's pretty high.'

'I know. The person who recommended you said you were expensive.'

'I'm good.'

'Will you take the case?'

Vanesco stared at the man and thought about why he was there. Could be he had a wife who needed finding, possibly he had that kind of cover, but not for a moment did he figure that was his real reason. He assumed Kohn had sent this guy to follow up on his letter bomb. Maybe if the explosion had taken off his fingers instead of the mailman's, Yeo wouldn't have climbed the stairs. There were questions bunching up, and soon he'd have to start getting answers. Possibly Yeo might bring him close to the source.

'I'm busy right now. It'd be a coupla days before I could get to it.'

The man nodded. 'March won't get lost any more than she is. I'd appreciate you're getting to it as soon as you can, Mr Vanesco.'

'Who was it recommended me?'

'My lawyer. Clark Cunningham.'

Good old Clark E. Cunningham. 'He tell you my policy of taking a hefty deposit? In cash.'

The thousand dollar deposit in hundred dollar bills was the

easiest grand Vanesco had earned. He figured he wouldn't have to do a thing.

What he did do was go down to the street to follow his would-be client. There he confirmed that the man was other than a soft drinks manufacturer. He headed into Chinatown, carefully covering his tracks. Vanesco let him go, knowing there was no way he could make a successful tail, for all the while Yeo was checking he wasn't going to tell the skiptrace any more than he had already.

With the grand in his pocket and the wolf from the door, Vanesco could afford some legwork on his own behalf. It wasn't enough to suspect the letter bomb was from Harry Kohn, he wanted to know it was, then he could do something about it. Like maybe breaking his legs.

Bombs in general, and letter bombs in particular, were a specialized area of crime associated with terrorism. Vanesco's own contacts were limited but easily extended by lunching a former colleague in the New York FBI. What the agent offered were three names, one with vague Mafia connections, if he could be found. None of them were exactly waiting around to be interviewed. After lunch Vanesco checked his own source in Brooklyn.

Burton Becker was a staunch Republican and owed no allegiance to any of the separatist movements he sometimes worked for. He hired out to anyone who could meet his price, made whatever kind of bomb they required, then sometimes informed on them if the pressure was too great.

'I've been outta that business longer than you know,' Becker said over his beer.

They were in a social club on 4th Avenue in Sunset Park commercial district. This was a neighborhood in transition. Over the last ten years or so the small stores had disappeared, along with their customers, while the vacancy rate and number of low-income minority residents had gone up. On the increase were incidents of felony, also clubs like the one they were in, the two often going together. Most weren't licensed to sell liquor or anything else, but nonetheless sold everything that turned a dollar. A lot of coke and heroin dealing went on, and not only dealing, some heads stayed at their tables and got off. It was an interesting reflection on the city's law enforcement agencies, Vanesco felt, that he could sit here in the middle of Brooklyn at two-thirty in the afternoon and witness the parade. Anyone who knew the place could get admission.

'I'm after some information.' He laid one of Yeo's hundred dollar bills on the table. 'I wanna know who made a letter bomb I got in the mail this morning. That's all.'

The bombmaker wasn't impressed. 'That don't buy much around here these days.'

'A coupla phone calls. The name gets you four more.'

'Where can I reach you?'

Vanesco gave him his number, finished his drink and caught the subway back to Manhattan.

His answering service had picked up two calls, both from Moyra Yeston, Brad Coley's lady, who was calling not from Canada, but New York.

'She leave a number?'

'She called from a phone booth. Said she'd keep trying till she got you.'

She got Vanesco at his office soon after, sounding like she was in trouble, and he told her to get into a cab and come over.

'Mr Vanesco, I don't have cabfare.' She was embarrassed.

'Find a cab. We'll take care of it when you get here.'

The cab driver had figured she was pulling a stunt when she climbed out with her son on Division Street and said she had to go in for the money, she explained afterwards to Vanesco. The driver had insisted she left her grip behind. Cab and grip had both disappeared by the time Vanesco got down to the street.

'Everything I had was in that grip,' the woman said. 'My clothes, Darren's clothes. They weren't much, but all we had. Jesus. What kinda asshole would steal that?'

'Cab drivers here'd steal an old sock off you,' Vanesco said. 'You check the name on his license, remember what he looked like?' She didn't. 'Never leave anything in a cab. Make the cabdriver come up and get his money. He'll give you an argument, is all.'

'What shall I do? I'd better call the cops.'

'Well, I'll tell you what happens. They listen to your story,

85

make sympathetic noises, put the phone down, finish.'

'But they gotta do something.'

'We'll take care of things.' He smiled like a reassuring cop.

She opened her hands looking for some articulate expression, but shut them, finding none.

He waited for her to get to the reason for coming down from Canada.

'I'm sorry. Showing up with these problems. I didn't know what else to do. Brad didn't have close friends. Jesus. . . !' Her sigh was close to despair and not far from hysteria. 'He didn't have anyone, 'cept me and Darren. Can you believe that? A man lives all his life without letting anyone near him. Discovering that I didn't know him came as a big shock. I mean, I didn't know a thing about him, not what went on in his head. That's real spooky, Mr Vanesco. I found out something real spooky up in Marathon. That's why I packed our bags and hitched down here. I couldn't think of anyone else who'd give a damn. Like I told you, I was broke. I figured there be something in the bank when Brad died. No fortune, but enough to live on while I got my head straight. He did okay with his boats, could afford to make those trips. I went to the bank. We weren't legally married, but I guessed Darren and me were entitled. There wasn't any money. The day he died he'd drawn out every cent.'

Vanesco took this in as if of minor importance. 'How much was that?'

'Nearly forty-seven thousand dollars. I mean, that's real weird, right? Almost like he knew something was going to happen. Like he knew he was going to die.' She hesitated and glanced at her son, before adding, 'Like he didn't die.'

'You think that's possible?' asked Vanesco. He glanced at the boy, whose silence was worrying him; usually five-year-olds would have been fidgeting and interrupting their mother. Zell's kid would have.

'Yes. But why'd he go through that whole number? He coulda just taken off. I guess I haven't got any right, and I haven't got any money to pay you, but I was wondering if you could find out what happened, as you had some kind of interest.'

Vanesco considered the woman and what she was asking.

86

He was a man who wanted reasons for doing the things he did, and a prime reason was that he got paid. That wouldn't be the case if he did what Moyra Yeston asked. But an equally compelling reason to get involved here was because he had been used, and walking away could cause him as many problems as staying in. Things were happening around him that indicated his staying involved was the only way he was going to get some answers and maybe get in control of the events.

'My interest ended with finding Coley. There was nothing else for me.'

'What if he's not dead?'

'That might interest the law firm that hired me. I'll scuffle around, Mo, see if I can come up with something. What do you plan on doing? You have a place to stay in New York?'

'No.' An embarrassed look came over her again. 'I didn't think too much about what we'd do when we got here. I went into shock when I learned about the money. There's a coupla of friends I figured we'd stay with, but I called, they're out of town. It's okay, we'll find somewhere. I used to hitch all over one time.'

'Are you kidding? This is New York, it's early spring, you got no clothes.' He reached for the phone and dialed Zell's number. 'I've got a friend, she comes up with answers to problems like this every day.'

'I don't want to be any kind of problem.'

'Either she can help or she can't. That simple.' He could have checked her into a hotel and added the tab to his expenses from Kohn – he planned on going back to the Mafia boss and telling him he was resuming the case – but didn't think it was a good idea to just plant her in a hotel.

Zell's phone was finally answered by Sam. His mother came on soon after out of breath. They had run up the stairs. Vanesco told her about Mo and son and asked if she could help.

'There's always something can be done, Jim. But most Welfare offices are closed up this time of the day. Look, have her come by here with her kid. Meanwhile I'll make some calls, see what I can fix up.'

'Thanks, Zell. I'll see you later, honey.' He replaced the

phone and scribbled out Zell's address. 'You know New York, Mo?'

'No. I think I can find my way around.'

'You wanna risk another cab?' He smiled. 'The guy'll take you right there. S'Charles Street, inna Village. Here.' He gave her three hundred dollars with the address. 'You're going to need a change of clothes.'

'I don't know what to say. I feel real dumb letting that cab driver steal my bag.'

'That's New York for you – it screws everyone. She's like an old whore – they want it bad, she does it bad.' He looked at the boy again. 'How you doing, Darren?'

The boy shrugged and looked at the floor.

'Is he okay?'

'He's tired. Aren't you babe?'

'I guess,' he replied in a whisper.

'You'll like Zell. She's got a kid his age. Who knows, maybe that's what he needs right now.'

Vanesco left with them, locking his office door. He walked them down to the street and put them in a cab, then took another to 3rd Avenue.

'What the fuck do you want, Vanesco?' Kohn demanded when he emerged from a door into his secretary's office where Vanesco was waiting. 'I'm inna middle of a board meeting.'

'I'm going back to work on those four other guys,' Vanesco said.

'Just like that.' He sounded amazed. 'You got some fucking nerve, Vanesco. So what the fuck makes you think I want you back?'

The skiptrace measured him with a long look. Getting to be as powerful as Kohn was didn't make him proportionally smart, if it had he wouldn't be asking such a question. Vanesco figured he wouldn't have left an important meeting to tell him personally that he wasn't working for him. Instead he was making sure of his commitment.

'You want the other guys. You, or whoever you're fronting for.'

'You got a big mouth, Vanesco.'

'I've also got a talent for finding people.' He waited. 'So,

88

do I go back to work?'

'What's your interest now?'

'Same as always. I want another five grand to cover my exes – I plan on going to Europe.'

'What else, Vanesco? There's something else.'

Vanesco smiled. 'I don't wanna be around to pick up my mail.'

The man didn't react.

'Draw a check for five grand,' Kohn told his secretary.

'Payable to bearer,' Vanesco told her.

She checked with Kohn, who simply said, 'I want some results.'

'That's all you'll get, Mr Kohn,' the skiptrace said.

When Vanesco reached Zell's apartment later that evening, Zell was on her own, Sam was across the street at a neighbor's; he was grateful to find her alone and embraced her like he hadn't seen her in a month.

'Hey, this is kind of nice,' Zell said, responding. 'What is this? You feeling guilty about extending my day?' She was in a good mood.

He didn't consider the letter bomb, but guessed that had something to do with his reaction. No matter how well people handled their surface fears, the inner fears were something else. Vanesco felt grateful for having Zell to hold right then. There was no percentage in telling her about the explosion.

'You manage to get them fixed up?'

'I made some calls, but it got too late. They can stay here, I guess.'

'Are you crazy, Zell? How can they stay here? The apartment's not big enough for you and Sam. What are you talking about?' He was getting angry.

'There's no problem. We don't need your kind of comfort. They can sleep on the floor. People do the whole time.'

'You can't just take people in like that, Zell. You don't even know them.'

'I didn't pick them up on 11th Avenue. She's your client, she's in trouble. You're helping them. We can't just dump them. Welfare can't cope any better than you or I.' She looked at him, her expression softening. 'You saw that kid, Jimmy.

He's in real trouble.'

'Jesus!' Vanesco exclaimed in dismay, but nodded.

'Why are you being that way?' she asked.

He knew why. He saw Mo as a threat to his relationship with Zell, just as Sam sometimes was. 'I figure it's a big problem for you in this tiny apartment.'

'It's okay. I'm glad you asked me to help. She can keep the scumlord busy when he comes by.'

'You been getting more hassles?' Vanesco understood the landlord's problem, and to a point sympathized; he would've liked Zell to move into his apartment. But she wouldn't let herself be pushed, nor would Vanesco watch it happen.

'The regular dirty phone calls. No problem.' She put her arms around him and kissed him. 'I like her, Jimmy. I think you're a nice guy helping her.'

'Nice guys finish last. Didn't you know that.'

'They get to heaven, is what.' In her good moods Zell was spontaneous and optimistic, despite the beating she was taking in her job.

'Where are they now?'

'They went to Canal Street to do some shopping.'

'Canal Street? Did you send her there?' He was surprised.

Zell misread his meaning. 'She knew about Canal Street. She'll be okay.'

Suddenly Vanesco knew she would. For someone who didn't know New York well enough to know not to leave her bag in a cab, he found it curious she should know Canal Street was the place for cheap shots. It made Moyra Yeston more interesting; maybe she didn't lose her grip, and wasn't as helpless as she appeared.

Possibly he was being his usual paranoid self, or maybe she wasn't what she seemed. Either way now that she had insinuated herself here she would get closely looked at.

BOOK TWO

Existence is a subjective reality

Twelve

The cry that rose through the cold, starlit night was almost human. A distressed sound of fear and pain. Had it been human it would have caused William Torbert no concern, but the cry was from a mare in foal out in the paddock, and the cause was dogs. Thinking about this made him angry, and hearing the mare in distress hurt him. Only he didn't move. He wanted to go to comfort her, but resisted; he wanted those dogs more.

The barking stopped. It was as if the delinquent dogs realized they had gone too far, or maybe the mare had gotten her heels into one of them, though it was doubtful. The dogs had been roaming the district for a couple of weeks, mostly worrying sheep and killing lambs; the local farmers did nothing, apart from laying poison, which the dogs were generally too smart to touch. They had been by his place two nights ago, causing another mare to drop her foal. She had been ready to foal and it wasn't the dogs' fault it was stillborn, but the distress they had caused was reason enough for Torbert to be up on the rim of the hill overlooking his farm on this frosty night with his Remington 700. There were five or six dogs, and if he caught them in the open he would kill all of them. He knew rifles, and his eyes were still good enough for night shooting.

As the mare cried again he had difficulty holding his position, but he heard the dogs headed in his direction. It was the only way they could come without going through the yard by the house; east there was a densely planted forest of young firs and to the west a small river with a swift current at this time of year. He had skirted around the paddock, knowing the dogs would head out south; right then he could have scared them off, wounded one or two, but he wanted more. He saw the first dog spring up and over the drystone wall that separated the paddock from the upper field. Torbert raised the rifle and put his eye to the Scopechief starsight. The dog was some kind of cross-bred German shepherd. Torbert's finger moved through the trigger guard. Over the

93

wall came two sheep dogs that had gone wild through neglect or bad handling. Local farmers didn't respect their animals, not even those they could drive to market. Dogs were just something that were always around the place, usually chasing cars passing their roadside farms, fed scraps from the table, and not missed when they strayed; there was always some bitch with a litter, dogs were easily replaced. Sometimes good dogs took up with bad for the hell of it, like the fifth dog to come over the wall; an Irish Setter that someone had paid money for and was doubtless trying to find. There were six, but one would live, for Torbert had only five shots. Back home he could have made Master's rating in the National Rifle Association, but then had had neither the time nor the inclination.

They were in the center of the field when the first shot rang out. The German shepherd fell, startling the others. Torbert dropped two more as fast as he could engage the bolt. The reports merged into one as they echoed across the valley. The remaining dogs fled in different directions, with panic clamped to their tails. Torbert swung the rifle after the Setter; it somersaulted. The rifle came to the right and the bullet found its mark. The last dog reached the wood and was gone.

Torbert didn't bother to reload but ran to the mare. She had started to foal early and knew she was in trouble. She was smart enough to have entered the loosebox, which had direct access to the paddock next to the foaling yard. The night was too cold for dropping her foal on the ground.

All his mares were brought in at night. There were eleven of them and each was about a month from foaling as they had been put to the stallion around the same time. Torbert liked to get his mares to the stallion early rather than late, so they would foal through the following spring; also the success rate in cover was only fifty percent, so if they weren't covered on the first attempt there was still time. This mare being blind was given the run of the yard paddock. She had gone blind after a fall and her owner had been about to sell her at a local fair to a dealer who bought horses for the Belgian meat trade. It wasn't sentimentality that made Torbert buy her, for he wasn't a bit sentimental. Horses didn't respond to sentimentality other than in temper. They appreciated being treated with dignity and respect. If anyone came by and talked baby-talk to his horses he told them to quit it, regardless of whether they were prospective buyers. What he had seen in this blind horse was a fine brood mare, and after she had gotten over her nervousness and had settled down, that was what she made, so far throwing two excellent foals, the second making champion foal at Dublin. Now she was in trouble on account of a pack of dogs; Torbert was mad at their owners and would have preferred them dead up in his field.

'Easy, Ruby,' he said in a calming voice as he threw on the stable light.

The mare was on the straw bedding unmoving. Her large, unblinking brown eyes were full of fear and she was sweating badly.

Torbert knelt beside her. 'Easy, Ruby. Take it easy, sweetheart. You're gonna be fine.'

Her udder hadn't started to bag up, nor had her teats waxed over, but every other sign said she was about to foal. This loose box would be okay for foaling but he would sooner it happened in a loose box in the yard where everything was to hand to deal with any emergency.

Right then he made the decision to hitch the loose-box to the Landrover and run it into the yard. He might not be able to get the mare into a foaling box, but she'd be close enough. Closing the low tailgate, he ran to the house and returned in the Landrover. Hitching up took no time. He slammed off the hydraulic stabilizers, then checked the mare again before pulling the plug on the electricity supply. The horse hadn't moved, nor had she by the time he had the box in the yard and the power reconnected. The dark patches of sweat on her chestnut neck had spread.

Crouching behind her shoulder, Torbert stroked her and talked to her, telling her to get up. At first she didn't respond. 'C'mon, sweetheart, try it. Okay. C'mon, you can make it, Ruby baby. Just try it.' There was no alarm in his voice, just firm reassurance.

Suddenly she threw out her front feet, and Torbert instinctively braced himself against her shoulder. She started up, trembling as she did so. Her legs began to buckle. Torbert pushed himself off the side of the box as he felt the horse's weight against him. He stood five-seven and weighed a hundred and forty pounds, but the sinewy strength he mustered prevented the mare crashing down. His help gave her a chance to push on the floor and take another shot at pulling herself up. Torbert hung in there, straining every muscle until they felt they were tearing. In one final effort the horse threw her neck out and was up, but shaking and uncertain she would stay on her feet.

'You're fine. You did just fine, baby,' Torbert told her.

Her ears pricked, maybe at a sound too far off in the night for him to hear; her eyes opened wider, straining to see something she would never see; her nostrils distended, she snorted a couple of times. Sweat broke out on her chest. The contraction passed. Another followed immediately. She was sweating heavily.

Most of the mares Torbert foaled on his own, but right then he could have used a little help, someone to watch her while he washed up ready to give a hand. Out of the mobile loose box, he grabbed the foaling kit he kept in the yard: disinfectant, rubber gloves, bandages for the mare's tail, scissors. He rolled his sleeves up and sprayed disinfectant on his hands and arms.

The mare's water bag slipped out, followed by one of the foal's legs covered in a white membrane. At once Torbert realized it was a hind leg and from its angle it looked like a breech presentation. The foal was coming out twisted. Ruby shuddered with the contraction, and threw herself down onto the straw to roll and ease the pain. The effort exhausted her, she lay unmoving after that, putting nothing into her labor. Torbert reached into her vagina to feel the foal; there was a chance that the force of this would damage both the foal and the dam, but it was a chance he had to take; the seventeen minutes it took a mare to foal were ticking away. The foal felt badly positioned, he knew the head and shoulders wouldn't come through the narrow pelvic area without some damage. Reaching into the mare past his elbows, he used his arms like forceps and levered the foal over, and straightened its exit. It took a lot of effort, throughout which the mare didn't stir. When he got done finally the mare took an interest, knowing it was now all right to bear down. After a few minutes the back half of the foal had emerged, but stopped. Torbert reached in again and eased the foal's head through the pelvic opening, and finally the whole thing slipped out. The mare didn't move she was exhausted. Torbert suspected she might have hemorrhaged, and there was nothing he could do about it.

Ducking out of the loose box, Torbert went to the comfortable sitting-up room and grabbed two blankets and a blowheater. The blankets he covered the mare with, then hung the blowheater on the wall and plugged in it; the foal would feel the drop in temperature when it broke the amniotic sac. He felt the umbilical cord to make sure blood had ceased flowing from the placenta. When the foal put its foot through the membrane and started to breathe, Torbert stripped the sac away. The mare wasn't going to get to her foal to lick it like she ordinarily would, she hadn't the strength. So Torbert dragged it across the straw within reach of its mother's head. Ruby put her nose against the stallion foal and sniffed, then feebly began to lick him. The licking stimulated the foal as it thrashed about, trying to get on its legs. But as that flicker of life in the premature foal rose, so the flame of the mother diminished. Thirty minutes later she died of exhaustion and internal bleeding.

By that time Torbert was giving the foal its first feed. The mother was dead and the foal needed feeding, next it would need a foster mother. He had a mare who had recently lost a foal but whether she would adopt this one was something else, even though it was her milk the baby was taking from the bottle. A mare's first milk was important, as it contained all the dam's antibodies which immunized the new-born against disease. Had her milk been running Torbert would have milked off the dead mare, but he had a stock of colostrum in the freezer from the mares who had lost their foals.

It was a long night for Torbert. The foal needed feeding every hour; it was in the heated foaling box next to the sitting-up room, and Torbert put the mare who had lost her foal in the box next door. Across the yard in a store shed the body of the foal lay awaiting disposal. The dead animal collection wouldn't hurry for a ninety pound foal. The unheated store shed would keep the animal in a tolerable condition.

With two sharp knives, which were kept for the purpose, Torbert carefully skinned the foal. It took over an hour, interrupted to feed the new foal, who was waiting at the loosebox door when he arrived with the bottle. When he had finished skinning the foal, he carefully tied the hide to the newest arrival, leaving only his head and face clear. The young foal was curious, but made no fuss—he had obviously inherited his dam's good nature. Tethering the fostering mare so she couldn't damage the foal if she decided to reject it, he took some of her milk and rubbed the foal's head to add to the familiar smell, then brought them together. That was an anxious moment for Bill Torbert. He had a fine strong stallion foal in need of a mother, and a grieving mare in need of a foal; the solution would make life much easier if it worked.

For what seemed like an age the mare sniffed the pelted foal, then pulled her head back on the halter to look at this strange animal with the familiar smell. At that moment Torbert feared she might try to kill it as frequently happened when a mare rejected a would-be fosterling. But she sniffed him again, then finally pushed his head on to her teats. That was all the encouragement he needed.

For the first time since hearing those dogs last night Torbert relaxed. It was now five-fifteen. Around eight o'clock his day help would arrive and he could get some sleep. He stepped out of the box and shut the doors. Along the yard he looked in on the dead mare, regretting her loss, and feeling angry that it had happened. Having taken care of the problem didn't make him any less angry at the people who took in animals yet weren't prepared to be responsible for them. He guessed the Irish weren't unique in that. He suspected the unconcern of the Irish, like the British, about the domestic animals that they let breed and roam the countryside came from their island insularity. Had rabies been endemic they'd think again.

The record showed William Rockwell Torbert to be a retired US Army colonel living on his pension, plus what he made out of his stud farm. He lived well. He had come to Ireland eleven years ago, living first in Dublin, then Kilkenny, before finally settling in West Cork. He bought the hundred and twenty acre farm, a fine Georgian house, in need of repair, with stables and coach houses, for eighteen thousand dollars. The work he had put into the place made it worth twenty times that on today's market, only he had no plans to sell. He had always been a rootless man, having no family in Ireland, America or anyplace else. Here his roots had sunk deeper, he had stayed longer, felt safer than he ever had in the past. That was because he had a lot of cover, believed his trail had gone cold, and was careful. He had been careful all his life. That was how he had gotten to be 46, when his life expectancy hadn't been much above 36. The reason he had picked Ireland wasn't on account of any romantic affinity, for he guessed the Irish were as much assholes as anyone else. But despite having no surviving relatives Torbert was second generation Irish-American, a fact that spared him hassles with immigration. The Irish claimed their own as far back as the grandchildren of those who had emigrated and automatically qualified them for Irish citizenship. It made life a lot easier when you didn't want to be traced, and Torbert had found few officials more amenable than those in Dublin. Once settled, that was the last of his official problems; Ireland allowed him to get lost in his little backwater.

The only problem he had, though one he could live with, was the local people. He sensed they didn't like him and he didn't give them an inch. The result was that they didn't know him, but they were curious about his living alone in that big house, and they just stood off and stared. People had an odd way of doing that in these parts, and it had worried him at first. They were always watching, wanting to know about him; their early inquiries had met cold rebuffs, and soon they had stopped asking questions. That suited Torbert. Had he lived in the US or in Europe people would have been concerned with how he sustained emotionally and sexually. But in Catholic riddled Ireland, where large numbers of people were selfsustained both sexually and emotionally, the question never arose. In fact the answer was simple, he had no need. Long ago he learned to live without sexual or emotional needs, when he realized they made him less of a survivor than he wanted to be. Never once had he deviated, or had any need of physical relief; he was strong, had a will that could resist anything. With him it was only a matter of deciding, then doing it.

Not once did he question the purpose of life in general or his existence in particular. Torbert was a physical person whose life was expressed in physical, explicit actions which he believed held no higher purpose, nor fitted any higher pattern.

The hot shower washed away the blood and exhaustion of the sleepless night, and he felt fine afterwards. He could get through the day without sleep, and probably the next night if he had to. He shaved slowly, pulling the razor in careful strokes across his brown, weathered face that was etched like an old cracked piece of leather. As faces went his was neither good nor bad looking, and didn't offend; his features were regular, his dark hair was flecked with gray. The only memorable thing about him was his right ear, which had a piece missing. That was both a bloody and a painful memory. A horse had bitten a chunk off it; Torbert had never broken that horse of nipping. Surer than hell the horse hadn't understood the beating it got when Torbert returned from the hospital. He fingered his damaged ear and thought about that horse. After the beating the horse wouldn't let anyone near him; a good stallion ruined, though Torbert didn't regret what he did.

While Torbert was eating breakfast after two hours sleep the man who helped with the farm arrived. There were oats and barley to plant, and grass. They grew their own food-stuffs for the horses. The help, John Hurley, lived in the town, preferring both the comforts of a modern home and the lack of final responsibility in working for someone else; he had once had his own farm and a damp, cold farmhouse without plumbing.

'You were after getting them, Mr Torbert,' he said, when his boss came into the yard.

'Five,' Torbert said. 'Not before they ruined a mare.'

'I know of course.'

He didn't know, it was a manner of speaking the locals had, which at first had infuriated Torbert. Now it irritated only if he was in a mood to be irritated. He could give Hurley the most abstruse information, or concepts that would amaze or baffle him, when finally he would say:'I know of course'.

'Put them in the pickup, John. I'll take them into the garda. Not that those guys'll give a damn.'

He discussed the day's work; a ten-acre field to be harrowed and sowed for hay, and some of the meadows manured. The stable girl sometimes drove the tractor, but with twenty mares, foals and a stallion to take care of she didn't have much spare time.

Eileen, the girl who worked the horses came to the kitchen to discuss her day when she arrived. Her liberated attitude had a lot to do with her age, and the fact that she had spent time in Dublin. She was in her mid-twenties, sturdily built, mannish in dress and not pretty, none of which concerned Torbert. The daughter of a local store owner, she had no wish to get married or work in the store.

He told her about what had happened last night as she drank coffee; they discussed the horses' day, which mares would have to be watched. All those in foal had their teats checked regularly for waxing, which was a sign birth would shortly take place.

Later that morning he removed the dead skin from the foal, the fostering mare was now content in her role.

The local town was a two-street affair with about fifteen hundred residents situated six miles due north of Torbert's place. There was a Protestant church and a Roman Catholic church, four schools two of each denomination, two lawyers, one for each persuasion; the same with the four doctors and most of the bars, which every other store-front in the town was. Yet there was no conscious separation as in Northern Ireland, and no noticeable tension resulted from religious preferences.

Torbert came to town maybe once a week. His food was bought in bulk; he collected newspapers whenever he was in; he drank alone. Most other requirements were filled in response to a phone call. On the occasions he went to town, whatever the weather, there were always people standing around watching him, exclusively it seemed, but he guessed it was anyone who happened through also. They stood outside the bars and stores in the town square, unblinking eyes in unmoving faces followed his pickup as he headed out to the garda station on the edge of town. Everyone knew why he had come, as nothing happened around there without everyone knowing. The ironical thing was, Torbert found, that whenever folks were like that nothing happened.

He carried in the two biggest dogs first, then the three smaller ones. The two policemen in the damp smelling station stood looking but said nothing as he piled the dogs on the floor.

'They won't kill any more of my horses,' Torbert said. He was angry with these cops for their non-reaction, their lack of action on the dog problem.

Finally one of them said, 'Grand job. You were after getting them, Mr Torbert, sir.'

They were unconcerned, despite now having five dogs to dispose of. He guessed they'd throw them on the garbage dump, where they'd blow up and stink and attract flies. Their attitude reminded him of a farmer whose dog had worried a mare of his, causing her to bolt and break a leg. Torbert had pursued the dog home and broken its leg while the farmer looked on, as if understanding the necessity of that.

It wasn't for the cops benefit or the need to tie up loose ends that Torbert had brought the dogs in, but to show that he wouldn't be intruded upon.

People in the newsagents were talking about Torbert when he walked in. They stopped immediately.

He collected the Irish Times and back copies of the Herald-Tribune. The front page item on the Tribune immediately stopped him thinking about the townspeople. It said the Senate Foreign Relations Committee had endorsed Lawrence Wallechinsky's appointment as ambassador to China. That indicated to Torbert that this man's low profile of his CIA and State Department days was over, the chrysalis was leaving its casing. Alarm bells began ringing. Torbert knew how paranoid Wallechinsky was, what a danger he would see him as.

The fact was that Torbert was a danger to the new ambassador.

He wondered now if his former confederates were thinking the same thing, and what he could do about it. He got his answer that evening when catching up with his newspapers.

In the classified section of the Herald-Tribune he saw a contact message suggesting a meeting in London for the following Tuesday. The newspaper was a week old so someone had been worrying about it longer than he had.

Thirteen

A man entered the barroom and stopped in the doorway, his glance flitting about anxiously. Seated at a table, Chuck Paley watched him go to the bar, where he asked the barman something before ordering a drink. Paley didn't hear the man's question, but saw it got a negative response, and watched as he turned and looked over each of the eight customers in the Inn on the Park barroom. This wasn't his contact, Paley decided, but was probably some guy who had arranged to meet a girl who had probably stood him up. Certainly she hadn't been and gone. He had been waiting since eight-thirty and there had been no unattached ladies. It was a quarter after nine, and his man was fifteen minutes late, a fact that caused Clarence Paley no concern. He had been told about 9pm. He raised his empty martini glass and caught the waiter's eye.

Paley's thoughts turned to the small ad, which had been in every edition of the Herald-Tribune for the past week. He wondered who placed it, maybe Ambassador Wallechinsky had placed it. The thought that kept on coming around was that. Each time he tried telling himself that the former CIA deputy chief couldn't have known about their early warning system, but any one of the others might have sold out for a promise of immunity. That promise would have been no surer than the original one Wallechinsky had given, only eleven years on it might have sounded worth listening to; Wallechinsky was always persuasive.

The question for him then to ponder was which of them had sold out. The only one he was certain hadn't was himself. Any of the other five could have gone over to the communists with Wallechinsky. His thoughts ran back to their time on that Texas ranch, considering who had been the brightest shade of pink. Lance Niles, he was pretty far left, with his talk of Christ being a true communist, how all people were created equal and should remain so. It was surprising that a red like Niles was on such a picnic; he had wanted to give America away to the niggers and underclasses. John F. Kennedy had been selling America along that road, and Paley was surprised that Niles didn't go right along with him. He had never really talked to Niles, nor any of the others, and in retrospect he realized that the people putting the job together hadn't wanted them exchanging ideas and views. Also he realized that each of them had gotten involved for his own reason, which had been exploited to the full.

A thin man with a whispy mustache came into the barroom, took the customers in at a glance and headed across to Paley.

'Mr Paley?'

He was in his early thirties, and Paley, who was the older, made him for a cop, despite his tinted eyeglasses and expensive haircut; city detectives in the US dressed stylishly, but not as a rule in England.

Paley's gray eyes measured him, then signalled the waiter. He ordered scotch.

'Sorry I'm late. Got delayed at another stop. Been here long?' His eyes swept the barroom, checking the other customers again.

Still Paley said nothing, and the detective looked at him, offering a tight, mirthless smile.

'Inspector Machin couldn't make it. Sends his apologies, said you'd understand. I'm Detective Sergeant Adams. You'll be dealing with me in future. We had a bit of a change round.' He shook Paley's hand.

The detective's hands were soft, the nails professionally manicured. He wore an expensive ruby ring on his pinkie. Being a cop in London, where as a rule hoods didn't carry guns, must have been an easy life, Paley reflected.

'We could step out to the gents. But it'll be as safe here. Know what I mean.'

Paley nodded and glanced across to the bar where the man whom he surmised had missed his date, finished his drink and left. 'Your boss should have let me know,' said Paley.

'What d'you want? A memo?' He reached into his pocket and brought out three envelopes, selected one and handed it to Paley.

It was fatter than usual.

'My guvnor bunged you a little present. Some grass to roll the hash in. He said you don't use tobacco.'

Paley smiled. He couldn't bear to take tobacco smoke into his lungs, and disliked even being in a smoky atmosphere. This wasn't what he smiled at, rather the disapproving attitude he sensed from this cop, who readily dealt on the dope market after knocking over the suppliers. Then everyone had double standards.

'That's kind of your boss,' Paley said. He put the envelope away and took one from his own pocket. 'Two hundred pounds.'

'S'what the man said.' He glanced into the envelope but didn't count the money. He would outside. 'I'm not trying to talk myself out of business, but you could score that for half the price in Gerrard Street.' He finished his drink.

'At considerable risk,' Paley said. 'And no guarantee it would be as good quality. I'll stay with Scotland Yard. You deliver.'

'You know where to reach us. Be lucky, pal.' The detective left.

It was a nice arrangement. He had scored two ounces of best quality hash, the grass being thrown in was unusual. He was only ever interested in the best of anything.

Chuck Paley was obsessed with perfection, it was his high, and finding himself with anything less was a bad trip. It was an expensive way to live, but he had settled in Britain in the early '60s with a great deal of money, which he had invested wisely. Perfectionism and poverty were incompatible. Had he been poor then there was no way he could have called in the decorator to paint the walls of his Mayfair apartment whenever they got marked, or have the rugs cleaned as often as he did.

The unaccompanied woman who walked into the barroom just then wasn't perfect, but in biological need Chuck Paley made allowances in such areas.

From her apparent disappointment, he deduced she was the date of the man who had recently left. Leaving his drink, Paley went over to her. Having figured why she was there gave him the advantage, also he had had more martinis than her, and that increased his advantage. He introduced himself, told her what had happened to her date, and invited her to his table; the alternative was to drink alone or leave, so she accepted.

The woman was a stewardess for British Airways, and had that tight primness which that airline went for. She was 29, called Carol, and drank gin. Both had a good line in small talk, and seemed equally aware of it eventually leading them, via dinner, back to either of their apartments.

Carol shared an apartment in South Kensington with three other stewardesses. She was reluctant to take him back there, but more reluctant to finish the evening alone. They ate in an Italian restaurant on Old Brompton Road, so her place became the logical destination.

She brought him in to the sitting room, while she went and checked the duplex apartment, which was situated on the first and second floors. A problem with bringing people back was that one of the other girls might be crashed out from a trip.

There was no one in, and Carol relaxed when she returned.

'A nice place,' Paley observed. He didn't truly think so, in fact, he felt uncomfortable here. The room was a mess, with too much odd furniture; it needed cleaning and decorating. Being a communal room it reflected their combined tastes in objects collected from trips to different parts of the world: rugs from India, masks from Africa; Mexican pottery, eastern bamboo work. All was chaos in Paley's eyes.

'Make yourself comfortable. Let me take your jacket.'

Their furniture didn't suit sitting around in jacket and tie, but he kept his necktie on.

She got him a drink, from the kind of fold-away trolley used on airplanes, stocked with the same variety of miniature bottles.

'I've something else here, if you're interested.' He reached into his jacket for the package of dope.

'God, I've never seen so much dope,' she said. 'Do you deal?'

'That's an impolite question. You got any cigarette papers?' He normally used a hash pipe, which he didn't carry around, rarely smoking other than in the privacy of his own apartment. He wasn't sure why he chose to now.

One of the other stewardesses used grass and had a whole box of papers. Carol got a packet and came and sat on the floor near Paley.

'What a surprise you are,' she said with a note of excitement.

He gave her a look as he crumpled some singed hash along the joint he had rolled. Possibly she figured he should be more staid at 49, that was the way he appeared. It didn't upset him, in fact he knew it was a measure of his success. If you looked the way people expected a doper, burglar, murderer, or whatever to look, then you invited attention. Chuck Paley held a low profile.

The joint was generous. The grass itself was good quality, probably Thai, and would have gotten them off without the hash. Paley could feel himself getting there unusually fast. Nowadays he smoked for the narcotic effect, being beyond hallucinogenic effects.

'That is one joint. Really something.' He inhaled deeply and passed it to her.

'It's too much. Really far out, Chuck,' she said after toking.

Why did the dumb cunt say that? The thought popped into his head. She was imitating the American drug culturists, and her words sounded phony.

She passed the joint back and rose, moving like she believed she was floating. She hadn't his tolerance and was getting up a whole lot quicker. She was affecting her swaying gait, he decided, and it irritated him, as she did. He watched her through the pale blue smoke, analyzing why this was. He was picking up on her tense vibrations, he realized, and they were making him tense, and so diminishing his pleasure. The music she put on made him feel more alienated; Rolling

Stones music was the last thing he wanted to hear then. It jarred, causing tension to start at the top of his head and run to the base of his spine. He brought his hand up to massage the pain.

The girl danced toward him through the chaos. 'What's wrong?' she suddenly asked, half reading something in his face. Paranoia swelled through her. 'What's wrong?' she repeated. 'Have I done something? Is it the music? What is it?'

Tell her it's the music, a voice inside said; another voice said, no, tell her she's a cunt. 'I've got some tension in my neck and back,' he said.

'I get that after a long trip. Massage relieves it. Would you like a massage?' There was apprehension in her voice as if she feared rejection.

He let her remove his tie and shirt with her dull, insensitive hands. He saw his tie on the floor and wanted to put it around her neck. He pushed the thought away. Her hands moved along his back. He rolled over to stop her. She wasn't pretty at all, he realized as he pulled her on to himself. He kissed her, but tasted something on her breath he didn't like. She kissed him. This wasn't going to work, there was no sexual attraction. He saw the makeup on her eyelashes, thick blobs of mascara clinging to fine lashes like matter in unwashed eyes.

'What are you doing?' she asked as he reached up to wipe it off.

There was an unpleasant edge to her voice.

'Take this off. I'll give you a massage.' He tugged her sweater. Beneath it she wore a bra; she had small breasts and a muscular body. What am I doing with this cunt? he thought, as he ran his hands over her body. Suddenly he felt abject loathing, as if he had known her all his life during which this hatred had been building. He could easily strangle her. She was speaking, but he wasn't listening; possibly talking about the Stones, as rock music was the emotional plateau upon which she existed. Killing her would be the simplest solution. An Indian tomahawk brought from some trip would split her skull. He would get blood on himself. He tried to force his crazy thoughts away, but they were getting stronger. He was getting higher and wanted to come down now and leave, but knew he couldn't. She was suggesting they go to bed in case her flatmates returned.

He woke with a start, a ghost crossing the channels of memory, stirring half-forgotten fears of when he had slept with a gun under his pillow. His hand was reaching under the pillow now, not being completely out of touch with that reality. He remembered what had happened in Washington recently, Wallechinsky's appointment, and that had brought the past back into focus. Wallechinsky had understood better than anyone what had been happening to America back then and he had trusted Wallechinsky more than anyone. Not anymore.

His eyes circled the room, trying to familiarize himself. He remembered the chaos in this apartment with its ill-assortment of furnishings, how he didn't enjoy being there. He shouldn't have gone to sleep. The place gave out especially bad vibrations. He had a problem moving, it was as though he was strapped to the bed, being drained by chaos. He instinctively knew he had to get away. Then he became aware of the woman, who might have been an insuperable obstacle. He wanted to leave without disturbing her, or having her see him again. Every identifiable point of contact could bring Wallechinsky one step closer.

She didn't disturb.

As he lay unmoving he became aware of the silence. She wasn't breathing, and turning, he saw her mouth forced open as if trying to suck air into collapsing lungs; her teeth were stained at the gums. He shivered with disgust. Her eyes were stark, terrified. He sat up and checked the room again, remaining calm. He didn't know whether her roommates had returned during the night, but he waited, listening, his own breathing getting faster. Wheels whirled in his brain. He had a situation that could cause him all kinds of problems. The thought ceased abruptly at the sound of someone up on the next floor using the john. Waiting until the building was quiet again, he eased himself out of bed. The time was 5am. Calmness came over him as he paused to consider the situation.

She deserved to die, he told himself, she was a wreck, and probably brought chaos to anyone she was with. Although society currently tolerated such people, he preferred they were disposed of by the simplest means; there were too many people in the world, most of them fucked-up. He felt no distress, but swiftly his mind moved back, seeking incidents that might link him to her. No one in the Park Lane bar would remember him picking her up, he decided; no one would recall them in the restaurant; no one had seen them enter the apartment. No one cared. People were too busy with self to notice anyone else. If he managed to leave unseen he would be clear, provided he cleaned up and left no trace of himself here.

After dressing he went quietly to check that none of the other stewardesses were around. Then he wiped anything he had touched;· he picked up all traces of the joint they'd smoked. From the bathroom he got a sponge and water and washed her vagina. His sperm might have identified him; forensic scientists could have made his blood group, not conclusively, but he wouldn't give them even that small advantage. Partial rigor mortis had set in and he had difficulty getting her legs apart. Only his body warmth in the bed had prevented full rigor.

After returning the sponge to the bathroom, he tidied up the woman, closing her mouth, eyes and legs. He arranged the sheet over her bruised neck so that anyone looking in would think she was asleep. Considerately he switched off the heating, as heat would accelerate decay, leaving a stinking mess.

Starting out of the apartment, Paley froze as someone came in via the street door. He pushed the apartment door closed and listened to a woman's footfalls on the Victorian tiled floor in the hallway. There wasn't a tense muscle in him, his breathing was slow, even. He knew what he would have to do if she came in. There was doubt about his not being able to do it, after all he had survived this long with the odds against him. The sound of the woman's feet stopped, and after a moment he realized she had stepped onto the carpeted stairs. He heard a door open two floors above.

He let himself out, and wiped the doorhandle. He didn't meet anyone on leaving the building, and from what he could tell no one saw him. There weren't many people on the streets of South Kensington at that hour, a couple of somnambulists huddled in their coats against the chill spring air, and a guy unloading a fruit and vegetable produce truck to a small store.

A thought occurring to him then was that maybe it was time to quit London, especially with Wallechinsky rising. Then he figured that quitting wouldn't be smart, for if an American was tied in to that dead chick, and one was missing from his usual routine, the cops would start looking for him.

Anyway he didn't plan on making any moves until he found out what was on the mind of his erstwhile partners when they met tomorrow.

Fourteen

The man with the small canvas grip was the first to leave the Alitalia Boeing from Milan and Venice, and first to approach the immigration gate for non-UK or EEC citizens. The officer glanced at the American passport, then at the holder and stamped the visa. Such moments were usually bad for Lance Niles, despite his valid papers. The cause of his apprehension was that Lawrence Wallechinsky had arranged this documentation.

Sliding the passport into his pocket, he shifted the overnight bag to his right hand and headed out past the baggage carousel. He had no other luggage and nothing to declare. The only reason he had this bag was because he believed international travelers without baggage were suspicious. When working for the Company the best cover on brief tours had been to go overloaded, the way the unwise traveler went abroad.

There was nothing Niles needed in the grip as he wasn't planning on staying, but catching the evening plane back to Venice. He checked the bag into left luggage and took the bus downtown.

London made him feel vulnerable. There were too many anonymous contact points, with people thrown up out of the past. So he came here only when absolutely necessary. He would like to have spent time in England, studying its religious architecture, having always promised himself a trip to see York Minster's medieval stained glass. But long ago had decided the risk was too great, and there were churches enough in Venice to last his lifetime. All his time was spent helping the Venetians restore them, a labor of love, one Niles anticipated spending the rest of his days doing.

Because of the physical geography of Venice, the insular nature of the people, Niles felt safe. Nothing surprised him there, and no one could approach him without he was alerted. If anyone came seeking him, someone would be asked who knew someone who would warn him. They were a people who respected privacy. Partly on account of the time he had been there and perhaps out of gratitude for his work, the Venetians had made him welcome. It was home. The annual tourist invasion was no threat, despite the smallness of the place. The Americans who came had an itinerary, being concerned to see as many churches as possible in their allotted time, few realizing that their entire vacation would be needed to look at just one church properly. Niles went back to churches time and again, forever making new discoveries.

Niles didn't know the Berkeley hotel on Wilton Place so didn't have the cab from the West London terminal drop him there directly. Instead he got out and walked around the block in case the hotel was being watched. It wasn't, as far as he could tell, but then he had gotten out of touch with such things.

The church on Wilton Place held more immediate interest for Niles than the hotel, where he might suddenly discover he no longer had a future. St Paul's Wilton Place was built in the early 19th century and would have been the center of the community when London was divided into parishes. The architect, who Niles wasn't familiar with, although no Wren, showed craftsmanlike stateliness. The west window was particularly attractive, but nothing compared to the glories of Venice. However, what St Paul's Wilton Place had over most Italian churches was heating. Lack of funding left the latter cold and poorly lit; it had distressed Niles when he found people had to put coins in slotmeters to get enough light to see the priceless art works. For tourists that was okay, but a lot of local people couldn't afford to pay, especially children, who he felt should have been given particular exposure to church art and architecture. He recalled his upbringing: it had been a poor Pentecostal church in the Yew mountains of West Virginia where he had done all his childhood praying.

This church was tranquil and had a good atmosphere, despite the roar of traffic along Knightsbridge. The altar, lit through a stained glass window depicting Christ and the twelve apostles, lay out of reach behind locked gates, at which Niles stood and closed his eyes. He thought about his own insignificant future in relation to Christ.

Throughout his thirty-eight years, Lance Niles had felt the power of religion, having been born with the sign of the stigmata on his stomach. The marks had faded before he was old enough to understand, but his mother had always told him how he was to be man of destiny, and would lead his country back on the path of righteousness. She had never said he was the second Savior, but had hinted every which way at it, and the preacher in their church in Fenwick had gone right along with her; the preacher had gone along with everything his Momma had to say. His Momma had been a strong willed woman, as a result Niles had grown up feeling a heavy burden. Everyone had expected so much of him. If he tried to be like other kids his Momma whipped him. 'I don't wan' you doing with that dam' foolery, boy,' she would say, then lock him away to study his bible. Soon he knew his bible better than anyone and that gave him prestige, and not long after had derived great comfort from it.

At fourteen he had been torn with guilt at his burgeoning sexual feelings, but had no friends to share this burden with, so no way of knowing that the desire to masturbate, neck with girls and get into their pants was common to all boys. His bible explained nothing of this, and so the pressures increased along with his guilt. Then one night he found his Momma with the preacher, who was doing things to her that even his Poppa didn't do within the boy's knowledge, and his Poppa was present and wasn't doing a thing to stop it. The boy realized he had got religion, had pressure on him to lead a moral crusade; he had taken his Poppa's rifle and he had killed all three of them.

No one had blamed him. They had put him in the hospital at Charleston, where there were a lot of crazy people, some of whom thought they were God. The doctors had tried to take religion from him, but that was his single refuge. He had no plans to let it go, nor to forget the cause he felt he was born to. He had wisely kept quiet about that while in the hospital and eventually they had let him out to join the army. Religion went with him. In boot camp he was called Holy Joe, even though he proved a most efficient soldier. He went into Vietnam believing God was both on his shield and at his side; his moral leader at that time was John F. Kennedy, and had been fighting the war for him personally. It was then that he had been brought to the attention of Lawrence Wallechinsky.

Lance Niles, as he later became, was one more person on the CIA deputy director's list who felt bitterly betrayed by Kennedy, after learning of the President's moral lapses. The President of the United States, the torch lighting the way for all those who stumbled, was no better than his Momma and the preacher. That was the truth.

Details which had since reached Niles about the private life of the former President gave him no cause to change his opinion; they confirmed what a liar he had been, how dangerous he had been to the people of the United States.

Niles remained kneeling, head bowed, praying that he would be able to return home and carry on his work, restoring churches.

Moving past the entrance of the hotel, Niles decided no one had it staked out. On entering the hotel he called the desk and was told that Mr Abatis, as Radulovic was known, hadn't checked in yet. Niles went to the reception desk and claimed the room.

The clerk was unconcerned that Niles had no baggage. After being shown to the third floor suite, he let the bellboy show him the facilities. He tipped him, then locked the door and made a thorough search himself. He was looking for microphones or bugging devices.

There weren't any that he could find, though he wasn't

sure he'd recognize such things now. He considered who might be interested in recording any conversation taking place between them. Wallechinsky was the only person and his interest wouldn't be in having a record of what they said.

Having searched, Niles relaxed. He settled in an armchair in the room that overlooked Hyde Park and opened the Gideon bible that had been placed there.

The telephone startled him. Abacus identified himself and asked if it was safe. Niles told him it was.

Chuck Paley wondered if that wasn't too easy when he put the phone down. His eyes swept the fawn and gold hotel lobby. He had gotten jumpy, and knew it was to do with his killing that air stewardess. There had been nothing on the news, but that was meaningless; the police here reacted differently to the media than they did in the States, if they could exclude the press, or ask for and get a blackout. But he figured he was being pursued. Pursuers were growing by the hour in his mind, everyone being a potential danger. He had burned all the clothes he had been wearing at the time – the girl was connected with the Inn on the Park, and an American, the cop from the Drug Squad would easily place the two together.

This distracted Paley, who failed to identify Aardvark sitting across the lobby, talking to a young girl and her mother. The girl had a keen interest in horses.

Torbert watched the man step into the elevator, the indicator stopped at the second floor.

Although proceeding with great caution, figuring he had the most to lose, Torbert was no longer as observant as he once had been. He hadn't failed to notice the man across the lobby, where he'd been since early that morning – Torbert had taken a room in the hotel – he simply failed to recognize him as Aardwolf. Shepard Erhart hadn't been hanging around begging to get made. He had three men to assist him in the public parts of the hotel. The people he now worked for offered as much assistance as he required. They wanted this operation successfully concluded; the East Germans didn't wish Ambassador Wallechinsky to take up his post in Nanking, as it indicated normalization of relations between China and America. If that relationship presented problems for the Eastern Communist bloc, under the active guidance of Lawrence Wallechinsky, it might operate to the definite detriment of Russia, and therefore East Germany.

If what Erhart planned was brought off, then no way would President Nixon's new ambassador take up his post. For his plan to succeed he had to convince the three men in that hotel room of the threat Wallechinsky saw in them and, as a result, the imminent danger they were in. That was a fact, but because of his own vested interest he wasn't sure they'd believe him.

He didn't get the opportunity. Leaving his room on the fourth floor, after being told all three men were in 211, he rode the elevator to the third floor where he planned to take the service stairs to the second. Someone else had the same idea. As the elevator door slid silently back he saw the small frame of a man move through the door to the service stairs. The figure was familiar, the fleeting glimpse of his moon-shaped face printed on his mind was run through the index of faces stored on his mind's eye. Erhart knew at once that the hotel room was a trap.

Working as he did for the East German espionage service he knew he was on the CIA wanted list, and certainly both the British and West German lists. Being in London was dangerous, but it was important he warned his three former colleagues, despite the risk of getting involved in foiling a CIA trap, otherwise he would fail himself.

Stepping back into the elevator, Erhart pressed for the fourth floor.

Fifteen

In suite 211 the three men found they had nothing to say, which wasn't surprising. The common factors were their being expatriate, having formerly worked for the CIA, and being involved in a deed each of them would have preferred to forget.

Niles called room service for a bottle as they tried small talk, but even that they had gotten out of the way of. Had they lived back home, these three prosperous, middle-aged men might have complimented each other about the fine shape they were in; they'd have played tennis or jogged, dieted; they'd have traded coaches or diets. Only Paley was overweight. Lance Niles was tall, and thinner than a Kentucky string bean, and when he was restoring churches he sometimes forgot to eat for days, forgot to sleep, then finally when tiredness overwhelmed him he would sleep sitting upright in a chair, and eat when he awoke. Torbert shared a similar casual indifference to food, which he had to cook for himself. After working all day with his horses it was sometimes easier not to bother. However, Paley, with little to occupy him, spent time in London's restaurants, and knew the best there was: Soho's unostentatious Italian restaurants where it was like eating in someone's front parlor. But he could no more talk to these men about such things than they could about horses or religion.

Each went to pay the waiter when he arrived with the scotch.

But Niles did it.

'How'd you like it?' he asked.

Paley took his with water, Torbert on the rocks.

There was an awkward pause.

Paley said, 'The future,' and raised his glass. He ran his hand through his silvery hair, and added, 'Whatever it may be.'

'There's gonna be one?' Torbert finally got to it.

'That's what we came to talk about.'

'Shouldn't we wait for the others?' Niles suggested.

'Who says they're gonna get here?' Paley looked at the other two. When he didn't get an argument, he swallowed his drink and poured himself another. 'It's a quarter of one. The meeting was set for noon.'

'For Christsake, this is Britain. Three-quarters of an hour don't mean a thing.'

'Sure. You're British, and you ain't got some mother looking to take you out,' Paley argued. His glance went from Torbert to Niles, who was uncomfortable with the language the argument was couched in. 'The way I see it, those guys ain't coming.'

'You figure Wallechinsky got to them?' Torbert wanted to resist Paley's conclusions for purely selfish reasons; if that was the way of it then the smart course was to move on. Letting out for new cover would be his last alternative.

'That's what I reckon.'

'We should give them a while longer. Abatis called this meeting.'

'Did he?' Paley emptied his glass again.

'If they are dead,' Niles said quietly from his chair, 'we've been set up.'

'Jesus, we really are some dumb assholes. We worked for the Company. Right. Put together what we figured was some kind of early warning. Right. What we didn't plan on was one of us selling out. That could've happened.'

Torbert looked at Lance Niles, who had been his choice. His presence changed that.

'I ain't running,' Torbert said. 'All you get to do is put it off. If Wallechinsky figures it's time he got this tidied up, it doesn't matter whether it's here or someplace else. He'll want it done.'

'You plan to go after him?' There was a sardonic smile on Paley's pulpy face.

'I'd like to know what happened to the others. Mexico seems like a good place to start.'

'We've had eleven years with God's grace,' Niles said.

The other two men became embarrassed and avoided his look.

'Maybe they decided it was safer to take off.'

'I figure Abalone and Aardwolf would've made contact. Somehow gotten word.'

The telephone bell caused each of them to tense. No one moved. Then Niles, who was the closest, raised the receiver. 'It's Aardwolf,' he said, covering the mouthpiece as Erhart identified himself.

The other two pressed in to hear the conversation.

'We've been set up,' Erhart said. 'Wallechinsky has a hit man in the hotel.'

'Where are you?' Niles said.

'You'd better get out of there fast.'

'Who's the hit man?'

'You'll know him. We've headed him off. Go. I'll be in touch.' Erhart hung up.

Paley had the switchboard check where the call came from, but it had been dialed directly.

There was an uneasy silence.

'Any of you guys got a piece on you?' Torbert asked.

After a moment Paley declared his. He carried a S&W Chief's Special, which was the smallest .38 around.

Paley's look challenged him. 'You figure I should cover your retreat, pal?'

'I think we should leave together,' Niles suggested. 'Take a cab, then separate.'

'We gotta stay in contact. Until we resolve this mess.'

'You still aim to head for Mexico?' Paley asked.

'We know Aardwolf is alive. I want to know about the other two. If they're dead I want to know how.'

'What good will knowing do you?'

'I'll know if I gotta run. You wanna give me an address or number I can reach you at?'

That commitment caused both men to hesitate. Finally they made it.

They left the room cautiously, checking the corridor and

the service stairs. Paley led the way, his .38 clasped in his pocket. They rode an elevator to the basement. There the parking attendant didn't question Paley when he called for a Rover 3500, whose license plate he'd memorized on the walk from the elevator.

They ditched the car on the north side of Hyde Park when certain they weren't followed. They split up. Paley headed toward Oxford Street, and Torbert went west, toward the subway station at Lancaster Gate.

There were no cabs around and Niles stopped and watched some horseback riders on a track on the edge of the park. That was a nice thing to be doing on an early spring afternoon, he thought, especially for its representing as it did a life without worries. The riders were mainly children.

When the horses were out of sight he crossed the street and entered Kensington Gardens, uncertain why what was essentially one park had two names. Narcissi were out there, and early tulips, thousands of them. He strolled past the flower beds, knowing he had time before catching his plane back to Venice. After a while he sat on a bench and questioned whether there was any point going back. If it was all going to end he might as well be in London. Possibly that would make things less complicated and embarrassing for the church authorities. He wondered about precipitating this by presenting himself at the American embassy and telling his story. But why would they believe him? They could run a check on him, he told himself, but that would only confirm he was Lance Niles. Lawrence Wallechinsky had been thorough with their new identities, so what point going to the embassy? Maybe he should go back to the hotel and wait for someone to show up.

Instead, as he rose off the bench, he decided to look at a couple of churches before returning home. There was still a lot of work for him to do.

Sixteen

Despite being out of the business for as long as he had, Torbert could still find his way around an investigation, especially in a town like Mocorito. The people there no longer had any need to protect Dios de las Abegas, and Torbert soon discovered that Radulovic was dead and buried; the locals had paid their last respects, and were getting on with their own lives. Radulovic's suicide didn't accord with the meeting he had set up in London.

What caused the local cops to hold back on their information was the fact that Torbert hadn't laid any money on them; West Cork had put him out of touch with that, and he soon remedied the situation.

Then whatever they had they readily gave him, and what they didn't have they invented, figuring it was what he wanted to hear.

'What was Señor Radulovic to you?' one of the cops asked. He was fascinated by the chunk missing from Torbert's ear and kept stealing glances at it.

'He was a friend. Did he commit suicide?'

'He did, señor,' the second cop told him. 'The other Americano didn't believe it.' He shrugged, suggesting the truth was important. It wouldn't bring him back.

'Tell me about this other guy.'

What they told about Jimmy Vanesco wasn't much, and Torbert mistakenly believed they were holding out on him; so he gave them more money. Then they started to invent things.

Torbert's next move was to find Vanesco, and so he headed for New York.

There were two Vanesco's listed. The phone on the West Side went unanswered; an answering service on the downtown number confirmed Jimmy Vanesco was a private inquiry agent; the woman told him Mr Vanesco was out of town, but was expected back in two or three days.

Was there a partner? secretary? wife? Torbert was insistent, said it was a matter of life or death. The woman wasn't impressed. 'Look, I've come all the way from Ireland to see Mr Vanesco,' he told her illogically.

There was immediate interest. 'Gee, I knew there was something about your accent,' she said. 'How about that. What part you from?'

He told her County Cork, and found a way to her heart. Her maternal grandfather had come from Cork City.

Anyone from Ireland might automatically have been blessed with innocence, so when pressed again for means of contacting Vanesco, the woman broke the strict company rule and gave him Zell's address.

There was no reply when he called her number. He figured she could have been at work, and decided to stop by her apartment later that afternoon. First he took a cab to the Herald-Tribune offices on Madison Avenue.

Their records didn't tell him who had placed the ad that called him and his former partners to London. All they told him was that it had been placed and paid for by cash in New York on March 15th. That detail increased Torbert's anxiety. It meant Radulovic couldn't have placed that ad, unless it wasn't him who had died in Mexico. He thought about the possibility as he left the newspaper offices. Those Mexicans he talked to had been all smiles and information, but he guessed the only way he was going to know for sure was to go back and dig him up. Then he'd be relying on memory, but what time in the ground would have done to Abatis was something else. That apart, anyway they probably lynched grave desecrators in Mexico.

The Cadillac Seville parked on Charles Street made Torbert shorten his step. Pimps and hoods had driven Cadillacs when he had been in touch with American sub-culture. The guy behind the wheel was watching the street, and not checking hookers, so Torbert guessed it was a hood's car.

What New York hoods were into held no interest, he wanted no contact with them. But wasn't sure that would be the way of it, for when he started into the building the man in the car thumped the horn a couple of times like he was signaling.

Two men ran down the stairs when Torbert started up from the hallway, where he had checked the mailbox. They looked like they belonged to the car outside; one wore a suit and a black fedora, the other a leather coat. As they passed him both tried to conceal their faces, but Torbert's trained eyes got a good enough look to have picked them out in a police line up.

They weren't burglars. He smelt what they had done before reaching the top landing. They had defecated outside the door, either that or had carried the shit up, but there was no kind of bag around. They had also smeared the door, buzzer and locks. He guessed they were lunatics.

New York was full of crazies, the cells at Center Street overflowed, especially when the moon was up and at its most potent.

He wondered why Zell Kleinbard had been singled out for this, whether it had anything to do with her connection with Vanesco.

He rapped an unsmeared section of the door, but got no reply. Maybe she was in but too scared to open the door. He considered going down to the street to call her when he heard people coming up the stairs. Two children who were racing each other to the landing stopped and looked at Torbert.

Zell, who wasn't far behind, jumped the gun, figuring he represented the apartment scumlord; then she saw the excrement, which Sam and Darren were now reacting against.

'You fucking asshole,' she screamed. 'You dirty fucking bastard. People are trying to raise kids decently in this neighborhood. You assholes take away all dignity . . .'

'Hey, take it easy, lady,' Torbert protested. 'You figure I'd pull a lousy trick like this then stick around?'

'That asshole Kali won't get me to quit my apartment.'

'You had visitors. They took off when I showed up.'

He told her about the two guys, then who he was; who he was looking for. Finally she calmed down. He guessed it was pretty upsetting to come home and find a whole pile of shit on your doorstep.

'You got any Kleenex?' he asked.

He wiped the locks so she could open the door. Doing it made him feel nauseous. Any amount of horseshit he could handle, but that was innocuous, probably because they were vegetarian. He persevered, figuring it was the easiest way to get her help.

She let him into the apartment, then bolted the door.

'Make sure you don't have crap on your shoes, Sam. You too, Darren,' she said as they started into the bedroom.

'Problems with your landlord?'

'We're rent controlled; he wants to hike the rents.'

'This is no place to raise a family. A city half-full of crazies and junkies,' he observed.

'It's doing all right. So Mayor Lindsay sold us down the river, but we'll make it. It'll be no place if all the decent folk give into pressures from assholes like Kali. We've gotta hang in, otherwise every neighborhood'll become a Harlem or South Bronx, people'll shut their apartment doors, won't give a damn what's happening on the streets, in neighborhood schools. Only single people will be able to afford these apartments, they won't care.'

'Yeah, you could be right,' he lied. He didn't believe the cities worth saving. The way for people to live was with space around them. 'How long d'you figure you can take this abuse?'

'It's been this way for a year now. What would get me spooky is if they started causing fire hazards. Kali's brother burned a couple of buildings down on Hudson. A mother and two kids died.'

There was a thoughtful silence.

'You ought to call the cops.'

'I report every incident. The NYPD have their own problems. How to get Kali to pay more into their pad; upholding the rights of his tenants won't do it.' She tried not to sound cynical. 'You wanted to reach Jimmy, you said.'

'It's important. You know where he is?'

'Not precisely. He's in Western Ontario.'

'You got a phone number?'

She shook her head. 'How d'you lose your ear?' she asked

with the inoffensiveness of a child.

Torbert pulled at the half-section of the ear, and smiled. He usually ignored such questions. 'A horse cropped it,' he said. 'It is important. You can't get closer than Western Ontario. I mean, I'd fly up there if I can't get him on the phone.'

'He'll be back in a couple of days.' She saw that was no good. 'Darren.' She went to the bedroom door. The two boys were playing war with plastic soldiers. Darren, who preferred being the Germans, was aggressively overrunning American encampments. 'Where is it Moyra has her cabin back home, honey?'

'Randle Point. That's where Pa got burned.' He announced this like it was information repeated off tv; then returned to his current war.

Zell considered the child before closing the door. Darren's problems were beginning to disturb her.

It occurred to Torbert then who the kid resembled. So he was dead too. He resisted asking the woman what her boyfriend was doing pursuing a dead man. Maybe he was just interested in what had happened the same as he was. Which left the question why. He wanted to talk to Darren about his Pa, but passed. Maybe he'd get some answers at Randle Point, even if they were those he didn't want. One thing looked certain, someone was active. Not for a moment did Torbert figure that Abatis and Abalone dying within days of each other was a coincidence, not after the warning they had gotten in London.

Stumbling across the skiptrace was inevitable in a place like Randle Point at that time of year. Maybe at the height of the holiday season they could have missed each other, but even that was doubtful when they were making inquiries about the same man, especially as he had recently died.

Torbert was at a table in the back of the general store drinking coffee and trying to thaw his hands when Vanesco came in with Moyra Yeston. Even if the man at the checkout hadn't nodded in his direction Torbert would have known who he was. He had an alertness which suggested he was a cop. His eyes took the place at a glance, making him, the clerk, and the two guys sitting by the stove.

125

'You wanna bring us coffee, maybe some sandwiches?'
Vanesco said.

He took the woman's arm and steered her through the store
toward the tables. There was a lunch counter that was shut
out of season, and instead of sandwiches in plastic displays
there were dismantled outboard motors, wrenches, oily rags.
It gave the place character.

Vanesco and Moyra had been to see the bank manager in
Marathon. The man was willing but unable to tell them why
Coley had withdrawn his money. It wasn't an everyday
occurrence, but the money had been Coley's and he had the
right to withdraw it. The manager had assumed he was going
after a better rate of interest, and had offered him a certified
draft, but Coley had wanted cash. He had confirmed that the
withdrawal was the same day as his demise, which put him
right in the frame.

'You were asking after Brad Coley,' Vanesco said when
they reached Torbert's table.

'I hear he's dead. Right.'

Vanesco glanced at the woman. 'That's his wife, Moyra
Yeston.'

Torbert told them his name and watched closely for some
reaction. Vanesco gave no indication that he knew the name
that was on Cunningham's list, but wondered what his
presence meant.

'Did you discover anything about the circumstances of
Brad's death?'

'You were friends?' Vanesco asked.

'Business associates, way back. I'm sorry he's dead, Mrs
Coley.'

She looked at him and said, 'We weren't married.'

Her face was empty, she had a listlessness which suggested
she had neither interest nor awareness of what was going on
around her. Vanesco got a feeling that she neither wanted to
find out any more about the man she had been living with,
nor wanted him to. Curiously he no longer felt any compassion for her. That feeling he experienced when first
finding her had vanished, along with her helplessness and
bewilderment that had engendered it. She reminded him of
people who hung around East 14th Street, trying to score,

126

needing to in order to get through the day; she was responding to every suggestion as passively as a head bottoming out. He had asked her if she had taken anything or needed to. She said no, but told him again that Coley had used a lot of scag. She said she snorted occasionally, not much or often. That wouldn't explain the downer she was on, and he didn't figure it was bereavement.

'What was your present interest in Coley, Mr Torbert?' Vanesco asked.

'I had some business he might have been interested in. I deal in farm machinery. I got the Toyota franchise for the North-Eastern territory.'

'Is that right?'

The woman got up from the table. 'I'm going to the cabin. There's things I need to do.'

'Sure. I'll collect you there later.' Vanesco didn't rise.

Torbert got up. 'If there's anyway I can help, Miss Yeston. Be a pleasure.'

She looked through him, offering no response.

Torbert watched her go out. 'She's taking it kinda hard.'

'You saw Coley recently, did you?' Vanesco said.

'We got out of touch. You know how it is.' He pulled at his damaged ear.

'About eleven years, I figure.'

That surprised Torbert. 'How much do you know?'

He waited while the girl brought his sandwiches and coffee. 'I know you didn't come up here to offer Coley a job. You got all the wrong information for that.'

Torbert thought about the situation. Finally he nodded. 'I came to find what had happened. How do you figure?'

'What made you think anything had happened? You haven't seen him in years.'

'He didn't show for a reunion we had. Nor did Radulovic.'

'You been down to Mexico?'

'That's how I know about you. I talked to your girlfriend. What's your interest?'

'Money. I was hired to find Radulovic and Coley.' He paused. 'And you. Along with three other guys. Chuck Paley, Shepard Erhart, and a guy called Niles. They at your reunion?'

'Who hired you?'

'A New York lawyer. A big honcho in legal circles.'

'He say why he wanted us traced?' Torbert asked. The cavity of his mouth had gone dry.

'I figured one of you guys were gonna tell me that.'

'The other two didn't tell you?'

'They might have, they hadn't died.' Vanesco drank some coffee and waited. But Torbert wasn't getting to it. 'You run across a man named Harry Kohn? He's pretty high in the Mafia, lately he's gotten smart, made contacts in administration. This one, the last one; the next one, no favorites.'

'I live abroad. Maybe I read about him in Time Magazine. I don't remember.'

Vanesco shook his head. 'He's in back of this lawyer. He tells it like Mafia business.'

'I never had any truck with the Mafia.'

'They aim to find you. You better believe it ain't to tell how you won on the numbers. They've either got the goods on you, pal, or mistaken you for someone else.' Vanesco saw from the look on his dark, creased face that this wasn't so. 'Whatever it was you and those other guys did, I'll find out. I'd sooner do that the easy way, being that kinda guy. You've got something buried back there, something that's getting someone in a lather. Now ordinarily I could live without knowing, I could've found you guys, made a phone call, collected my money. No problem. But things started happening I didn't like. I traced Radulovic; next day he's dead. Same thing with Coley. What I don't like is that I don't have control. I don't know or really mind who's out there waiting to take you out, but when it's done, maybe he gets to me.'

'Why d'you figure you were hired, Vanesco?' Torbert knew who, but couldn't figure why. He could see how the combination of Mafia, a lawyer and a New York skiptrace would distance Wallechinsky, but having some notion of how he thought, the ambassador would subsequently see each of those as a risk.

'Because I'm the best.'

'You believe someone's following you?'

'That wouldn't be difficult. Let me tell you something. I call New York now, tell them I found you, you better start

128

looking over your shoulder.'

'I've been doing that a long while.'

'They, whoever the fuck they are, haven't been looking, pal. They knew you were around only you weren't a problem. Suddenly you're a problem. Whoever it is coming after you is good. So you wanna tell me why you're suddenly a problem? See if we can work something out?'

The invitation was one Torbert would like to have taken up. There was an earnestness about the skiptrace, but he wasn't prepared to trust him. He couldn't give him the answers he wanted, because that might create a greater danger. If he overcame this immediate threat he wouldn't have to quit Ireland or disappear. Leaving the life he had made wasn't something he wanted to do, so was prepared to take risks to keep it. It was the only permanence he had known; possibly it was a mistake to put roots down, but they were there now, and they nourished him. If he were to answer Vanesco's questions there was no telling how the skiptrace would react, but it was certain he wouldn't share the interests of those so far concerned in keeping the secret.

Slowly the horsebreeder shook his head. 'The person with the answer is the man who comes after me once you call New York.'

Vanesco nodded. This was the best he was going to get. He accepted that by letting himself be set up Torbert was making a big commitment, especially as Vanesco couldn't guarantee to keep the hitman from reaching him. He wondered what Torbert had planned. The chances were that the killer wouldn't know what Torbert and the others had done, only who had hired him. However, there was no other route.

'You going to make the phone call?'

'Give me your address. And when you're going home.'

The details were easy to work out. Vanesco called New York and reported his lead on Torbert.

When he got to Coley's cabin the woman wasn't there, nor was the car he had rented. It looked like she had lit out rather than taken a drive, clothes she had brought with her from New York were gone. So too had some of the things from the cabin: the rest of her clothes, some of Coley's clothes also. Coley was alive, of that Vanesco was sure, and he was coming to believe that Mo Yeston was in contact with him. But questions kept jumping up in his mind; why would she come to New York, drag him back here?

He'd report the car, get a ride back to Thunder Bay, and head out to Cork with Torbert. There he'd see who showed up. He had a feeling it was going to be Brad Coley.

Seventeen

Setting foot in Ireland for the first time, Jimmy Vanesco immediately understood why Torbert wanted to hang in there, it was a different world to any he had known. What struck him most was the attitude of the Irish and their pace of life. Someone had once told him that in Ireland you could always find someone who didn't care, not about anything; it made a welcome change. Things happened in their own time, no one forced the pace. A woman in a store talking to another about a third, finished the conversation before she got to him. He had stopped to check his directions, feeling he had taken a wrong turn; the roads weren't what he was used to, and there were few road signs. The woman set him straight, then gave him an alternative route should he not care for the first, which was quicker, she said; the second woman said the other way would get him there just as quick, to which the woman behind the counter said, it would of course.

In the bar he later stopped at to ask directions to Torbert's place, a customer bade him good evening at 3pm; commented what a bad day it was, how it had been a shocking winter altogether, and inquired if he was on holiday, like Vanesco hadn't asked his question. He soon learned that there was no hurrying the process, you either accepted the pace or were frustrated by it. In New York people got iced for not answering inquiries fast enough.

At first Vanesco thought he had gotten the wrong place when he arrived at Torbert's stud farm, despite stopping twice more to check his directions on the way out of town. He sat in his rented car at the top of the long driveway lined with enormous rhododendron bushes, which were in bud, and looked at the house and stables in the valley. It was a pretty sight; with the surrounding hills it looked like the work of a landscape gardener, with a lake and a wood beyond, and a mountain in the west where the sun was headed. A mare and foal in a paddock completed the picture. The set-up seemed inconsistent with the way Radulovic and Coley had lived – it was as though they had been camping out, while Torbert had become a permanent resident.

'You like the layout?' was how Torbert greeted him.

Vanesco would have expected him to ask what kind of trip he had, whether he figured he was followed.

'Looks good.'

'I put a lot of work into this place. I practically rebuilt those stables myself. You can't get builders to do damn all here. Or else you gotta keep cracking the whip. You want to see over the place?'

Vanesco did, but not for Torbert's reason. Instead he wanted to see the strategic layout, for when he sprung his trap he wanted something in the net.

The house had sixteen rooms, excluding bathrooms and kitchen, but basically Torbert used only two of them, which made life easier as he didn't have a housekeeper.

'D'you get yourself a hotel?' Torbert asked.

'Yeah, in town.'

There was only one hotel, and Vanesco preferred to stay there, but thought it strange that Torbert didn't offer him a bed, when a lot of the bedrooms were furnished. He assumed this man didn't want him that close, where he could maybe find out about his past. Though Vanesco got the feeling that nothing of this man's earlier existence lived in this house with him. The place was really neat but as impersonal as a dentist's waiting room, and like that everything was orderly and in its place. Vanesco's own apartment was a mess most times. When it got too bad he called an agency cleaner,

131

got it cleaned up, then started over. This place hadn't been just cleaned, it had never been untidied. Bill Torbert was, he decided, someone with a compartmentalized life, who could only deal with things once they were pigeonholed. Why did he live this way? Vanesco was questioning not his neatness, but this grandiose permanence. Had he dealt with his past, locked it in its compartment never to be allowed out? It was however going to get out, Vanesco was sure.

'That's a nice rifle,' Vanesco said, picking up the Remington leaning against the kitchen wall. 'You get much use for it?'

Torbert looked at him, reading more into the question than there was.

The sound of a car coming along the drive caused alarm to flash in Torbert's face, like he was caught off guard.

'Were you tailed?' He went to the kitchen door that led to the yard.

A small man in a heavy sheepskin coat climbed from the car and spoke to the girl, who was filling haynets. Torbert watched them, a feeling of anxiety sliding over him. He stepped across the kitchen and unlocked a drawer, he removed a Colts automatic, he pushed it into his belt and pulled down his jerkin.

'You have a piece?' he said.

'No,' Vanesco said. His Browning was in his grip in the car.

'Stay outta sight. I'll find out who he is.'

From the kitchen window Vanesco watched him head across the yard. Their conversation was brief; they went along to loose boxes and looked at some horses.

It was at this point that Vanesco believed there was someone in the house. It was more a feeling he had than the noise he heard, which could have been caused by a draft. This was a time when Vanesco wished he hadn't parted from his Browning. He checked the drawer for another piece, but found only boxes of shotgun cartridges. There were some .30.30 shells for the Remington, but that wasn't a weapon to go searching for an intruder with; it was doubtful that he'd get off one shot with the bolt action.

Cautiously Vanesco moved from the kitchen into the hall.

132

The sun was way down by this time, leaving the wide corridor to the heavy main door shrouded in half-light. He resisted using the lights, as he had good vision, so if anyone was there they'd have no advantage. The first room he reached was a study, which was one of the two rooms Torbert used. There was a faint out-of-place smell, which Vanesco hadn't noticed earlier, but now realized was gasoline. It wasn't strong, strong enough to represent a danger, and he thought maybe Torbert had cleaned a gun there. The door directly across the hall was locked. This was a dining room and Vanesco couldn't remember if Torbert had locked it. He checked the next door, a sitting room, which was deserted; the fourth room downstairs was also, and Vanesco began to think that what he had heard were mice or rats. He moved back along the hall and started up the stairs, carefully placing his feet to avoid setting off creaking treads. He got to the third stair, when a gun was slowly cocked. Spinning round, he found himself facing Torbert's Colts automatic.

'What d'you figure you're doing?'

Vanesco recognized fear behind the man's anger. There seemed no point telling him he thought he'd heard someone. He returned the Remington to the kitchen.

'That guy's from Kentucky. Said he's looking to buy foals,' Torbert said of his other visitor. 'Did you recognize him?'

Vanesco shook his head. He didn't fit the details on Coley's record, and he hadn't seen him any place before.

'Calls himself Alfred Stimson. He knows enough about horses to buy a kid's pony. Says he's looking for bloodstock for a breeding syndicate in Lexington. I think what we've got here is a hitman.'

Vanesco nodded. 'You told him you'd sell him horses?'

'He's coming back in the morning.'

Something was wrong, Vanesco realized, but couldn't decide what. Someone coming after Torbert this way was too obvious. He thought about how Radulovic had died, and Coley; he considered again the gasoline he had smelt, the possibility that someone was already in the house.

'If he comes back it'll be tonight,' Vanesco said.

'S'what I figured. I told the help to get the horses inside. If there's shooting I don't want any of them in the way. You staying here?'

'Makes sense. You wanna get my gun from the car? Might be good if the opposition doesn't know who's here. Stimson'll be watching the place.'

Torbert brought the gun from Vanesco's bag in the car and watched him check it.

They ate dinner in the kitchen; a stew that Torbert took straight from the freezer in its crock and put on the stove. It had a blurred taste, suggesting it had been around awhile. Lately Zell had been giving him vegetarian food, which he hadn't resisted. Her objection to meat-eating was moral, she didn't believe man had dominion over animals or the right to inflict the kind of suffering inflicted by factory farming; Vanesco's objections right then were that he figured this would poison him, so didn't eat much.

Things started happening around ten o'clock when Torbert went to check on the horses. Stimson was waiting in a darkened stable, and pushed the barrel of a .38 into the side of Torbert's neck. Evidently he wasn't going to die from a .38, or he would have been dead.

Vanesco watched the small, round man steer Torbert toward the house. Torbert's skin had turned to parchment, his face suddenly old-looking. Vanesco realized that his move was too early the instant he made it; he took Stimson as he came through the doorway, but knew he should have waited to see if a partner appeared.

With a shriek of alarm Stimson begged for his life; afterwards Vanesco knew this had been warning to his partner. With the barrel of the Browning Vanesco slapped the fat man across the head, possibly fracturing his skull, then suddenly dove out of the kitchen and ran at a crouch through the hallway. He turned at the stairs. In the lighted kitchen Torbert watched, puzzled by the move. Vanesco realized he had misjudged the situation, and felt foolish. The house was silent. If there was someone around, he was being smarter.

'What the hell was all that?' Torbert said when the skiptrace returned.

Vanesco shook his head. 'I thought I heard something.' He didn't expand on that. If there was someone around then he wanted to reach him first. He figured Torbert knew who was coming and why, and would stop that person talking.

Stimson didn't know a thing, and Vanesco's questions didn't advance him. The fat man had no single piece of identification, and neither label in his suit nor laundry mark on his shirt.

Pushing the muzzle of the Browning into his eye, Vanesco said, 'You got five seconds to come up with some answers...' He pulled back the hammer.

Sweat broke out on Stimson's moon-shaped face and formed runnels down his temples. His lips moved without words emerging. Vanesco knew he wasn't going to pull that trigger, not like this, and something had communicated that to Stimson. But he was scared, for it only needed Vanesco's thumb to slip off the hammer.

'I'll make him talk,' Torbert said. 'The stallion out there could do with some exercise. That old boy'll drag him.'

Stimson didn't believe it, and Vanesco wasn't entirely sure.

The stallion, a solid-looking hunter, stood a foot taller at the shoulder than most of the quarter-horses Vanesco had seen. It had a powerful neck and muscular hindquarters that could pop its rider over any fence. The horse became nervous when Torbert led him into the floodlit paddock. There he tightened the girth, which the stallion didn't care for. He fixed a lunge rein to the head collar, and turned back to Stimson.

'How about that name?' Vanesco said.

'I don't have it.' This was no more than a dry, tense croak.

Torbert bound Stimson's wrists with a strap, then fastened the other end to the inside stirrup.

'I don't know,' Stimson insisted. 'You gentlemen have got to believe me. I jes' don't know. That's the righteous truth.'

Vanesco didn't believe him.

Torbert moved the horse out on the twenty foot lunge, and Stimson started to run, but his short, bowed legs weren't designed to pace a horse.

The horse trotted, nervous of this movement in his rear; when Torbert cracked the lunge whip the stallion broke into a canter, throwing his head. Stimson put in two paces before he was dragged over, and the horse gave a couple of bucks, trying to kick free of his impediment. The leather strap kept Stimson out of reach of its hooves.

There were cries of pain; for pity; to God.

Vanesco stood in the center of the circle the horse was describing, watching Torbert, whose look suggested he had no plans to stop this. He could kill Stimson like this without any kind of hassle from the cops.

'Why don't you give him a break?' Vanesco said as he ducked under the lunge. 'See if he wants to talk.'

Torbert cracked the whip again. The stallion thrust its back legs out at Stimson, this time the left hoof caught the strap, the force of it hauling him closer. Then, kicking again, a blow caught Stimson on the shoulder, causing the horse to take off, spooked by the contact.

'Easy, fella,' Torbert said. 'Easy, boy.' The words calmed the horse, and Torbert reined it in to a standstill. He gave him a piece of apple from his pocket.

Stimson lay in a whimpering, unmoving heap; his face muddied and cut, his clothes torn. In case Torbert started the horse again, Vanesco released the strap. If Stimson had anything to talk about, right then was the time.

'How about it, Stimson? Who sent you?'

The man opened his pain-filled eyes and tried to focus, he didn't say anything until the skiptrace reached out and grabbed his shoulder. 'My shoulder's broken, it's broken,' he hissed.

'Can you make it to the house?' He planned to work on him through that shoulder.

Vanesco couldn't tell if the shoulder was broken, but when he stripped his coat and shirt there was a red, inflamed area where the hoof had hit him. Vanesco caught hold of the arm and Stimson knew what he was going to do.

'The man who hired me is called Erhart,' he whispered.

The name didn't mean a thing to Vanesco, and Torbert gave no sign.

In the next instant Stimson ceased being a priority.

'Gasoline!'

Suddenly Vanesco became aware of the smell.

Torbert wrenched open the door onto the corridor and saw the shadow of a man disappear into the empty sitting room.

He ran, calling to Vanesco, who was right behind. On reaching the door of the sitting room there was an incendiary explosion behind them, a large whoomp of oxygen being sucked into a gasoline flash. Flames swamped the hall, licking through the old oak paneling, running up the stairs, engulfing the center of the house in seconds. Whoever had set the match knew about fire raising. Had a fire crew been waiting outside there would have been no way they could have saved the building. Vanesco and Torbert were unable to get back to the kitchen through that wall of flame.

'Jesus Christ, it'll spread to the stables. I gotta get the horses out.'

Torbert went out the main door and ran through the yard, he flung open the gate of the paddock, then ran to open the stable gates. Nothing could have stopped him right then, not the thought of someone out there trying to kill him. 'Get those stables opened,' he shouted to Vanesco.

Windows popped in the house as flames pushed through. The clatter of hooves filled the air along with frightened cries as horses tasted the smoke and heat and sensed the danger. As soon as stable doors were opened horses charged out, some shepherding foals. When he got to the stable opposite the kitchen Vanesco remembered Stimson.

The door was open and at first he thought Stimson had made it out. Flame had swept the length of the hallway, and the kitchen was filled with dense, yellow smoke, which the draft from the open door was making worse.

Stimson was on the floor by the table. Pushing farther into the smoke, Vanesco knew he hadn't taken a large enough breath to reach him, and when he gulped more air he drew in the searing smoke and started to cough and had to get out. He went in again, this time with his coat over his head, wondering what he was doing trying save this guy.

Stimson was dead, he could tell immediately. He hadn't been in that bad a shape, he had been killed. The thought had barely formed when someone covered with a wet blanket came at him out of the dense smoke, knocking him off balance.

By the time Vanesco dragged himself out into breathable air, the killer had gone. He saw Torbert with a horse blanket over his head working close to the flames, which had spread to the haylofts above the stables. He was getting the last of his horses out. Vanesco wondered whether he'd have had time to kill Stimson, and what purpose it might have served.

'You see a guy come out here?' he said.

'That's the last,' Torbert told him as a mare cantered away through the yard.

The two men moved clear and watched the house burn, silhouetted against the flames that lit the sky like day. Vanesco's eyes scanned the surrounding darkness, aware of someone out there watching them. They could be picked off like quails, but he guessed that wouldn't happen. Anyone dying connected to this would die in what looked like an accident; a bullet would leave too many unanswered questions, even in Ireland.

'That's like a lifetime's work,' Torbert said.

'You got insurance?'

'I got my horses clear.' He looked round at them herded in the paddock. 'What happened to the fat man?'

'He's dead.' Vanesco waited, but Torbert didn't seem concerned. 'I'm no closer to finding out why I was hired or what it was you did.' He paused, not expecting Torbert to come in with anything. 'This is your big chance, you wanna vanish again. Stimson's going to be pretty burned up in that. No one's gonna identify him. You could take off, let everyone believe it was Bill Torbert burned out there. No one's going to know.'

Torbert looked at him. 'How about you?'

'Give me the information I need.'

He thought about the offer. 'I made quite a life here,' he said. 'Took a lot of time and work. I've got some of the best horses in Ireland. Yes, sir, I got some real fine horses. People come from all over the world to buy Irish blood stock.' He stopped talking, the hiss and crackle of the burning building filling the air. 'I read somewhere that in China scientists are working on a drug to make people smaller, so they won't need so much food, so many clothes, so much land to live on. Can you believe those Chinese, for Chrissake. There's no future for them. Here there's a future. We've a population in relation to our land mass, it's a country that's not over-developed. You've gotta work to make your way, sure, but a man can buy a piece of land here and do his thing without bureaucratic interference. There's little crime. You know the biggest incident of crime here? Stealing bicycles. Can you believe that? No one's gonna mug you, break into your house, rape your daughter, then plea bargain it away because the courts can't handle the volume. No sir, not here, they don't have to make the people small.'

There were arguments Vanesco could have given him, but saw no point. 'What about the sectarian troubles?' he said.

'That's Northern Ireland. It's Britain's problem.'

Vanesco thought about that statement. It reflected this man's unrealistic, isolationist attitude. The belief that a man could stand alone, an heroic figure in an inhospitable landscape was unrealistic. Vanesco knew, he had been there.

A fire engine was heard now. Vanesco found that funny considering the state of the fire, there would be embers to damp down, and a body to find. Torbert didn't stir, he had made his decision. Maybe he was being realistic, for even if everyone else could be convinced that Torbert had died in the fire, he guessed whoever had hired Stimson would know different.

Although Torbert had no plans to help him get the answers he wanted, Vanesco wondered if the same went for his warning his former partners. One thing was sure, whoever was in back of Stimson would send someone after the others just as soon as they were traced. Simply not finding them now wasn't enough, Vanesco decided, for it would leave him not only with his questions unanswered, but in real danger.

Eighteen

The Persian rugs had to be worth a lot of money, Erhart decided, not knowing a thing about them; there were a number on the brightly polished wooden floors throughout the apartment. Persian rugs and antique furniture, works by painters whose names were recognizable was one way of investing a quarter of a million, Erhart reflected, but the permanence it suggested was insane. His eyes roamed freely over the large room, thinking how Chuck Paley had good taste; then he had come out of a wealthy New York Jewish background, and although the black sheep who had severed all connexions with his family, in his early years he would have been exposed to such things. Erhart had no aesthetic appreciation of Chippendale or Wedgwood, instead he got along fine with the stunning ruggedness of modern chrome and canvas furniture, and sturdy, practical pottery.

What Shepard Erhart had done with the quarter million dollars he had received was put it in a numbered account in a bank in Zurich. Either that or spending it fast, had seemed the only smart thing to do, because he hadn't anticipated surviving this long. Maybe the others had. Looking back he realized the numbered account wasn't so smart, the money had just sat without earning a cent, while depreciating through inflation. He had always been a careful man, and Switzerland with immediate access to cash seemed the most careful move. So he hadn't earned a penny interest, but his money was intact. In other circumstances he might have put it to work, but he hadn't figured on getting hooked up with Birgit Heller.

He had always expected to go behind the iron curtain,

knowing he would be safer there, but he had been surprized in Geneva when Birgit Heller had picked him up. In retrospect it seemed a hackneyed, clumsy approach, and Erhart smiled, enjoying the memory of the sexual interlude. Had he not been interested in going over, warning lights would have flashed. Birgit was a tall, honey-blonde with large breasts, and a feeling for sex beyond the call of duty. The casting was clichéd, she even had black lace underwear. Everyone had been considerably more naïve in the sixties, and the Company had made as many booboos. After that brief love affair, when she had passed him on to her boss, she had gone out of his life. Then by chance he had met her in Munich where she had been helping to look after the East German Olympic team; he had been a guest of the West German Interior Department. They had been brusquely polite, and no old flame had rekindled; she had gotten big, and severe-looking, only that wasn't the problem, the years and growing up meanwhile had proved too big a gap. There would have been precious few opportunities anyway, the watchers were watched also, and he was apparently working for the West Germans. The next day Black September had struck in the Israeli village.

Thinking back, he realized he had been watched from the moment he arrived in Switzerland, probably before. Just as they had been keeping tabs on the other five. In East Germany someone was always watching someone, so six Americans with a past they needed to hide were no additional problem. It hadn't been constant surveillance, that wasn't necessary, from the reports Erhart saw he was amazed at how necessary it was for his former colleagues to have an identity. He would have expected them to keep moving, stay unencumbered by emotional or property ties; this indicated to a large degree how Western urban man needed objects which gave him a relative identity. Coley was the only one who stayed loose, but even he committed to a woman with whom he lived and fathered a child by. However, Erhart doubted it was an emotional commitment. Brad Coley was totally without emotion, for him everything and everyone had a price, some merely a higher price than others. He was the single person among them who had gotten involved for money rather than ideology. Erhart was better able to understand Coley's attitude than most of what motivated the others, none of them had believed in their reason as resolutely as Coley had his; had this been the case they wouldn't have accepted the money that had been put up, nor the anonymity they were offered afterwards. Himself included.

He spent a lot of time thinking about that burning summer out on Colonel Parker's ranch, and all that had happened since. Then when Wallechinsky had been appointed ambassador to China, the first since the stoning of the embassy in Nanking in '49, Erhart suddenly knew he was going home. He had stayed too long in the field. He wanted to leave his office in West Berlin, cross into the eastern sector and not return. Wallechinsky's appointment had given him the opportunity, those tabs on his former partners would finally pay off. Exposing himself wasn't important with him safely on the other side of the iron curtain. Wallechinsky wouldn't take up his post; the State Department wouldn't appoint another ambassador; Sino-American relations would plummet to a depth lower than at the height of President Nixon's bombing of North Vietnam; by comparison tension between the East European Communist Bloc and China would pale to insignificance.

Erhart sometimes wondered why political gamesmanship was so important. It was all ego, yet he was locked into it and played the game. Maybe it was because no one had learned any better way to live.

Success now, he knew, depended on an essential important element: bringing one or more of his former partners over with him to corroborate his story.

This was proving more difficult than he had figured. He had underestimated the danger Wallechinsky had seen in these men, and the speed with which he was moving against them.

Erhart checked his watch, then glanced at the brass carriage clock on the mantleshelf. Both read seven-thirty-three. The light had gone outside now, leaving the room deep in evening gloom. Erhart hadn't turned on the light, but wondered if he should as he rose for another drink. Maybe Paley carried a gun and would shoot first; with the light on maybe he wouldn't only shoot first but get off the best shot. He poured himself more sherry from the crystal decanter, and left the light off. He didn't use ice in his drink, had he then he would have found in the kitchen the icebox defrosting, water running out over the Italian ceramic floor.

Feeling uneasy in London, Erhart was uncertain how long he should wait. His earlier uneasiness over having stayed too long recurred and he wasn't sure why. Possibly it was nothing more than a primal response to vanishing daylight. Although he had been at risk too long, he knew his endangering himself would have been pointless if he left without contacting Paley.

He had to wait another hour and had his third sherry before Paley showed up. By which time all the ice in the freezer had melted, causing a shallow pool of water to leak across the floor in the kitchen.

Paley froze as he turned on the living room light. In the next instant he was reaching for the tiny .38 special, but stopped as Erhart drew the hammer on his gun.

He stared at the man in the leather chair, not recognizing the face, but seeing something familiar behind the taut, unwrinkled skin, in the eyes, around the mouth.

'Who are you? What are you doing here?'

'That's good, you didn't make me. The money I paid that surgeon wasn't wasted.' He smiled.

'Aardwolf! Right.' He came forward, his manner more friendly. 'What happened back at the hotel?'

'You almost fulfilled your destiny.' He waited, then said, 'To die violently.'

'I plan to live a long while, and die in a comfortable bed – with my leg across a pretty girl.'

Erhart considered him. His pulpy face indicated a liver condition which he probably didn't know about. Erhart studied faces, and their danger signals.

'How the hell d'you get in? I got alarms here.'

'I guess you forgot to switch them on.' The alarms hadn't been set when he picked the locks, and he wondered why that was.

'Can I freshen your drink?' he offered when he went to fix one himself.

Erhart shook his head. The sherry had given him heartburn and he wished he hadn't drunk it.

'How did you find me?'

'Through the people I work for.'

Paley arched his dark eyebrows.

'The East Germans.'

Paley sipped his drink. 'What's their interest?'

'Habit, I guess. Surveillance is the biggest source of employment in East Germany,' he observed drily.

'Nice that you kept your sense of humor. So what do you want?'

'You got a nice sense of humor too. I want you to live a long, comfortable life, maybe bed that last cute little girl.'

'Things are okay. I enjoy the life.' He indicated his apartment.

'It's coming to pieces.' He waited. 'I want you to go over. I'll guarantee your safety.'

'The price is too high.'

Erhart said nothing.

Paley nodded, not accepting the proposition, but acknowledging its necessity. 'How about the alternatives?'

'There are none.' He told him about the man Wallechinsky had looking for him. 'If he doesn't reach you, the cops here will. The chances are you'll only get life for murdering that airhostess. I guess they're not far behind.'

'Your people have been staying pretty close.'

'They had a lot of practice. There's no extradition treaty between Britain and East Germany.'

'All I do is sing for my supper?' He straightened a jewelled snuffbox on the table. 'You know how much that is worth?' he asked.

'Nothing at all to you right now. You want to come over with all this stuff, fine.'

'How soon do you need to know?'

'Soon. Friend Wallechinsky hasn't lost any of his efficiency.'

'How do I reach you?'

From his vest pocket Erhart took a cheap business card of a toy import company in Mornington Crescent, a suburb in North London. 'Identify yourself, tell them you want some

German dolls. They'll make the arrangements.' He considered this man, sensing that he was then getting nearer to going home himself.

As his unexpected visitor was on the point of leaving, Paley said, 'It was an accident, the hostess. We were stoned. It just happened.'

'Sure,' Erhart said. It made no difference to him, only the effect was important, that was the lever.

Erhart's departure left Paley feeling disturbed. There had been little in the newspapers about the killing, and he wondered how far from him the local cops were, whether this man would call them to get more pressure on. Maybe he'd already done that. He thought about Wallechinsky. If he were brought down in flames, then most of his serious problems would be over, Paley realized. Or maybe they'd just be starting. What use would he be to the East Germans afterwards, especially if wanted on a murder rap? Either way he'd lose, so it was a question of which way he'd lose the less.

Arriving at a decision wouldn't be easy, cold sweat broke out over Paley as he considered the problem. He ran his eyes around the room. Maybe he could transfer some of his lifestyle with him; but then East Germany was a sparse, utilitarian society, and like most of the communist bloc countries there were acute shortages – to get oranges often meant queuing half a day. That was for working stiffs, he argued, he could manage. But more important he would be safe.

Paley decided to sleep on the decision. He guessed he'd buy the proposal, if only to bring Wallechinsky down. He decided he'd call the number in the morning, as he slid the card in his pocket. Collecting up the used sherry glasses, he went to the kitchen, still puzzled how the man got by the alarm. He'd have to check it out.

'Shit!' Paley saw the pool of water in the kitchen, and thought the sink had overflowed; then he discovered the problem was the icebox. He figured a fuse must had blown. The plug was okay. He went to the kitchen cupboard where the fuse boxes were. Positioned close to the floor and at the back of the cupboard meant he had to crouch in an awkward position to reach them. When he plunged the switch on the metal box into the off position in order to open the fuse box, there was a flash. Chuck Paley never knew what hit him; it was five hundred volts from the head supply that had been connected directly to the on/off contact on the box. Crouching on the wet floor, Paley had made the perfect earth. To make certain a roll of baking foil had been leaned against the fuse boxes and floor. The electrical charge continued to run down that until finally the main fuse burned out.

Five hundred volts didn't amount to the electric chair, but was enough to ensure Paley wouldn't get up again.

Nineteen

There was a plainclothes cop watching the apartment building in Mount Street, and Vanesco wasn't sure if Torbert had seen him. If he had he didn't comment. The cop didn't necessarily have any connection with Clarence Paley, but chances were he did, and the skiptrace feared the worst as he rode the tiny cage to the fifth floor.

The elevator, which had been tacked to the rear of the buildings as an afterthought, stopped at half-landings and they had to walk up the last flight of stairs. The door was ajar, the lock was broken. Vanesco and Torbert exchanged looks, as if uncertain how to proceed.

Vanesco thought about the probable connection of the cop in the street with this; knew instinctively now that he wasn't going to get to talk to Paley.

'Come in, gentlemen.'

A tall, barrel-chested man addressed them from the bottom of the long corridor. He had a red face that suggested his booze intake wasn't helping his high bloodpressure. He stood in the kitchen doorway and watched them approach, giving

146

them no opportunity to actually see into the kitchen, which ran at a right angle to the door.

'Can I help you in some way?'

He had a harsh voice like he had long ago damaged his throat. His yellowing, bloodshot eyes continued to bore into them.

'We're looking for Chuck Paley.' Vanesco suspected this was no run of the mill cop. Had he been then the first thing he'd have done was explain who he was, why he was there. 'That ain't you.'

The man's smile looked as if it caused him pain. 'Was he expecting you?'

'We planned to surprise him.'

'That'll be different now.' He glanced at Torbert, then back at Vanesco. 'Who are you?'

Vanesco produced his investigator's license. 'That's Bill Torbert,' he said.

'He a private investigator too?'

'You wanna tell us who you are?'

'Kelvin's my name. I'm a detective.' He quite obviously held rank. 'What was your business with Paley? If you don't mind me asking.' There was sarcasm in his tone.

'Just hired to find him, was all.'

Kelvin looked at him, his face remaining blank.

'You found him, Mr Vanesco.' He stepped aside and motioned them into the kitchen.

On the wet floor was Paley's body, an angry, protesting expression set in his face.

'We estimate he died sometime yesterday evening. I suppose you can account for your whereabouts at that time, gentlemen?'

'No problem. You saying someone killed him?' Vanesco said like he didn't know any better.

'He electrocuted himself. But before that someone had wrecked some fuses and rigged the wiring for whoever came to mend it.' He gave Torbert another look, as if his face was unlocking a memory which he hadn't yet identified.

'You sure that's how it happened?' Vanesco asked. He was sure that whoever had gotten to Radulovic and Coley, and Stimson in Ireland, had been here. Only now whoever it was wasn't picking up threads from his lead but had gone ahead of him.

'Three things about chummy,' the detective said, jerking his thumb at the body, 'make us certain. He dealt in dope – he used it, but we suspect from the amounts he bought he was a dealer. He killed an airline stewardess, so he was due to be picked up. Further he was about to disappear behind the Iron Curtain. All of which doesn't bode well for longevity, nor death by natural causes.'

Kelvin's people hadn't found Paley, nor had they been interested in his dope deals. Detectives investigating the homicide of the airhostess had found him following an anonymous tip-off. They had found the dope at his apartment. When they searched the body the business card given him by Erhart was discovered. The phone call to the toy importers had been routine, endeavoring to establish facts about the deceased. It had been intercepted by Inspector Kelvin's people, who were tapping the toy importer's lines, knowing it was a contact number for East Germans operating in Britain.

'Would you mind telling me why you were hired?'

A smile wrinkled in Vanesco's mind, and he wondered if he shouldn't refer the question to Torbert, who hadn't said a word but looked quite ill. Maybe that was a way of putting pressure on, but then if Torbert were to open up, this detective was certain to question him in private. Right then Vanesco saw an advantage in protecting Torbert, even though he was certain to try and prevent information coming out. Torbert knew where Lance Niles was in Italy, and possibly the whereabouts of the sixth man. The biggest obstacle to Vanesco finding the answers he wanted was the fact that someone was out there, making sure the men with the answers wouldn't ever talk.

'That I can't tell you, pal.' He watched the cop, noticing that his expression didn't change, nor had it from the moment they met. 'Not because it's privileged information or any of that shit. I don't know. I don't get told. I don't ask. A firm of New York attorneys hired me to find a bunch of guys. A respectable law firm. I figure these guys're due some kind of inheritance.'

'It's not going to do him a lot of good. Who are the other people?'

'Can I claim privileged information?' He was smiling.

The detective wasn't smiling when he said, 'I could make life very fucking difficult for you.'

He nodded. 'A man called Niles, another's Gavin, and Torbert. I was hired to find them.'

The detective looked at Torbert for a long time. 'What connection did you have with chummy, Mr Torbert?' Kelvin said with a contemptuous politeness.

'I never saw him in my life.' The lie came out smoothly.

'What about the other man?'

Torbert shook his head. 'Name doesn't mean a thing.'

'Why the fuck are you here then?'

'Mr Vanesco invited me along.'

Still the detective's expression didn't change. 'How about Gavin? That would be George Shepard Gavin, also known as Shepard Erhart, of the East German secret service?'

The information surprised both Vanesco and Torbert.

'Gavin, or Erhart as he's now known, was in this flat last night. Probably the last person to see Paley alive.'

'You figure he burned him?' Vanesco asked. That made sense. Erhart was the name Stimson had given him. Identifying the killer would have simplified matters; however, it would have clouded the issue if it was subsequently proven he was working for the East Germans. What could the contact between them and Harry Kohn be?

'It's unlikely. Erhart wanted something from him. Otherwise there was no reason for him to be here, at risk.' He considered Torbert again.

Another detective appeared from along the corridor, he had a large brown envelope containing fiber samples for the forensic scientists.

'That's everything in there, guv,' he said. 'S'not a single thing to identify him.'

'He seems like a careful sort of person. When you've finished come on down to West End Central. Have one of the others hang on for the ambulance.' He turned to Torbert. 'You sure you can't identify him, Mr Torbert?'

'I'm sure,' Torbert said.

Kelvin nodded. 'All right, let's go down to the station.'

'I'm not going to come up with anything there, friend,' Torbert said. 'I don't know this guy.'

'We simply want to go through things with you, get a statement. S'nothing more than a formality.'

His tone was almost friendly, but still he didn't change his expression. Suddenly Vanesco knew who he reminded him of, although there was no physical resemblance as such, it was Michael Yeo, the soft drinks manufacturer who had asked him to trace his wife and kids. The habit of not showing anything at all in the face indicated a profession where feelings were best concealed.

Knowing cops like he did, Vanesco knew that there was no difference between their few formalities to set the record straight and direct interrogation. Separating them into different interview rooms at the police station on Savile Row was inevitable. Vanesco didn't go for Kelvin's one cop to another routine, but kept to the bare facts: hired by Cunningham to find four men whose names he offered; he hoped Torbert would hang in with the same story. In such situations Vanesco always found it best to give some of the truth.

The problem was that Inspector Kelvin was a political cop, a member of the Special Branch, and wasn't buying what Vanesco was selling.

'You know what I think, Mr Vanesco?' the detective said, sitting across the table from him in the small, bare room. 'I think your friend Torbert is a dangerous man. He's scared, he's probably a bit psycho. A man like that, s'no telling what he's liable to do.'

'You got a good eye, inspector.'

'Been at it a long time, pal. D'you carry a gun, by the way?'

Vanesco had wondered how long he would take to get to that. He reached under his coat for it.

'That's an impressive tool. I don't suppose you thought to apply to the Home Office for a license?'

'Would they have given me one?'

'They would not,' he said. 'We must have a talk to your airport security. Nice, I imagine that would cut a man in half.' He removed the clip and put the Browning aside. 'Let's start at the beginning, Mr Vanesco, shall we.'

Vanesco knew it was going to be a long day, and felt a sense of impatience, had a feeling of frustration. He knew he should have been on a plane, headed for Italy, trying to reach Lance Niles before the killer.

'Why don't you put a call in to Clark E. Cunningham?' Vanesco ventured.

'We did. We're waiting for him to get back to us. Meanwhile I'd like to know as much as you know.' He smiled.

Twenty

Lance Niles no longer looked a well man. Neither his overcoat, scarf nor gloves kept out the cold bite to the spring air, and the wind off the lagoon cut through him as if he were naked. At one time he had barely been aware of the cold, his work sustained him, keeping him glowing with an inner warmth. Since Aardwolf had found him a chill had settled over him and he couldn't get warm.

Fear was his problem. Panic had risen through him the moment Erhart had approached him in the nave of San Sebastiano. Having gotten over his surprise – convinced as he was that no one could reach him without he got prior warning – Niles had mentally started running. Moving among the lunchtime crowds in the alleyways and piazzas, his eyes darted around, seeking the face of the person who had come to kill him, a face out of place among the round, well-fed Venetian faces. Once more he was doomed to be forever looking over his shoulder; he had been condemned to that eleven years ago, only he had believed the sentence was miraculously commuted.

During the decade he had lived in Northern Italy, he had become like the Italians, adopting the customs and rituals governing their lives. Lunch was to the average Italian a two and a half hour love affair with the belly. It was a habit Niles slipped into when work didn't totally distract him; minestrone and breaded veal and a couple of glasses of wine in a trattoria he used since working on this particular church. He had eaten hardly anything today, and on returning to the church had worked without concentration. When the diocesan bishop visited the site to inquire after progress of the restoration, Niles's dull, mechanical response caused him to ask if he was well.

Niles had to get away or he knew he would be next on the list to die. He thought about the others who had been killed. There was only himself and Aardwolf left; Aardwolf couldn't be reached, having the entire East German security network to cover him.

He didn't want to die, Niles realized, and would do anything to prevent that. It was odd that he should feel this way, always believing that when his time came he would be ready, for he was one of the chosen and death for him was but a beginning, a rebirth to a higher existence which he had earned by his work on earth. But after Erhart's warning he had become scared, like someone who had suddenly discovered he had been worshipping the wrong god. The question that surfaced through his thoughts was: Have I contributed enough? He didn't know the answer, and wanted more time to make certain. He thought about Erhart's offer. Maybe the only safe place was behind the Iron Curtain. But would he really be safe, and would he be able to carry on his work? Communism was a relatively new religion, Christianity and its churches had been established in those countries long before; there could be work for him, churches to restore. He would be sorry to leave Venice, knowing he might never return.

An image of Lawrence Wallechinsky loomed before him, and he recalled what that man had done, and what his desire for personal power made him capable of. Wallechinsky was the epitome of evil, and deserved not to live, the fact that he would be brought to account after his death seemed insufficient.

As he moved through the alleyways toward his apartment

on Campo San Domini, Niles concluded that he should do all in his power to destroy the American ambassador to China before he was able to perpetrate more evil.

Approaching the ponte that crossed the rio San Polo, he saw a man leaning on the parapet. Fear took a firmer hold of Niles. There could be no other reason for him standing there like that on such a cold evening other than waiting to kill him. There was no view here, for the canal, which joined the Grand Canal, curved, while buildings, themselves of no especial historic interest, protruded. The light was fading anyway. The man was dressed like most Venetians in a dark green raglan style overcoat, which was currently fashionable, and a cloth cap. Niles stopped as two girls passed him and headed over the ponte; the would-be killer turned in Niles's direction, causing him to backtrack into Campo San Polo, where people were going home out of the cold. No one noticed his haste until turning to glance over his shoulder, he crashed into a woman. He apologized in Italian and she cursed him out as he hurried on. He glanced back again on reaching Calle Forno, and saw the man come up over the bridge. Niles started to run. He had walked these narrow streets thousand of times, knew them better than he knew any city. In winter the alleys smelled of urine, the city cats having no earth to scratch, while in summer the cats' smells were masked by those of the canals; none of this detracted from a city that was free of traffic and carbon monoxide. He had felt at home here, and now he felt threatened, estranged, as he turned out of one alley into another, hurrying from his pursuer; for the first time since arriving in Venice he lost his sense of direction. Instead of finding himself in Campo San Cassiano as he expected, he found himself by San Silvestro on the Grand Canal. He stopped, confused by this, and tried to clear his thoughts and work out how he got here, but the man whom he still believed was following him dominated his thinking.

Turning back, he ran into Campo San Aponal. He had helped restore the 15th century Baroque church there, it had three fine Tiepolos, but was rarely visited by tourists. He tried to recall when he had worked on that church as he turned along Calle del Sole, but his thoughts stopped abruptly. Across the thoroughfare the man in the green overcoat stood looking in a jeweller's store window. Niles stopped, struggling for breath, undecided which way to go. Suddenly he veered to the right.

People turned and looked as he ran, only Niles wasn't aware of them. The single thought in his head was of getting to his apartment safely.

The apartment where he lived was situated on the corner of Calle Chiesa, overlooking the 15th century church of Santa Maria Mater Domini. The square where it stood was mostly old and crumbling, but the apartment house had been well restored.

Niles paused on the bridge over the rio delle due Torri and watched the square, trying to determine whether anyone was waiting for him. The square was poorly served by a single lamp and he approached the house cautiously. Once through the street door he felt easier, but ran up the two narrow flights of stairs. In his apartment he leaned against the door, there to have creep over him an enormous feeling that whoever it was pursuing him was already there. He froze and listened, but nothing stirred. He switched on the lights, then checked the bedroom. There was no one, nor in the living room nor his study, which was filled with books and drawings of religious architecture. He had amassed one of the most comprehensive collections in Europe. Historians from all over wrote him for information. His collection served a practical purpose, it wasn't collected merely for information on mankind's past but to help save that legacy and hold it in trust for future generations. He found the thought of leaving Venice without all this sickening, but knew he had to depart and quickly, tonight if possible, and he wouldn't be able to take more than a few books. He would ask Bishop Storti to arrange for his things to be forwarded. He could trust Storti with that.

After closing all the blinds in the apartment, Niles called Erhart at the hotel Danieli.

'I'll take your offer,' Niles said. 'But let's get it done right away.'

'You got some kind of problem?' He sounded concerned.

'I was followed this evening. How soon can we get out?'

'There's a plane for Milan and Paris at ten tonight. Can you

154

make that?'

Niles said he could and arranged to meet him at the airport.

When he rang off Erhart smiled, without sharing the joke. His Venice contact sat across the room, still in his coat and wearing his cloth cap, drinking his way through a bottle of Valpolicella. Of each of his former associates Erhart had read Niles the clearest, had known he would spook if some pressure was put on him.

He got up off the bed and extended his glass to the man in the green coat. 'I figure we've about wrapped this up, Peter.'

The reason for his optimism was that he believed he was ahead of the field.

The leather grip which Niles had filled was deceptively large, and more packed into it than seemed possible. It was heavy but there wasn't a thing in the bag that he couldn't immediately do without. Maybe he could leave some of the books, but finally decided he couldn't. He had eight books in the bag, big books but still only eight out of about eight hundred. He hefted the bag, deciding he could handle the weight. He wouldn't have to carry it far, only across the square where he would call a water taxi to take him to the Piazzale Roma, there he'd take a regular cab to the airport.

A noise outside the apartment door stopped Niles as he brought the bag from the bedroom. It sounded like someone trying to get in.

'Yes. Who is it?'

Whoever it was had gone by the time Niles got the door unlocked. He cracked the door open and peered onto the landing. The greencoated man who had followed him came to mind, and panic began to rise again. They were closing in. Whoever it was didn't want him making that plane. Right then Niles wished he had the gun he had dumped in the Grand Canal back in '64 after deciding he had stopped running.

He had to get out, take his bag and get himself to Marco Polo airport; it didn't matter if he was early, he'd be safe at the airport, there would be too many people around for anyone to harm him. Also Aardwolf would be around.

There wasn't a single person in the square. That made Niles feel uneasy. Even the bar in Calle Chiesa was deserted. Where were the bar flies? He hesitated in the apartment house street doorway, afraid to go on, believing illogically that his pursuer had got everyone inside so they couldn't witness what was going to happen. That was crazy, people were eating dinner, watching tv, it was a cold night. It wasn't unreasonable there weren't too many people around. There weren't any!

A young couple came over the bridge, they were huddled together either in affection or against the cold.

Niles saw his opportunity. He moved out across the square, past the church and into Calle Tentor, deciding to take the waterbus from San Stae. Ordinarily it was a few minutes walk, but the weight of his grip pulled on his right shoulder, he leaned to the left to counter the weight, and when he tried to hurry it banged against his side. He found himself trying to hurry, hearing someone running behind him. Niles stopped and turned, the running disappeared. A door banged. A shrill greeting in Italian was heard; a snatch of a tv soap opera. Then silence except for his heavy breathing. He was sweating from the exertion with his bag. Half the stuff he'd brought along could have been left behind, especially the books. He wasn't going to do any work on churches in East Germany for a month or so. He'd be fully occupied with the Wallechinsky business, and would have received his belongings by the time he was done.

He set off again, checking behind him. San Stae lay at the end of the Salizzada, but Niles turned into the tiny Calle Albanesi. It was a mistake. The alleyway was dark, the single street lamp being busted. It had been busted on purpose; that was crazy, no one could have guessed he'd turn off there, but this didn't make him feel any better. Turning right onto Calle Tron, he saw a man in a green coat and a black cap pass the intersection ahead of him. He was convinced it was the man who had followed him earlier.

Some people overtook him and he followed them back into Salizzada. His arm was aching and he was sweating heavily. He had to hurry.

At night the waterbuses ran on schedule and not frequently. The bus to Piazzale Roma was due in, which was why people around him had suddenly appeared. If he missed the bus he'd have half an hour to wait, and with no one around, apart from the killer. He struggled on, and considered abandoning the bag and running.

In the arched doorway of the church of San Stae Niles saw a face he knew and it made him go cold. It was that of a ghost, and disappeared in ghost-like fashion. At first he thought he had imagined it, until he dug through the layers of memory to that ranch in Big Springs, Texas. That was where the face belonged. He felt sick now, knowing he wasn't going to make it. He tried to identify where the man had gone. Other people were heading through Campo San Stae to the bus stop. If he stayed closed to them nothing could happen to him, but his eyes darted about, looking for that threat of death.

The boarding point came in sight and he saw the bus heading across the canal. He quickened his pace. He was safe. He was going to make it. He reached the gate of the bus stop, excitement causing his blood to pound. The bus slid up to the stop, thumping and scraping along the floating dock with the swell. Niles paid his fifty lire fare and moved onto the pier. There panic clutched at him when a figure ahead in a hooded parka turned. The moon-shaped face inside the hood was oriental and was looking directly at him. Then the oriental waved to someone. Niles surged forward with his bag, pushing past the porter who was securing the bus with a rope around the mooring post. The porter screamed at him to wait, but he made it, he was on board. At that point he noticed the oriental was a student who had been waving to his girlfriend.

Niles stood by the disembarkation gate on the opposite side of the bus and counted off the four stops to Piazzale Roma, with each he felt more safe. A few people bustled around him to get off at stops. Not many got on. Finally the entire busload of passengers stirred to disembark.

Fear left Lance Niles briefly as he watched the lighted terminus pier slide closer, and he concluded that he had imagined most of what he had seen and heard. Venice was full of shadows and noises, the street lighting was bad, and equally the alleys had a strange acoustical effect, especially with so much water around. He'd miss Venice even though in theory their politics weren't so different where he was going. He had been happy here, and was determined that somehow he'd return. In many ways he'd never leave, his work would remain. Memories crowded him, friends he'd made, favorite eating places, particularly fond walks, smells that were so evocative; sudden bursts of sunlight penetrating washing strung alleys or flooding a darkened square. Most of all he'd miss the evening light, the westerly sun running out over the laguna, its transparent brilliance elevating both body and spirit. He would come back.

People were pressing in behind him now like they could get off before the bus reached the dock. The Italians' impatience was something he had never quite gotten used to. He turned to speak, but couldn't. His face froze as the man immediately behind him smiled. It was a cold, unfeeling smile, the eyes remained unmoving. Niles was about to speak his name when he felt the pain of something sharp penetrating the small of his back and he cried out. Niles was only aware of the instant paralysis he felt, and that cold, smiling face.

The needle had by chance hit a vein, which made its effect almost instantaneous.

Hands that appeared to go out to catch Niles eased him over the rail. He dropped between the boat and concrete pier as the waterbus slid into the terminus. The porter shouted and the pilot slammed the vessel into full-astern but the screw didn't bite fast enough.

Lance Niles was dead before the boat and pier made ground meat of him.

Twenty-one

Marco Polo airport, overlooking Laguna Veneta, was small and windswept, with a series of single-storey buildings where the departure lounge doubled as arrivals hall, depending whether there was a plane coming in or going out. Air traffic wasn't heavy, but come Easter in a little over two weeks things would get busy. There were few formalities on coming into Venice, everyone was a tourist and Italian immigration was smart enough not to hassle them.

The airport was suddenly a hive of activity with just one plane having arrived, to shortly be departing. Erhart considered how it would have been with a dozen flights trying to get in or out with fog rolling in off the sea. He disliked airports, especially waiting around at them. Ordinarily this wouldn't have been his choice of airport to be delayed at – it would have taken about five minutes to get done with the distractions—but this evening he would have welcomed any delay to Alitalia's flight to Milan and Paris, hoping Lance Niles would make it.

Erhart checked the time again as the final call was made. His Italian could get him through a menu and onto the right bus. He didn't stir as he watched the last passengers straggle through the gate. Niles wasn't coming, he decided, and not because of any change of heart. He had been too scared to have changed his mind. Erhart knew he had made a mistake in not bringing Niles out himself, but resisted getting angry over it.

He considered simply getting on the plane himself, seeing little point in going back to find out what had happened. He had failed, and discovering how Niles had died wouldn't mitigate failure, but he felt he had to go back.

After he informed check-in that he wasn't taking the plane he had to struggle to retrieve his valise which had been loaded. It was the gun he wanted from it; then when he checked the bag into a left luggage box, Erhart found there were no cabs to take him back to Venice; nor were there any downtown buses, as they only arrived to meet flights he was told. The car rental desks weren't open either. That was small city airports. His feeling of frustration and anger increased.

An official told him that another flight got in soon, there would be transport arriving then.

Erhart wanted to get back to Venice immediately. He called his contact to have him get a cab and collect him, but couldn't raise the man. He called a cab company out of Pizzale Roma. They told him they'd get a cab to him directly; saying the same ten minutes later when he called back, again ten minutes after that. He was still waiting when the Alitalia flight from London arrived.

As the passengers came through the arrival hall Erhart saw Bill Torbert, and instinctively drew back behind the information counter, even though he had no expectation of being recognized. He second-guessed Torbert's reason for being here: he was resisting giving up the life he had made for himself.

He watched the short, dark man collect his case and pass through the immigration and customs, who shared one long table. By the time passengers were clear, ground transport had arrived; three buses. Two were for package tours; Torbert boarded the third and paid his fare downtown. Erhart waited for a few more people to get on the bus, then boarded himself.

Torbert sat next to Jimmy Vanesco, even though there were vacant seats and they had come through immigration separately.

Glancing up as he did at each of the boarding passengers, Torbert tensed as Erhart met his look. He didn't recognize him but there was something familiar about the man, maybe just that he had caught his eye. Torbert was puzzled, something in those eyes said he knew him. A shiver ran through him. He glanced around at Erhart, who took a seat at the back of the bus.

'You know him?' Vanesco asked.

'Was he on the plane?'

'Didn't see him.'

'Something tells me we're not going to reach Niles.'

Vanesco said nothing, but shared the doubt, which had persisted throughout his investigation; it had been reinforced in London when he, along with Torbert, had been interrogated by the Special Branch. The detective came on heavy until someone in New York had talked to someone, either Inspector Kelvin or his boss. The detective's attitude had changed, and he had obliquely referred to their having a guardian angel. He hadn't been at all pissed off about letting them go, but accepted it as though a fact of life in his job. Vanesco had recognized that same political imperative he had known in the FBI; there deals were made for political advantage, when agents had been simply pulled off investigations, no explanation given. There had been nothing he could do about it, no way to carry on the investigation alone, and no reason to anyway, for agents rarely saw the whole picture to begin with. Political expediency, whether in the FBI, or that to which Kelvin responded in London, Vanesco found disturbing. They were after all supposedly safeguarding society's freedoms, and all their actions theoretically were taken in the taxpayer's name. He thought about the call that would have been made about himself and Torbert, the instructions to release them could only have come from the State Department. That complicated things further.

After checking into the Danieli Royal Excelsior Hotel, a former palace on the Riva degli Schiavoni, they headed by water taxi for Campo San Domini. The driver stood at the helm, steering with one black-gloved hand, a cigarette clenched in the other; he wore an expensive camelhair tie-belted coat, a felt hat and expensive pointed shoes. Most of the taxi drivers plying the canal were similarly dressed in this Italian macho uniform. Vanesco and Torbert huddled inside the cabin out of the cold and the spray as the long motor craft thumped along over the wash of a waterbus.

At Niles's apartment they found policemen looking for some indication of next of kin. Niles was at Santa Chiara hospital, the uniformed officer told them, in the morgue. He gave details of the accident, and his inquiries ended when Torbert said there was no next of kin. He had discovered the connection with the diocesan bishop, and would inform him of his death; an easier task than breaking the news to a wife or mother.

Vanesco's frustration increased when he stood in the morgue while Torbert identified what remained of Niles, a bloodied mess of stripped skin and flesh. Torbert couldn't be sure who it was, and Vanesco was less sure, but said it was Niles. Things were complicated enough, and he saw no reasons to leave complications here. The Italian authorities would convolute things unaided. Looking at the body was, Vanesco felt, like watching the six o'clock news, not a damn thing he could do about it.

The satisfied smile that fell over the man's face as Torbert and Vanesco emerged from the lighted exit of the hospital was chilling. He had expected Erhart to arrive at Niles's apartment, and saw these two as a bonus. He would have gotten to Vanesco sooner or later, so it might as well have been sooner. Maybe someone would start to add things up, question the deaths of these Americans in Venice within hours of each other; they might just wonder about the apparent heart attacks they would sustain, even though there were no next of kin to make a noise; they might find the skin puncture, but that was all they would find. The large-molecule poison would have been absorbed so fast that unless a toxicologist knew what to look for it wouldn't be found.

What about Erhart?

The question loomed large as he watched the two men cross the canal de Santa Chiara and move along the quay past the bus stops and taxi berths. Erhart wasn't a target; however, his concern was that he might recognize him and prove a danger. Erhart would know at once who had gotten to Niles; he wouldn't like that, and despite his being a professional he might try something foolish.

He watched Torbert and Vanesco climb aboard a waterbus that would take them along the Grand Canal, he assumed, to one of the hotels around St Mark's. He considered whether he could move against them on the bus. There wouldn't be many passengers, so at best he'd only get one of them, and would immediately alert the other. He might not get clear himself. He took a taxi.

The call Vanesco got as he stepped out of the shower surprised him. He assumed it would be Torbert, who was right next door. The voice was muffled as if through a scarf. The caller wouldn't give his identity, but said he wanted to talk about Niles.

'Fine,' Vanesco said. 'Why'n you stop by the hotel?'

'I don't plan to die in the same way. You have to meet me.' He gave the address of a printers and book binders on Calle Monti, off Calle Fabri, which led almost directly out of St Mark's Square to the Rialto Bridge. He could walk it in five minutes.

The caller hadn't said to come alone, that was Vanesco's assumption, but he had no plans to go without Torbert.

Calle Monti, a wide alley that stopped at the rio San Salvador, was no better lit than any of the other alleys and squares. The yellow gas lamp near the bridge cast a small circle of light, leaving the print shop in darkness.

There was no one waiting when Vanesco and Torbert got there early. They had met only four people on the way and three of those were in St Mark's Square, which was flooded and had wooden trestles down for people to walk on. The other person they met was in Calle Fabbri, an old Italian shuffling home. The two men searched Calle Monti. Torbert crossed the bridge into Calle Bolletta, where a footpath ran alongside the canal. The lighting was worse here, and a damp mist on the canal where boats were tied up didn't help. Torbert stepped into a doorway on the narrow footpath, keeping Vanesco in sight on the other side of the water.

Vanesco turned his watch toward the street lamp, it was a few minutes before three. The caller had said three am. It was a dumb meeting, Vanesco thought now, an obvious trap, and he wondered how reliable Torbert was. He remembered how he had been back in Ireland, but then he had had his horses on his mind; now he had something else on his mind.

The sound of two cats in a brief skirmish rose across the river, startling Vanesco, the narrow buildings giving it an eerie quality. There was quiet after that, only the water lapping against the boats. The cold and damp stole through him and he buried his hands deeper in his overcoat pockets. He felt the Browning there, but got no reassurance from it. For a gun to be of any use he had to see someone. He could see nothing; he felt a presence, only resisted acknowledging it. That was Zell's area; when she got a feeling about something she went right ahead and acted on it. It was amazing how often those feelings came out right for her. But still Vanesco resisted his feeling.

He heard something, and strained his hearing, but the only sound was the ever present water washing against the brickwork, causing boats to gently bump the sides of the canal. He heard footfalls; then someone clearing phlegm from his throat. He assumed it was a man, never having heard a woman do that. He saw an enormous fat man come over the bridge and waddle down the shallow sloping steps onto Calle Monti, not missing a beat on seeing Vanesco.

This wasn't who he was waiting for, Vanesco decided, as the man spoke to him, bidding him goodnight. Vanesco watched him go. That was nice, he thought, here people were civilized; he considered such an encounter in New York or Chicago, and knew it couldn't have taken place. In American cities if you saw someone waiting around in a darkened street at 3 am you didn't approach, for the chances were they'd mug you.

His thoughts stopped abruptly at the sound of swift movement, someone running, two, maybe three steps, followed by a surprised cry.

Vanesco ran over the bridge in the direction. He could see nothing, but heard a splash as something went into the water. Torbert sped into his thoughts. He caught a glimpse of a retreating figure, and the noise he was making echoed off the water between the buildings, but vanished the instant he stopped.

'Torbert?' There was anger and fear in his voice. The sound of someone on the move reached him again, and Vanesco started along the dark path, his gun in his hand. The movement stopped and so did he, trying to locate it. He couldn't. Light from Calle Monti reflecting on the green oily water showed Torbert floating face down amid the garbage of orange peel and Coke cans and fruit boxes.

Vanesco stayed where he was, crouched by the water's edge, oblivious to danger then. He didn't particularly like Bill Torbert, wouldn't have sought him for a friend, and ordinarily wouldn't have cared much about his dying, but he had gotten used to him, and his dying like this represented another failure. He was both running out of chances and people to give him answers. Now there were only two men who could give him the answers he wanted, one was the person who had Harry Kohn hire him; the other was the guy who killed Torbert. Somehow he planned to get to one, or maybe both.

A noise farther along the path brought him up. He didn't rush, but moved slowly, keeping close to the buildings, his eyes trying to penetrate ahead. From what he could tell there was no way off this path, other than by water or back the way he came. Somewhere down there was the man who had killed Torbert; the way Vanesco figured things was that this guy could see no better than he could.

The movement he saw to his left was too sudden and too close for him to avoid it. An arm from a doorway grabbed him. Vanesco started to bring his gun up until he felt the cold rim of someone else's gun muzzle in his throat.

'Stay quiet,' came a whisper close to his ear.

Vanesco sensed less danger here than he'd first thought. He relaxed when the man said he was going to put his gun away.

'Who the hell are you?' Vanesco noticed he was sweating now.

'Be quiet. He's up there, near those boats. Just stay loose, he's gotta come back this way.'

They both saw the movement as a figure dove into a boat, but didn't hear any sound of someone landing; they were out of the doorway and running in that direction. Before they reached the boat, a figure in black leaped out of a doorway and hit them with a powerful flashlight beam. He followed through with a fast sprint, that gave them no time to recover themselves.

Vanesco had one chance at a shot, he leveled his Browning at the figure retreating and could have dropped him, but Erhart pushed the gun aside and the shot went wild.

165

'What the fuck?' Vanesco's words were lost as the retort echoed across the water.

'Too many problems. Let's get out of here.'

'What about Torbert?'

'He's not a bit of use to either of us now.'

The man started away. After a moment Vanesco followed.

Twenty-two

The cocktail lounge piano player had gone home by the time Vanesco got back to the Danieli with Erhart, but the barman who was clearing up seemed to welcome more customers, and would have preferred fixing them something more elaborate than bourbon.

Vanesco studied the face across the table now they were out of immediate danger. From their brief conversation the questions he had gotten answered, he felt he knew more about Erhart than he had any of the others. Erhart was on his list as George Gavin, the sixth man, and the most practical, the skiptrace decided. Both plastic surgery and his stopping his shooting Torbert's killer said as much, as that would have caused problems for them.

Paranoia started up again, maybe Erhart had been working with the killer, and that was why his death would have caused problems; it couldn't have been coincidence that he happened to be around. In fact the more he thought about that the more distinct probability it seemed. The same set of questions kept recurring.

Who was it killed Torbert? And Niles, presumably. Who hired him? And more important, why? He had to get answers to those questions before he got any further.

'You've got to get the answers,' Erhart said after hearing

the questions. 'I know them. There's not a thing to stop me walking right out.'

'I could call the cops.'

Erhart shook his head. 'I'd say you're a man who solves problems, an American archetype. You move in, identify the trouble, ask questions, find the answers.' His tight skin concealed the smile.

'I'm not making too much headway, pal.'

'Maybe you're asking the wrong questions. If you find the right one I think maybe you won't like the answers.'

Vanesco conceded the point. 'You get to like the answers less and less, along with a lotta assholes you ask the questions for.' He swallowed some bourbon and held Erhart's look. 'What happened back there, I figure you were a part of it. S'why you let the guy get clear.'

'I had no reason to kill Torbert, less reason to kill Niles. They were more useful to me alive.' He waited. 'How much d'you know of what you're investigating?'

'Absolutely nothing. I was hired to find six guys. No one knew why these guys were wanted, if they did they weren't telling. Then when they started dying I began asking a different kind of question.' He saw Erhart's look. 'I get hired because I don't ask embarrassing questions. But I got this feeling I was sucking for someone.'

'There were more efficient ways of finding these people, only the risks are greater, especially for the person who did the hiring. Your scuffling around on your own would distance him, whereas the CIA wouldn't.'

'You're the man with the answers, pal. So unless our friend comes in here and takes you out, I expect some of those answers.'

'The man who killed Torbert,' he paused and again offered that tight smile. 'It was Brad Coley. I guess he's on your list.'

'Sure. He was supposed to have died in a burned out boat.'

'Coley was an expert with both boats and fire. You can be sure whoever died in that boat it wasn't Coley. He's alive and back working for the CIA.'

'What's their interest?'

'They've always had an interest. Until summer '63 we all worked for the Company. Niles wasn't Lance Niles then, nor

167

was your friend called Torbert. Their names don't matter. We severed all connection with the CIA in November '63. The twenty-second to be precise.'

'Kennedy,' Vanesco said. There was an odd feeling in his stomach, it wasn't nauseous, more like a palpitation. He remembered how he had felt on hearing about the President being shot: sick and empty and despairing, even though he hadn't been a Kennedy supporter – in the FBI Republicanism was almost mandatory – he knew the President was doing good work. That whole feeling flooded back.

'The veil of secrecy was never lifted. Our official contact with the Company had safely ended, before that each of our deaths arranged in unrelated incidents. None of us had relatives to ask questions.'

'Okay, now let me get this straight. You're saying the CIA killed Kennedy?' He sounded more incredulous than he was. he had heard all the rumors, even the one that Hoffa had got it done to stop Robert Kennedy's threat to his autocratic rule over the Teamsters and their entrenched connections with organized crime.

'Who was in a better shape to set it up? It wasn't policy – Dulles was the only reason it wasn't, the director in those days wasn't sure enough of his powerbase. He amounted to little more than administrator for the Seven Sisters who run the US, and not just its economy. They wanted it done all right, but getting round to actually saying the word that was something else. Then deputy director Lawrence Wallechinsky was contacted by the rightwing pressure group based in California, that was a firm within a firm. The ramifications are endless – circles within circles. The question is how big is the circle. That's what you're trying to discover.'

'Hughes?' Vanesco suggested.

'Not any more, not directly. That point in time he no longer existed other than as a business appendage to Aristotle Onassis. But I'm getting ahead of myself. The people in California had their fingers put in the crusher by Kennedy's administration – they had openly backed Nixon for President in the fall of '59. After the Cuban fiasco they had gotten active. Their apparent intention was to do something about this crazyman who was sitting in the White House and giving

America to the communists, the liberals, the blacks. It wasn't coincidental that their objectives complemented the American economy. Look how the market reacted after the assassination. It went up, when every kind of logic says it should have gone down.'

'Why would Wallechinsky get involved in a deal like that? He didn't go anywhere fast.'

'He didn't need a weatherman to tell him which way the wind was blowing, Mr Vanesco. He put himself in possession of facts most people got scared just thinking about. True, his career didn't rocket, but it consolidated. He could've made Director of the CIA, probably Secretary of State, but he worked away behind the scenes, building power, getting owed big favors, from both Republicans and Democrats. He could have had Kissinger's job, but didn't want it because he plans to have Richard Nixon's job. The ambassador to China is his emergence, he earned that more than any other ambassador earned any position.'

'Why was it necessary to kill the President? If I read you right the public were manipulated into voting him into office. The same could have been done to end his reign?'

'He was becoming dangerously popular, and it wasn't foolproof. The CIA was, and still is, a powerbase. One of the most powerful in the world, one that had been designed and built up by some very important people, but primarily Aristotle Onassis. It was in effect the executive arm of a huge cartel headed up by Onassis and Howard Hughes, until '57 when Hughes disappeared only to be replaced by a look-alike. Then some populace-jerk of a President comes along and says, "hey you motherfuckers, you pull a stroke like the Bay of Pigs on me again, I'll annihilate you." You think a real powerbase working for the biggest corporations in America, used by them as an expeditionary force in any part of the world where their commercial interests were threatened, you figure they're going to stand around and allow themselves to be wiped out? What Kennedy was doing was downright unAmerican, and no way accorded with the deal between Onassis and Joseph Kennedy when his son was promised the presidency. The problem was Joe had a stroke and lost control of the family. Jack and Bobby started to rebel, started to believe their own rhetoric, they figured erroneously that power in America lay in the people. That was when Walle-chinsky came into his own, talked to the people in LA, made a perfect marriage – means and necessity.' He paused. 'Every-thing is possible in the United States, Mr Vanesco. There you need only two things to make that satanic leap from the un-thinkable to the practical, money and imagination.'

'Why involve this pressure group in LA? If Hughes was now under Onassis's control and they were a circle within the Hughes circle, why increase the danger by having more people a party to the conspiracy?'

Erhart shook his head. 'It's a fallacy – a common one – that more people increase the attendant risks in a conspiracy. What happens is they reduce it. If enough of the right people are a party to it then it ceases to become a conspiracy but the status quo.' No obsessive paranoia was driving this man, he spoke in a calm, matter-of-fact way. 'These people deal with possible destruction of half the world as a matter of daily routine, they had no problem making the leap. As to poten-tial material, America's a melting-pot of all the peoples and cultures of the world, they've been thrust into a collective-progress that's faster than most can deal with; the collective cortex is fatally damaged, but the pressures are too great for them to stop and resolve the fundamental problems that afflict their society – the ritual hatred of the blacks; of Jews; communists; cancer, finishing last. People want ready-made instant answers. They seek analysis, expecting to short circuit living, experiencing, questioning, a process which takes an entire lifetime in an empiric culture just to begin to get even a few answers. There was no problem finding malcontents to stand up and shoot down the President. They didn't need to look further than the Company.'

'Aren't you overreaching for Onassis? What motivates him? What need for Christsake?'

Erhart studied the weary, beaten face before him. He sipped his drink, then said, 'Ego. That's about as far as you need look, I guess. He's a man who wants everything for himself, and I do mean everything. Possessing gives him pleasure; he becomes greedier because his design is having and the more he is the more he has; he feels hostile toward everyone, cheating customers, destroying competitors, exploiting workers. He's never satisfied because there's no limit to his wishes; he envies anyone who has more than him, and is frightened of everyone with less. Most of the time he has to keep the lid on these feelings because he's an international businessman, he has a social and public image.' Erhart fell silent.

'I guess you just described everyone who ever bought a car or tv or cared a damn about the way he lived.'

'Precisely. About one third of the world. But Onassis is the supreme egoist. His active philosophy is the synthesis of capitalism.'

Thoughts were going off like machine-gun fire in Vanesco's head. He felt no need to defend the American way of life here nor attack communism. A lot of what Erhart had said about the American system was true, he had come to that himself. But the fallacy of the alternative, communism, was that it ended class struggle by eradicating classes, while the western system remained based on the principle of unlimited consumption. All the while people wanted more there would be exploited classes, class struggle, which in world terms meant international friction. However, in that recognizably flawed system within which he lived, people could openly question, and with a few notable exceptions it could take that without having to hit back. Vanesco saw no percentage in laying that on Erhart.

He thought about Lawrence Wallechinsky and the six men he had been hired to find. Although he had been given some answers to some questions, along with reasons for what had happened, he still wasn't convinced.

'Why did Wallechinsky wait all this time to go after you guys?' Vanesco asked.

'The simple answer is that now he's gone public, we've become an unacceptable threat. That's not the entire answer. We've always been a threat. The fact is we weren't supposed to get farther than the plane that was to fly us out of Dallas. We switched planes at the last moment, figuring on some move against us. The aircraft we should have been in came down in the Black Mountains, a real neat accident. There were no survivors. By then we were clear, each of us with the quarter million dollars we'd been paid.'

'Outta petty cash?' Vanesco said.

'That was petty cash to those people. We were professionals, they knew we wouldn't die easily, not then. We'd each
been at our peak. This far on, well, those guys had gone
downhill, lost touch.'

'Sure. Wallechinsky's not dumb. Right. It's eleven years,
the threat had gone. I talked with Radulovic, he was
harmless. Torbert was obsessed with horses.'

'Paley was into dope, Coley was dealing shit. Niles had got
religion, I work for the East Germans. We were no problem
aside from the fact that we were still around.'

'So why would the ambassador to China want to stir it all
up again?'

'He heard I was looking for the others. Looking to bring
them to East Germany. That was a serious miscalculation on
our part. We fed him that information in order to get pressure
on the others to have them run in our direction.'

'Wallechinsky moved too fast for you?' Vanesco said.

'Something like that. The plan is to sabotage Sino-
American détente, shred it so fine it takes another twenty-five
years to get started.' He said this in a logical manner as
though it was the only direction after weighty deliberation.

'You some kind of fucking crazy. Nixon's going to China,
whether it's Wallechinsky, Kissinger or Nixon himself who
made the deal, it's the best news there is for peace.'

'Whose peace? Not the Eastern Communist bloc. The cosy
arrangements the Chinese and Americans will be making
with Wallechinsky out there could do the Russians a lot of
harm.'

'In their heads,' Vanesco said.

'Nothing exists outside the imagination. Even the possibility of America selling the Chinese arms isn't ruled out, as
incredible as it may seen. The problems over Vietnam have
resulted in your country overcompensating and starting this
dialog with the Chinese. What we see happening now is the
East-West cold war beginning again, the strategic arms limi-
tation talks breaking down. That's not too drastic from the
US viewpoint, having acknowledged communist China; the
thinking is that the Russians would be fully occupied with the

Chinese. If we can disfranchise Wallechinsky we halt the dialog with China.'

'That makes Wallechinsky pretty important? Assuming he did fix up the Kennedy assassination, why would the Chinese care?'

'They wouldn't. But they would worry about Wallechinsky's Onassis connection. He's important. He's the lynchpin holding that fragile relationship together. There was more involved than merely bringing one of the others over and blowing the whistle. By the time we got through there would be no Sino-American relationship.'

'Well I guess God's on the side of the righteous, pal.' He finished his bourbon, and flapped his arm at the bartender. 'If Sino-American relations start and finish with Wallechinsky, why not just kill him?'

'We will as a last resort.'

'Okay, so I buy this story of yours about six guys shooting the President. Seems I recall a little guy named Oswald who took most credit. The prestigious Warren Commission confirmed it.'

'If you believe that, my friend, you must be in a minority of one.' He waited while the barman brought their drinks. 'Oswald was a plant. His purpose was to stop people thinking about the unpalatable alternatives. He was just one of the countless disaffected Americans who needed only a suggestion and an opportunity to attempt the satanic leap. The secret service files are full of Oswalds. Wallechinsky set him up.' He laughed. 'The irony was that Oswald couldn't have made those shots if the car had been stationery on Dealey Plaza. Even we couldn't do it right, and there were six of us, all experts. We had him on a cross plot from the moment that limo came up the hill. Oswald! Jesus. The public outcry was so great that the first guy who looked like a suspect was all anyone wanted. What the public didn't know about was that four other suspected assassins were gunned down in Dallas that day, by cops and secret service men. Or the recording accidentally made by the Dallas police from a car that was parked on Dealey Plaza. All the shots were recorded via the mike in the car. So it goes.'

Vanesco waited, and thought about the Warren Commission, the doubt placed on its findings in recent years. The two dissenting voices of its members were those of Senator Russell and Congressman Boggs. Both died shortly afterwards.

'There were two conspiracies in Dallas that day. The one to kill the President had taken a lot of planning; the other was improvised right after the shooting. It was the second conspiracy, not the first, that they most needed the Warren Commission to conceal. The first one had been put together too well for there to be any mistakes which would show up in the climate that followed the shooting. Sure, we shot the President in Dallas, as everyone saw. The problem was we didn't kill him.' He paused, as if for dramatic effect, but he needed none. 'He got to Parkland Memorial hospital alive, that's a matter of public record, what isn't is the fact that he stayed that way. They got him into the trauma room and went to work on him, and when medical expertise goes to work on the President of the United States, nothing's spared. I guess that's democracy. The inhibiting problem they found was that half of his brain had been shot away. There was so much brain damage that although the miracles of medicine could keep him alive, what they had left there was vegetable. There was a lot of pressure on the people in that emergency room, and a lot of external pressure from this rightwing organization out in California. They had an alternative in the form of a strongman waiting to take over. It was believed by the administration that such an organization could and would do just that if there was any kind of constitutional crisis. Wresting control from the democratically elected government of the United States is unthinkable, until someone succeeds. Venturing into the unthinkable is all a matter of timing; they should have moved the moment Kennedy was shot. Only when Wallechinsky learned what had happened he didn't initiate the moves he was meant to. He saw a safer way of consolidating his own position. In retrospect he was right not to have made his move, for Hoover had details of the whole plot. Maybe you knew something more of that.'

Vanesco didn't. There had always been rumors, and if you worked with any expectations of promotion you didn't get caught with them on your lips.

'Hoover didn't move against them for his own reasons. I'm sure he figured on politically strongarming all those guys involved. And for all I know he did.'

'What was the second conspiracy? You telling me Johnson killed Kennedy?'

'Not quite. What Johnson did, and, ironically, with the help of Wallechinsky, was to keep Kennedy alive, and fool the world. They did just that. The conspiracy involved letting the world think he had died so the executive branch of the government could go on functioning with Johnson stepping up and taking the oath. That's why the autopsy evidence is strictly guarded in the National Archives. It's an invention based on a plausible prognosis. While Kennedy was quietly shipped out alive to the tiny Greek island of Skorpios, where he remains to this day. The island was owned by Aristotle Onassis. The connection was complete. Full circle. We come back to the nature of your original inquiry: how big is the circle?'

Anger was starting to build in Vanesco. Had he gotten this information over the past decade he could have handled it, but all at once it was too much and the obvious course was to reject it; however things had happened that now made this impossible. Part of his anger came from fear, which lay just below the surface. He wasn't exactly naive, but this information was hard to take. Sure, Erhart could have invented it, Vanesco argued, by why would he have? Because he was crazy? It was too simple, and he was sitting in this hotel in Venice with a trail of dead people behind him, people who had died because of what they knew about that assassination in Dallas. Now he had the same information and saw clearly his position. His fear surfaced. Someone, Wallechinsky ultimately, would try to kill him, unless he struck first. But against who? The ambassador to China? But how? Knowledge was power, that was evident from the power J. Edgar Hoover had wielded in his office at the FBI, only the trick was to finish holding the right kind of information. Vanesco held the wrong kind, the kind that would get him nothing but danger; it wasn't directly related to Erhart telling him all that he had, Vanesco had set himself upon this course the minute he had inquired after the man behind Kohn.

Vanesco stared at his bourbon as if staring into a crystal ball. 'Let's get a couple of things straight here. Why would Wallechinsky go along with this deal to ship Kennedy out to Skorpios and keep him alive? He was working for this outfit who wanted him dead.'

'Your ambassador to China only ever works for himself. Rather than risk some sort of reward from any new regime, he settled for being owed a big favor by the new President. Lyndon Johnson was known for returning favors.'

'Johnson coulda had them ease up on intensive care, let Kennedy go.' It was a dumb proposition he realized.

'He had neither the balls nor imagination to make that leap. It would have meant telling the medical people, actually saying the words. This was the President of the United States we're talking about.'

'Yet they must have known about the other deal.'

'Some did. Those who did are now dead.' He held Vanesco's look. 'A matter of public record. They died of natural or accidental causes, in unrelated incidents. The only common factors are that they were all in the trauma room at the Parkland. Their deaths help to form a part of the 9 billion-to-one odds against all those witnesses to the assassination and related events dying as they have within the last decade. That's a hundred and forty-nine to date.'

'What?' The number shook Vanesco.

'I've done my research. Kennedy had threatened the powerbase for the last time. No way could Wallechinsky lose now. He was political, everybody's man and nobody's. He did favors on both sides of the fence. Now he's ahead of the field, almost.'

'You can blow the whistle.'

'Working as I do for the East Germans? Who'd buy it? He knows that. Could be he won't trouble sending anyone after me.'

Anger burst out of Vanesco. 'Why the fuck are you laying all this on me?' He knew. He was being driven along a path that Erhart couldn't go himself. Maneuvered into a position where he could only go forward, seek answers to his questions. There was no point stopping now, he was already marked by his limited information, and even if he never got to tell about it he was determined to know the truth. He had to head on down to Greece, check whether there was a conspiracy bigger than the one that apparently killed the President.

Outside the sun was climbing over St Mark's Canal, touching the terracotta roofs, and church domes, making them glow with a pale brilliance. The quay was beginning to stir as Vanesco stood at the water's edge, trying to get his thoughts straight. He wasn't thinking about the trip he had to make to Skorpios, nor what he might find there, instead he was considering how he might kill Lawrence Wallechinsky. Right then it seemed unthinkable that he should try and take out a politician with no direct connexion to him, but he thought about the expression Erhart had used, taking that satanic leap, when the unthinkable became the possible. Looking back the leap seemed predestined from the moment Clark E. Cunningham had called him, and Vanesco accepted that there was no way he could not take it now. He no longer had a choice.

Twenty-three

The woman had been in his thoughts all the while he had been out of town: what to do about her? The question remained unresolved. The idea he must come to terms with was that he had to kill her. But he liked her, and at times it was fun having her around; and the kid? Well he didn't think too much about him one way or the other. The boy was his, but that didn't mean too much to him. In the field he had undergone a whole new conditioning, there regular loyalties didn't exist; the Company had been his family, his only loyalty, and since his departure he had refined the caring process to self, to ensure his personal survival. How Mo had gotten to be a specific problem was that she knew he existed; whereas up on the Lake she had been useful cover, here she would be a liability. She had led Vanesco back to Randle Point so he could kill him, and that was information about him he would rather she didn't have. Although he was freelance and his employers didn't dictate how he did their work, he guessed they'd be pretty steamed about the woman being mixed up in it. His second mistake had been to leave Vanesco with his suspicions about his death. The skiptrace would have passed that information to Torbert, who he guessed told the others. Jesus, his burning that dumb tourist up on the Lake had all been for nothing. What he should have done was stayed cool when Vanesco came looking, told him what he wanted to hear, got him off guard, then burned him. He had been in bad shape then, he had had all kinds of problems. He would redeem himself today. His contact had set it up for him. Vanesco was bringing a parcel of scag. What could be more natural than his dying after the exchange? A smile wrinkled in his mind. Dealers were always getting iced for good news they brought. It was such a regular occurrence that the cops considered it death by natural causes, and scarcely bothered to investigate. Another smile wrinkled in his brain. He was feeling good. Not only would he square himself with his employer, but also get himself a parcel of dope. Good news!

That still left the problem of the woman. Coley knew the smart thing to do, and wondered why he was resisting it. Maybe he was getting sentimental. He could fix her up, have her OD: she'd go off like a baby.

The man was thirty-seven, and killing came as easy as farting, he did both unselfconsciously. It started as a kid in the backwoods of Vermont. He killed and butchered his first hog when he was eleven. His Daddy had been showing him how for as many Christmases before that as he could remember. You just laid Daddy's .44 against the pig's skull, and gave it to that big old boy right between the eyes. Then you ran your knife that you'd been honing for two days across the hog's throat before he was dead so his big old heart would pump all the blood out; nerves made him do that, for he never died instantly, the bullet into that two-inch-thick skull would only stun him. Then you hoisted him rearend first on the block Daddy used for hefting engines out of the automobiles people brought to the woods for him to fix. When the last of the blood was drained, the big old hog went into the vat of boiling water to get off all his bristles. Next you removed the urinary tract before butchering him. The only reason the boy hadn't done all this earlier was that he wasn't big enough to handle a 400-pound hog. He had taken no pleasure in killing pigs then any more than he did in killing people now, but nor did he find it distressing, it just had to be done. Then, as now, it was an act of survival. He had never killed for the sake of killing like some of the hunters who came into the woods up around Lancaster. When his existence was threatened then he killed, if that held the answer, as it often did; also when he was given money to kill, because he had himself an expensive habit. The habit hadn't been no problem when working for the Company fulltime in Saigon, from there they had shipped heroin to the US in the bodies of GIs; with their guts removed they could take ten kilos. With bodies going home to all parts of the US it was the perfect method of distribution. There had been no wardodging customs inspector so indecent as to unstitch a dead GI. With scag to spare, to fool around with, he had gotten a taste for it; then he had been pulled out of South East Asia and offered the job in Dallas. The price had meant surviving with his habit for a long time. When finally told who the target was he hadn't baulked, to him doing it had been necessary to survive, he had had no grudge, saw no cause to identify with, nor injustice to right, not like some of the spooks. His prime concern had been survival, and the only real problem with hitting the President that he had foreseen to some extent was the furore that followed. But Wallechinsky had said that was being handled. Rather than reassuring him, Coley had realized that the last people the conspirators would want picked up was anyone who could start talking, that meant they'd all be rubbed out once clear of Dallas. But he had made sure he survived.

He moved the gearshift into low as he came off the Rochambeau Bridge onto Maine Avenue and made a left turn onto G Street. He planned to drop the Hertz car at National Depot on G in the SW district rather than at Alexandria

Station where he originally intended to. He was making sure he wasn't being tailed. He wanted to go on surviving.

After leaving the car he walked along 3rd Street to Independence and picked up a cab. He jumped out at a red light at Constitution, dodged through the oncoming traffic and took a cab in the opposite direction. He checked the rear window, no one else did the same, he was clean. When he turned he saw the black woman driver watching him. He read the no smoking notice she had – on account of an allergy – and wondered how she'd react if he fixed himself here. He could wait, but not too long. He took a third cab and headed for his meeting.

An hotel on New York Avenue down near 1st Street in the North-East section of Washington DC was where the meeting had been set. The neighborhood was black, the dwellings and apartment buildings were in a bad state of repair. The streets were littered, being cleaned less frequently than those in the NW section. Coley wasn't interested in stuff like that. He concentrated on who was around, what faces weren't black, out of work, on stoops or outside of bars because there was no place to go and couldn't afford to step into the barrooms. No one face leaped off the wall, but eyes followed him. He was whitey and easily made as such, which was why he had had the skiptrace set up here.

The room, on the second floor of the four storey building overlooking New York Avenue, was noisy. Trucks rolled past the whole time, this being the main route out of the city for Philadelphia. Coley put on a pair of leather gloves and checked both bedroom and bathroom. There he stopped and looked at himself in the mirror. He avoided having mirrors in the places he lived, not caring to look at himself; the face behind the mask he had once seen in the mirror had frightened him, and a dark well of fear had opened inside him. He preferred keeping that lid down. Seeing that image had revealed to him what he was, and he had become scared because he knew he had no control over that darker side. He resisted mirrors to prevent him searching for what he had once seen, knowing it might prove a fatal distraction.

Here the face looking back at him was lopsided, the cause wasn't glass distortion. His left eye was an inch lower than his right and he had a habit of tilting his head to make it less noticeable. People noticed and stared at him. When he first began dating girls he had felt a freak, and he hadn't stopped worrying about it until reaching South East Asia he had seen more freaks than regular-looking people. His eyes were all people noticed about him which was some kind of compensation; they never remembered the color of his hair, his build, height, how he dressed. He always wore a sport jacket and Levis, comfortable and practical. But no one remembered.

His eyes were clear now, the pupils smaller than usual, the whites showing on three sides of his eyes gave them a bulging effect. There was no one in his eyes today, nothing that frightened him. He thought then about Moyra Yeston again, and decided he'd help her OD, that was his only practical course.

The tap at the door caused Coley to look at his watch. He was sitting on the bed with the Washington Post covering his .38. One minute after four pm. Coley smiled, he thought it funny that a man should be so punctual to die.

'The door's open,' he said. He watched the handle turn. He didn't immediately see the man's face as he walked in, concentrating on his hands. If there was danger it would show in his hands. The left hand held an attaché case, the right was empty. His eyes moved up to the face and he was unable to keep from showing surprise.

The man in the doorway smiled at his surprise, his top teeth clamping over his bottom lip. 'Vanesco isn't coming, Brad.' He closed the door. He had no fear, knew there was no problem about turning his back on Coley, despite the gun he guessed was under the newspaper.

Disappointment chased surprise off Coley's face. 'Some problem?'

'No problem. We've got other plans for Vanesco. Put your gun away, I got something for you.' He set the attaché case on the nighttable.

Coley watched his contact, making no attempt to put up the gun. The thought occurred to him that he might have stopped by to kill him, but if that were the case he gave nothing away in his actions. Coley knew this man was good, but didn't believe he was that good. Why hadn't he called up

181

to say the meeting was off? His failing to take care of Vanesco loomed; his using Moyra Yeston was another black mark. Maybe he should shoot this guy and run, but then he'd have the Company after him, and he'd be left with his expensive habit and no employment. He put the gun in his belt, within easy reach.

'Why didn't you call?' Coley said.

'Vanesco was bringing you something.' His small hand gestured toward the case. Inside were glassine bags of white powder, a factory, and money. 'We gotta another job for you, in Chile.' There was no option.

Coley relaxed. They weren't retiring him. 'Fine. Anything you wanna give me.'

'This isn't the best shit around,' he said. 'Those sons of bitches cut it so much we'll soon be shooting up pure sugar milk. It'll get you where you want to go, I guess.'

Joy lit Coley's eyes. 'I could use something.' He fingered one of the glassine sacks. 'This all for me?'

'You'll be in South America a spell.' He took out the factory to fire up.

Right then Coley felt only goodwill toward this man; a wave of guilt over fucking up on Vanesco swamped in. 'I'm real sorry about missing that guy up in Canada. Jesus, I wouldn't want that to stand against me.'

'Don't worry about it.' He tipped the contents of a sack into his burning spoon and put some heat from his Dunhill lighter under it. He saw Coley's look. 'It ain't gonna get you as far as you figure.'

'The motherfuckers,' Coley said, thinking about the rip-off merchants who cut the scag. 'The girl's not gonna be any kind of problem.' It was an apology.

'She's not?' He sounded disinterested.

'She's gonna OD. I decided.'

'That's drastic.' His attention was on the heroin he was cooking.

'I want to keep things sweet with you guys.'

'You decide what's best. She in town?'

He gave the address, she was at a motel in Alexandria, said she was expecting him to pick her up.

'What about the kid?'

Anxiety touched Coley's face. He hadn't expected that his kid would be demanded also. 'I figure he got a free ride. He's with Vanesco's girlfriend.'

The man's teeth came over his bottom lip. 'Sure,' he said. 'What's down in Chile?' He put his gun aside as he removed his belt and tightened it around his arm.

'A problem with Allende, the Marxist president they have down there. He's costing people a lot of money. We just need someone reliable to do the number our people are setting up.'

'Be glad to.' He flexed a fist, pumping up a vein. 'You shooting up?'

'Right along with you.'

He took a second envelope and started the burn-up – this one contained pure sugar milk, the only one of the thirty sachets. The white stuff in the other envelopes was, in fact, ninety-seven percent pure Chinese, the best the Company chemist had seen in a long while. The amount Coley was shooting into his arm was enough to cause anyone, even a high tolerance, to OD.

The man watched the last of the blood and heroin admixture run out of the hypodermic into the vein. Coley released the strap, and jerked violently as the dose hit him, his body jumped as though hit with a jackhammer. The man looked at his watch as Coley tried to settle into his load. His hands and hips moved rhythmically like an old man in sleep, his eyes blinked a couple of times, he convulsed, then suddenly went still. The man knew he was dead, it had taken forty-six seconds. Longer in fact than he thought it would.

He smiled with his even, slightly protruding teeth. This neatened things off; he would do the same with Coley's old lady, and that would close the chapter. Then all he'd need to take care of was Vanesco, until Larry Wallechinsky got paranoid about someone else.

As he cleared away the evidence of his presence, leaving only the factory Coley had used and the empty glassine envelope, he wondered when Wallechinsky would get round to seeing him as some kind of danger. Right then he was the ambassador's source of security, so represented no threat. But what about when everything was done, and he was the only person between Wallechinsky and his past? It caused a ripple on the surface.

As he left the room he hung out the Do Not Disturb sign. No one would ever disturb Brad Coley again. The thought amused him, and relieved his feeling of anxiety.

BOOK THREE

All that we imagine is real

Twenty-four

Athens was warm, and a relief from the cold of Northern Italy. Vanesco was enveloped in heat the moment he came off the plane, but still felt chilled. He was running a cold and figured the best option was bed with a lot of booze to sweat it out. Only he knew that wasn't in prospect. He couldn't sit illness out even when there wasn't any pressure on him. Right then there was pressure. He was driven to discovering everything he could about the John Kennedy assassination, and what happened afterwards; he wanted to remove the shroud of secrecy then confront Wallechinsky, if there was anything to confront him with finally. He thought about Erhart's reason for telling him all that he had, it was in the hope that he would trip up the ambassador. Vanesco didn't care about that, nor about the truth for its own sake – he had found he could live with other people's truths, provided it didn't affect him personally – the reason he had to explode this lie now was in order to go on surviving. To do that he might have to kill Wallechinsky, and so needed a real motive, something more than the word of an ex-CIA man now working for the East Germans. It was reasonable that in the position he had held within the Company Wallechinsky would have been responsible for people dying; but that alone wasn't sufficient motive for Vanesco, no longer could he unquestioningly handle stuff like that. The death of Peter Radulovic had finally brought about this change; although Radulovic had possibly been involved in the President's murder, it would have been a different person to that man Vanesco had seen in Mexico, one who, despite his past, didn't deserve to die. Wallechinsky's death would end it, he decided. The pressure would cease.

'How long will you be staying in Greece?' the immigration officer at Athens Airport asked as he scrutinized Vanesco's passport.

'A coupla days – depends how much I get to see.'

The man smiled, recognizing the first of the season's dollar-bearing tourists. He stamped his passport. Welcoming his dollars was one thing, being polite was something else when America owned Greece as it did through bankloans and the US Government giving money for Greece to buy US arms.

Vanesco didn't know Greece so his cover as a tourist was for real. All he could do was buy a map and stumble around. He took a cab downtown and checked into the Acropole Palace on Patission Avenue. That wasn't his choice of hotel, but that recommended by a tourist official to provide the unchallenged standards that Americans demanded away from home in an unknown city.

The ride was the worst, Vanesco thought, as he braced himself against the side of the cab and stared out of the window, trying to ignore the maniacal drivers hurtling vehicles around them. He was prepared to bet that nowhere in the world did people drive with the same crazy impatience, not in New York, Paris or Rome. There was a continual blare of car horns, screeching tires.

The poverty so apparent on the streets struck Vanesco forcefully, and he wondered if the driver had taken this route purposely to make him feel bad. Crumbling, decaying dwelling houses were a feature of urban living, here as in America, but whereas all American cities were ringed with garbage, junk that no one wanted, least of all the poor, on the outskirts of Athens there was a shanty town; on the streets were raggedy, unwashed kids begging, along with parents, who looked as though they didn't even make Welfare. Vanesco didn't know if Greece had a welfare program, he knew that last year a consortium, headed by the Crocker Bank, loaned the Bank of Greece $70,000,000, but he doubted that the underclass benefited from it. The most accurate indication of street-level poverty in any country was its domestic animals, and here the dogs and cats on the street were raw-bones, with matted, mangy fur, and mistrustful.

The worst was a tip he saw off the road for unwanted kittens. There they were emptied out of boxes and left to die of heat and hunger and thirst in a struggling heap. The sight made him feel angry and sick.

Four years ago Vanesco wouldn't have noticed such things, despite being no less observant. Then his priorities had been different and his eyes had swept the streets editing out such things. Zell had made him conscious of street poverty. He thought about the four grand he carried in cash, the five hundred dollars he made a day, the man whose private island he was trying to reach; besides Skorpios, Aristotle Onassis probably owned half Greece, while half the population lived below the poverty line. Vanesco drew no particular conclusions; there was something wrong with the system, but he was a part of it. He had been born in South Bronx in '32 and abandoned by a mother he never knew. They hadn't been easy times, but he reflected that they had probably been made easier by the fact that the city had raised him. The problem with most kids born into the underclass, whether their poverty was urban or rural, was that they didn't get dumped on the state, instead parents struggled against hopeless odds. They had a better chance of surviving in the US than Greece or Italy or Mexico, but it was a myth that there were equal opportunities in America for those trying to break out of the spiral of poverty. The way the poor mostly got out of the ghettos was through crime, and what happened then was that they usually increased the misery of their own kind upon whom they stepped.

Zell had some of the answers, or thought she had, while he didn't even pretend to. Like the majority of the privileged class, those with a job, an income, his inclination had been to wilfully ignore the problem, go on supporting the status quo until it collapsed.

The men with the keys on their uniforms in international hotels were very important people, as any seasoned traveler knew, especially when needing anything besides a bed. Hotel porters knew where everything from a three-dollar-whore to a hundred-dollar-chip poker game could be obtained. The porter at the Acropole was no less well informed. Vanesco called him to his suite, gave him a hundred dollars and told him he wanted to find a boatman who knew the islands, spoke English that Vanesco could understand and wouldn't ask questions. Neither the request nor the tip surprised the man. He said he would find such a boatman within the hour.

It took two hours in fact, during which Vanesco ate lunch. The porter didn't deliver a boatman, but an address in Piraeus, along with an escort. They rode the subway out to Piraeus, which was five miles from Athens. The old and rattling wooden cars, that seemed as though they would come apart when they hit the worn points, made the New York subway a joy.

The address was an untidy restaurant by the docks, there the air was breathable, Vanesco found, unlike Athens, where the pollution, or the Cloud as Athenians called the smog that enveloped their city, caused his eyes to smart. Across the quay fishing smacks were tied up, their day's work ended, nets out to dry. In the bay pleasure craft were moored along with ocean-going boats. The boatman was Yannis Drettakis, who was grossly overweight and wore a cap with the badge of an English Naval captain, his goatee had all but disappeared into his unshaven cheeks.

'Ello, Jack,' he said and offered a chair to Vanesco, who was identified by the man with him. Drettakis was still eating lunch, even though it was four in the afternoon, and Vanesco got the impression that he hadn't sat down late. He called across the restaurant for another bottle of retsina, which was brought by a woman who was his size and had nearly as much hair on her face. Drettakis turned a glass over and poured Vanesco a drink, then passed the bottle to the guide to pour his own. 'Cheers, Jack.'

'Here's to you, pal.'

The man's accent interested Vanesco, he sounded South African, having that kind of singsong Africaans sound.

'You want to hire my boat, Jack?' he said.

'Along with someone who know the islands.'

'You a smuggler? Only thing I don't run is Turkey dope. If this is your business it bad business.'

At first Vanesco believed this was a moral standpoint, until Drettakis explained that much bigger operators had that sewn up, and if he tried encroaching he would become fish food.

'What you want my boat for, Jack?'

The boatman wasn't as discreet as Vanesco would have liked. He looked at the third man at the table, being reluctant to talk in front of him.

Drettakis said, 'Anything I know about he know about. He my crew.'

'I want to get to Skorpios.'

Drettakis pushed the last of the pastry into his mouth and washed it down with some wine, acting like he hadn't heard what he said. He had heard, Vanesco could see his brain working, figuring the price.

'Why you want to go there, Jack?'

'The deal is you don't ask questions. Right.'

'I don't take the job yet,' he said, and wet his fat finger to pick crumbs off the table. 'I could get into plenty trouble taking you. I don't mean from armed guards who patrol the island.'

'Let's say I was a journalist after a story.'

'You wouldn't be paying me enough, Jack.'

'Which gets us nicely on to how much?'

'A long trip. Take all day – if you can get on and get off the island. Some don't make it. Pressmen not welcome, nor anyone else. The family is mourning its son, for Greeks an important time.'

'It'll be at night, without the welcome mat,' Vanesco said. The captain pulled a face. 'How much?'

'I could lose my boat if caught. Could get jailed. You know what Greek jails are like, Jack? The colonels didn't get around to modernizing them?'

Vanesco nodded. He figured this man wanted the job and was making sure of the price. 'What I asked for was someone who knew those waters.'

'I know the waters, Jack. I point out the risks. Twelve hundred dollars.'

'S'lot of money.'

'If I lose my boat, nothing. I want two hundred for myself and one hundred for him. When you want to leave?'

'Right now,' Vanesco said, giving Drettakis the only surprise of the meeting. He saw no advantage delaying; the disadvantage was that the captain or his deckhand could talk to someone.

Reluctantly he agreed, the reluctance was over leaving the restaurant, the immediate source of food.

They gassed the boat up, the cost of which was extra to Vanesco. The guy had him over a barrel and there was nothing he could do, other than take the money back when they set down on mainland again. He wouldn't do that, regardless of the outcome; however, he thought he might get problems if the captain figured he was carrying more than he was springing for. Vanesco didn't trust him.

Seated in the restaurant Drettakis had concealed a lot of his size. He was close to three hundred pounds, Vanesco guessed, and about fifty-five. How that body had worked against those odds for so long; Vanesco hoped his coronary didn't arrive halfway across. He watched the man in the wheelhouse as they headed across the Saronic Gulf. He saw Vanesco looking at him.

'A long trip, Jack. You want to use the cot below?'

Vanesco said he had no need of sleep right then.

'D'you know the island well?'

'I've been on it. Been past it a lot.'

'Can you set me down unseen?'

'If I can't, Jack, I not set you down. If we get seen I not put in.' He called to his mate to take the wheel. Then went below on the converted PT boat.

In what had been the mess, and was now an all-purpose space, Drettakis spread maps of the island on the table. His fat finger prodded Skorpios.

'Here. This the only place I set you down, Jack. The westside. All the beaches are broken up, filled with rocks to stop boats landing.'

'Where's the main house?'

'Up here, on the bloody top. But the main house we not worry about. The guards who make patrols and have houses down here on quay.'

'Are they there?' Vanesco asked. 'The Onassises?'

The fat man gave him a look. It was an odd question when the assumption was that he was going to try and reach Onassis and his wife. 'They didn't tell me their movements, Jack. If they not there, less problems. The patrols go out less.'

It was 1 am before they reached the island. That was three hours steaming plus an hour and a half coming in on the tide so that the engine wouldn't be heard. The dingy was lowered and the deckhand climbed down ahead of Vanesco.

'How long you need, Jack?'

'Who knows. Maybe an hour, maybe four.'

'It gets light here 5 am. I gotta be out by then. I'll come back for you at seven. If you're not here, Jack, I not wait.'

Vanesco nodded. 'Make sure you're here, at seven. If I ain't here then I won't be needing a lift back. Which way do I reach the house?'

The captain waved his arm. 'Straight up.'

The deckhand didn't say a word as he rowed him in. He beached the dingy against the broken rocks, and the moment Vanesco stepped out, he shoved off. Vanesco wished the Greek was going in with him, for right then he felt desperately lonely. He watched the dingy draw away until he could no longer see it, then he couldn't hear it over the waves. He watched the phosphorescence, and thought of other foreshores he had seen that on. Turning he considered the dark shape of the island rising in front of him. As he picked his way through the rocks on the narrow foreshore he tried to analyze his reluctance, deciding it wasn't simply fear. He had been in equally dangerous situations. Or had he? He realized he had been in none where the threat was so pervasive. But that wasn't the problem, he decided. Possibly in common with a lot of Americans he didn't truly want to know the truth he was seeking; he didn't want to believe such a conspiracy could flourish, along with its participants. Still he went forward, started to climb.

The terrain was rugged here, and from what he could tell in the dark it had been arranged that way. He hoped Drettakis proved right about the island's strategic geography, that this was the unprotected side. If the boat had been heard then they'd know anyone trying to land on this side was uninvited. There wasn't much of anything he could identify growing on this side of the island apart from some cypresses at the summit. The climb took him longer than he expected, and when he reached the brow of the hill he was sweating, despite the chill of the early morning.

Across a slow incline was a dark, regular shape stretching beyond his vision. Vanesco knew it could be nothing other than a wall surrounding the villa. Drettakis hadn't told him about that, and he wondered what else the Greek might have neglected to tell him: such as the wire set atop the wall. Vanesco hadn't seen it as he pulled himself up, and the shock of it, even though he realized in the next instant that there was no current going through the wire, caused his heart to falter. Nothing appeared to happen as a result of touching that wire, there were no lights, no sign of life. This made him feel better, but he remained unmoving atop the wall, watching for five minutes. If anyone was there, he decided, they were real good at waiting. Finally he dropped into the enclosure where some low buildings surrounded the three storey villa. An odd feeling accompanied him as he set one foot in front of the other; he was being drawn to a place he didn't want to be, to discover something he didn't want to know, yet found he couldn't turn from it.

The grounds here had been elaborately landscaped, the bushes and trees and grass wouldn't have grown without a lot of attention. A darkened shape loomed at him. Vanesco reached for his gun, then realized it was a statue of an angel. He didn't put his gun away.

A chapel standing among cypress trees was the first building he came to. The door wasn't locked. Vanesco didn't risk the light, there was no need, the chapel would tell him nothing; a door led to an annex where he found an elaborately marked grave. Kennedy's? Even he wouldn't have rated this; burial inside a church was reserved for saints. The grave was recent, and the building around more recent still. In fact it wasn't finished, Vanesco realized, and risked using the flashlight Drettakis had loaned him, masking it with his hands. The tomb was Alexander Onassis's. Vanesco remembered reading how the plane he had been piloting out of Athens had crashed on take off, Onassis was convinced sabotage had been the cause. He risked letting the pen-sized shaft range wider. Building onto the chapel was one way of elevating your progeny to sainthood, and he was surprised Onassis couldn't simply have purchased such status.

The third building Vanesco reached wasn't locked either.

He guessed none of these doors would be. Who would dare to come to Skorpios to rob one of the world's foremost robbers, especially when he had the power of life and death over such perpetrators? Also if Drettakis was right about guards on the island few people would risk their lives coming here. Those guards, Vanesco suspected, weren't there to prevent theft but protect essential privacy. What of these guardians, how was their devotion to secrecy secured? Maybe it never was, which was how Erhart knew what he did. The antiseptic smell of hospital emergency room hit the skiptrace as he entered a small cloakroom area. A closet held surgical smocks and rubber boots. A door beyond this revealed a stronger antiseptic smell, and Vanesco could feel his pulse quicken as he stepped through the door and carefully closed. He realized he was holding his breath and the light probed the room, picking out stainless steel and plastic emergency life support apparatus. An electrocardiograph machine, anesthetic equipment, an operating table; there was monitoring equipment that Vanesco didn't recognize but guessed any hospital in the world would have been grateful for.

There was a bed with a ventilator close by; an electro-encephalograph for measuring brain activity also. Possibly this had been used for Alexander, but it was unlikely he would have been brought over alive. Perhaps it awaited Onassis in the event, but why so much oxygen, Vanesco questioned as he ran the flashlight over the dozens of tanks. This had to be for keeping Kennedy alive he decided; the location of this emergency unit tended to support his assertion, it was set apart, to the north west of the villa. Had this been for Onassis, it would have been close to hand.

Voices from across the grass quadrangle startled Vanesco. He didn't need the language to know what was said. The voices were shrill, excited, two of them; then a third closer by. A dog barked. Unsure how they had discovered his presence, he slipped back through the cloakroom, and once outside he ran. Not knowing what direction to take, he made for the shrubbery and immediate cover. Although Vanesco hadn't seen anyone he figured he had been seen, especially when floodlights bathed the whole enclosure in a brilliant, whiteish-blue light. A Doberman pinscher barked furiously as it passed with its handler. Vanesco had no fear of dogs, but was glad that one was leashed or he might have had to kill it. A second man appeared. Erhart's information about guards was correct, one had a machine carbine. They headed for the emergency unit. Vanesco moved in the opposite direction, circling the villa. It took him an hour, keeping tight to the greenery. He felt relieved when the lights were switched out, but not especially safe.

The villa was built, Vanesco guessed, to a Byzantine pattern rather than genuinely Byzantine, the kind of place Americans dreamed about retiring to in Florida. From a small vineyard on a south slope, Vanesco considered how he might get inside the house and take a look round, whether the President had been moved up there. Why would he? Because they knew he was coming? How? And would they have let him land? It was nonsense. Kennedy wasn't in the house, If still around, and Vanesco began to take seriously the notion that he had been, he would be in one of the other buildings. He wouldn't find out just standing around.

Cautiously he set off to check every building around the main house. Where he was able to he kept within the cover of the greenery. Either there weren't too many people on the island, or they weren't early starters, certainly they didn't get up with the sun. All of these buildings serviced the villa; generator house, workshops, store rooms, servants quarters – there a woman prepared food. He completed a circle and arrived back at the life-support unit, planning to take another look. As he opened the door from the cloakroom, he heard the single click of a machine carbine, and didn't wait to ask questions. No hail of bullets pursued him as he ran, only voices. A dog barked, then another; someone cursed them out as they strained at their leashes. Vanesco sprinted through the enclosure and leaped at the wall. As his hands went out for a hold he prayed the current hadn't been switched through that wire. It hadn't. The thought of keeping an intruder in had probably never occurred to anyone. Dropping off the wall, he lit out down the slope in the direction he had come in. Scrambling through the rocks, he slid into a fissure and fell a short distance to a sandy floor. He was unhurt and ran the only way he could.

Whatever his belief in fate before encountering Zell Vanesco had tended to deny it, but things happened beyond coincidence. It looked pretty much as though that was what had brought him here: the long fissure ran through the rock face and looked directly out over the Mediterranean. In this sandy clearing was a grave with a small unmarked cross in gray polished granite. The sun was coming up over the rim rock behind it, but as he stood there Vanesco shivered, even though he was sweating. This had nothing to do with the cold he was running, it was that recurring chill he had felt at the news of John Kennedy's assassination. The grave could have been there for a relative of Onassis, or a favorite pet, but Vanesco knew instinctively this was where the 35th President of the United States lay, without the eternal flame, or any kind of epitaph. It was ironical that perhaps one of the best known men in the world should finally be so anonymous.

The charitable institution that had raised him had done so in the Catholic faith, but even then he had known that the church was the biggest hype there was. Now he didn't reach back into those early teachings; nor did he respond like a detective looking for hard evidence to take back. What was there without he became a grave-robber? He moved away to the opening in the rockface where he sat in the sand and looked out over where he had landed. The stretch of beach had disappeared, the sea was against the rockface and there was no sign of Drettakis's boat. It was just after six, and despite knowing the fat guy wasn't coming to pick him up, Vanesco sat there waiting till well after seven am, watching the empty blue horizon and occasionally glancing round at the grave. Finally he climbed out of the fissure and headed back in the southeasterly direction. The terrain on the opposite side of the island was less rugged; there was a harbor and a pier with some low dwelling houses nearby; small craft were tied up, but nothing as big as the *Christina* was anchored.

Without warning a Doberman appeared around some bushes and hurled itself at Vanesco, who froze. The dog stopped, and snarled uncertainly, holding him at bay.

'Get outta here, you mother,' Vanesco growled, ''fore I break your arms.'

197

The dog obviously didn't understand English.

The dog handler approached at a run and spoke in Greek to the dog, but still it took no notice. A Doberman that didn't obey its handler Vanesco didn't find encouraging. The man spoke to Vanesco.

'I don't understand you, Charlie. I came to see Mr Onassis.'

'American?'

'I'm a journalist. I came to interview Mr Onassis.'

'How did you land?'

'By boat. Maybe I'll talk to Mrs Onassis.'

'Go to the house. Walk slowly, or the dog will tear you.' He rapped more instructions to the dog.

A man with a carbine watched as they approached the villa on the long open drive. The gunman didn't speak English and everything Vanesco said was translated by the dogman. They wanted to know who he worked for; how he got there. The gunman wasn't satisfied with the answers and hit Vanesco, who didn't have time to avoid the blow. The odds didn't favor retaliation.

'You're trespassing,' the dogman said under instruction. 'We could shoot you.'

'The world press wouldn't sit still for that, Charlie.'

'Why are you here?'

The question came again and again. When it was obvious they weren't going to progress, the gunman went to telephone. The result was Vanesco being shipped off the island under armed escort.

The police were waiting when they landed at Pirgos. There were few formalities. He was handcuffed and bundled into a hot and stinking panel truck. Vanesco protested, demanded to see the American Consul. He continued to do so throughout the long, hot ride across Peloponnisos to Athens police headquarters. They searched him, removed his possessions and put him in an interrogation room and left him for over an hour.

Later a man came in with Vanesco's Browning, minus the bullets. He was a precise man wearing a gray suit and starched collar, he had a mustache, which looked as if it got a lot of combing in front of a mirror.

'You requested the assistance of the American Consul, Mr Vanesco?' His English was faultless.

'You bet. Why am I being held like this?'

'Trespass is a serious crime in Greece. You are fortunate not to have been shot.'

'It don't amount to all this attention.'

'Then let us examine the real purpose of your landing on Skorpios.' He smiled, showing his white even teeth. He indicated the gun. 'It is believed you went there to murder Mr Onassis and his wife.'

'Horseshit.'

'Perhaps you'd care to tell me your story. We know it wasn't a journalistic pursuit. You're not an accredited journalist. Attempted murder would mean a long prison sentence. There'll be no difficulty persuading Yannis Drettakis to cooperate with us.'

Vanesco wasn't exactly surprised that they had the boat owner. 'Why don't you call the consul?'

'The only inconsistency is your incorrect information about the movements of Mr and Mrs Onassis. But no matter.'

There was no way Vanesco could see them progressing, this man was playing with him, for what he had really been after, knowing it was neither a story nor murder. 'Why don't you let me call my client in New York. He'll straighten this out.'

'Your client?'

'Clark E. Cunningham, attorney at law.'

The policeman thought about this. 'He hired you to kill Mr Onassis?'

Vanesco smiled. 'Why don't I make the call? Collect.'

'Will he be in his office?' He checked his watch. It was 3.40 pm local time, that made it approximately 8.40 am in New York.

'He likes to get started ahead of the pack. You wanna put in the call?'

The connection took twenty minutes, by which time he had persuaded the Greek cops to get him some coffee. It was cloudy and bitter, and made him more aware of the fact that he hadn't eaten since lunch yesterday.

199

The policeman didn't say the call would be listened to, but Vanesco assumed that would happen.

'Vanesco,' the New York lawyer said in what sounded like a formal tone to the skiptrace. 'What precisely is the situation?'

Vanesco told him the problem. Then added, 'I've wrapped the case up. Call Lawrence Wallechinsky in Washington, tell him where I am. Tell him I know how big the circle is now.'

'Then why don't you tell me? I'll call our consular department, see about having you released.'

'Call Wallechinsky.'

'Why should this interest our ambassador to China?' Cunningham asked, anxiety entering his voice.

'You gotta have been where I've been to know that, Clark ol' boy,' he said. 'Make the call.'

Vanesco was gambling. Maybe he was way off course in taking the direction like he had from Erhart, for although what he had told him in Venice had in someways been confirmed, nothing was conclusive. Neither the life-support unit on Skorpios nor the unmarked grave proved anything by themselves. The prospect of anyone going out to examine the body in that grave officially was nonexistent. Having Wallechinsky take the next move was the only way he was going to get enough confirmation to satisfy himself. The biggest risk was that the ambassador would do squat, which would make Vanesco a solid candidate for a Greek jail.

The lawyer made the call, which resulted in a call to the American embassy in Athens; here unclaimed favors were owed by both the Greek police and government. Suddenly Vanesco was treated deferentially, even his gun was returned to him. Vanesco smiled to himself, figuring Wallechinsky was now struggling for breathing space. But still he wasn't released, and within half an hour two men arrived from the American embassy. From the moment they stepped into the room Vanesco had a bad feeling about these guys. He didn't doubt their credentials, or that they had diplomatic status, but in a pig's eye they worked solely for the State Department.

'What's the story, pal?' Vanesco said to the older man, who was about his age.

'The story, Mr Vanesco? Aren't you going to tell us?'

'What happens now?'

'We go to your hotel, check you out, put you on a plane to the States. Before you embarrass the American Government.'

'S'what I figured.' He considered the Greek policeman. 'You want to come along, captain?'

'I think you are in safe hands, sir,' Captain Yiotas said.

'Might save me taking these guys off somewhere between there and the airport,' Vanesco said.

'That'd get you a lot of problems, Mr Vanesco,' the younger man warned.

'What if I make that plane? That gonna cause you problems?'

'I think you have a totally erroneous take on this situation,' the older man from the embassy said, trying to reassure him.

'How about it, captain?'

'Gentlemen?' the Greek cop said.

'Be our guest.' They tried to be gracious about inviting him along.

The plane was a TWA 707 to Paris. Getting off at Orly and switching flights would have been pointless for there would be someone watching for him, and this gave him a single alternative, he didn't resist. He knew from here on he was a marked man, so all he could do was go forward, play his hand to its conclusion, or run, try to disappear like the six men he had originally been hired to find. But Vanesco had been around too long doing what he did best to know that wasn't possible. If someone wanted him badly enough they would find him. He would stay on course for New York, now he had identified the main antagonist.

Twenty-five

The feeling of being watched was never stronger than when Vanesco came through the gateway to the freest society in the world; he felt very paranoid. If he turned, he figured he would see his tails lit up like beacons. He didn't turn, he was too weary, and identifying them almost inevitably meant trying to lose them. They'd pick him up again at his apartment or office. He had made his decision back in Athens, he wasn't running.

Cabs were scarce outside the TWA terminal, and Vanesco took an offer to share a ride.

'How much is he rushing you?' the fare seated in the cab asked. He had his feet against the back of the driver's seat. His shoes were expensive two tone.

Welcome to New York, Vanesco thought. No good afternoon, did you have a good trip? 'Four bucks to the Lower Westside.' The man had been asked more.

'What is this, pal,' the passenger said when the driver returned with a third passenger, 'strokes for folks? You charge me six and him four. What you rushing that guy?'

The Spanish driver laughed nervously and mumbled about his going uptown. Vanesco was more interested in the third passenger, figuring he was part of his tail. He was medium build, with a dark weathered face that reminded him of Bill Torbert. Vanesco could have got his gun from his bag and pushed it against the guy's neck, checked his piece. The cab driver and the other fare would figure he was crazy. Maybe he was; he did nothing.

Climbing from the cab on West 23rd, two blocks from his apartment, Vanesco didn't look back to see whether the dark guy got off also.

Burglars had been in during his absence. Vanesco dropped his grip on the floor and let his eyes wander over the mess that had spilled into the wide hallway. He had no fine porcelain, rare stamps, old masters to worry about, and sound insurance, so the loss was never as important as the invasion. Moving from room to room, checking out the wreckage, he thought about trying to tell himself this was just part of the diminishing law and order in the city, but knew it wasn't. There were a lot of crazy burglars who sometimes smashed up apartments out of frustration, but that kind weren't capable of opening triple locks as if with keys; and the apartment had been systematically wrecked, couches slashed, drapes torn, rugs lifted.

After showering and finding a change of clothes from those scattered from the closet, he began to question why; he knew who, but did Wallechinsky think him dumb enough to leave evidence here. What evidence? His discoveries had been made in Europe, and weren't in any tangible form. Maybe there was some documentation stating how involved Wallechinsky was, and he had missed it. But Erhart would have known about it, Vanesco argued, he seemed to know about everything else worth knowing. The proposition was insane, there was no such evidence. The only reason Wallechinsky had this apartment taken apart was in the belief that he had put some evidence together.

Vanesco collected shells for his Browning and left the apartment and headed across to Zell's. She wasn't home, and he guessed she was meeting Sam from school. He fixed himself a sandwich and took some tomato juice from the icebox. As he shook the jar the top flew off and juice slopped out.

'Goddamnit!' he said, leaping back to avoid the splash. Zell drove him insane with her habit of never screwing jar tops shut. He never once thought to check before shaking them. He considered the mess on the floor, the splashes on his brightly polished boots.

As he reached for the sponge mop, he heard someone outside the apartment door. Instinctively he reached for his gun, assuming that it wasn't Zell but the people who had been tailing him. He regretted bringing them here, but there was no question of their not knowing about Zell.

Wrenching open the door, Vanesco startled the two men outside, the gun startled them more. One was squatting with his pants down, defecating on the doorstep, the other man's stupid grin vanished.

It was him Vanesco hit first, laying the heavy Browning across his face.

'You fucking scumbags!' The words were out the moment he realized who they were. Outrage bubbled through him.

As the second man rose, pulling up his pants, he hit him on the return swing. Flesh peeled back, exposing the cheekbone and he started to scream. Anger was still rushing at Vanesco, and he released some of the frustration he had felt over this past week at helplessly watching people die without being able to do anything; the fear he felt at having to go forward, knowing he was only just staying on top; also his loathing for such assholes as these who were choking this city to death. There was no way he could pull himself back, he was screaming abuse as he swung on the first man and hit him again with the gun. Bone shattered with the noise of gunshot. He laid the barrel across his face a third time, driving him down the stairs. The man stumbled and ran, then fell. Vanesco swung round and the other man begged for mercy.

'Don't hit me, don't kill me,' he screamed, pain and hysteria in his voice.

Vanesco wanted to do both. He laid the gun across his head again, catching him only a glancing blow through trying to kick him at the same time.

'Clean it up!' he shouted, manhandling him through the shit like a mop.

He would have beaten him more, but saw Zell on the half-landing clutching at the boys, trying to keep them from seeing. She succeeded with Sam, not the second child, who watched avidly.

'Tell Kali he's dead.' Vanesco released the man.

Zell shrunk back as the hood stumbled past her, leaving a trail of blood and faeces. They stood unmoving, listening to his painful descent, finally the street door banged.

The woman was stunned when Vanesco brought her and the kids into the apartment.

Darren was saying, 'Jesus! Did you see that? Did you see. Real neat.'

Vanesco poured the woman a drink. 'It's okay, Zell, it's done.' Her reaction surprised him. She had lived in New York all her life, had been in social work these past three years, dealt daily with the realities of homelessness, drug addiction, alcoholism; guided the victims of crime through the iniquitous Welfare maze. Maybe it was the level of violence so close to him that disturbed her.

Zell took to bed in the room the boys were using. Vanesco cleaned up the tomato juice, the mess outside the apartment, cooked dinner for the kids. He would have preferred taking them down to a restaurant but it would have meant leaving Zell. He didn't expect the landlord, Abi Kali, to send any more hoods, but he might.

'Where's your Ma, Darren?' Vanesco asked.

'She ain't coming back,' he replied.

'Where'd she go?'

'Dunno.' The pizza he was pushing into his face took priority. 'You figure you killed that guy?' he asked around the food. Like most adults this kid wasn't interested in an answer. 'I betcha did. You whipped him pretty good. Boy, I betcha that fucking asshole's dead.'

Vanesco realized the size of the problem he'd brought Zell here, and knew he had to trace the mother. Only he wasn't sure that would be easy. He glanced at Sam who was sullenly eating his food, his emotional problems reduced to nothing alongside Darren's. He guessed the boy wanted to go to Zell, but was scared to, knowing he didn't give in to him like she did. Part of the trouble was that Zell was afraid for the kid's affection, believing she might lose it unless she continually overreached, to a point where she lost any sense of balance between her own needs and those of her son. While his ever refusing Sam was always an implied criticism to Zell, over which she would always defend Sam, whether he was right or wrong. It was something Vanesco knew Zell would eventually have to deal with if the boy wasn't going to have intractable emotional problems.

'How you making out, Sam? Not the best pizza in the world.'

He gave Vanesco a quick look. 'When's Mom gonna get up?'

'Give her a break, hey? She needs a rest.'

Sam dropped his head and pushed his plate away. 'Don't want that.'

'Fine.' He wasn't going to pander to him. There was nothing wrong with either the food or the boy.

As if she was listening behind the door, Zell appeared on cue. 'Don't speak to him that way, Jimmy. Can't you see he's upset.'

Fulfilling his role, Sam burst into tears, and fled to his mother.

'He wasn't until you told him he was,' Vanesco said.

'I'll finish his pizza,' Darren said, grabbing for it. Food was a compensation he found for the emotional disturbance surrounding him.

Life remained an unaltering pattern for Zell and her child, Vanesco thought; she comforted Sam and defended him regardless. There might have been nothing beyond their walled-in relationship; no pressure from a landlord; no crumbling urban existence; no Jimmy Vanesco who wanted to stay around. That depressed him. He didn't expect admiration from Zell for the way he got his living. The level he dealt with life on was different from Zell's, different again from that she wanted for Sam, and Vanesco wasn't sure it was realistic. He had changed during the four years of their relationship, and accepted that a lot of those changes were for the better and hadn't affected his efficiency. But he couldn't make the ultimate sacrifice and stop being a detective, if only because that violent world she so detested wouldn't stop intruding on their lives; violence in return was his only real point of reference, his only way of dealing with it, despite Zell.

Later that evening, when the children were asleep, Vanesco lay next to Zell in bed, both were naked, only he failed to find the passion he had expected to be there after so long apart from her. The fault wasn't entirely Zell's. She was tense, thinking about the violent scene she had witnessed, the effect it might have on the children, but Vanesco was probably more tense. He was thinking about Wallechinsky and how he was going to reach him; what if he did; about how they would come after him, the probable outcome; about Zell's landlord, who was pressuring hundreds of tenants on the Lower Westside, a lot of whom couldn't deal with it as well as Zell. He thought about maybe taking Abi Kali for a ride and not having him come back.

'You shouldn't have that gun here, Jimmy,' she said when he reached out to her.

Vanesco knew that all the while it lay so close to hand she would be unyielding, it affected her in the same way a third person in the room would. He stroked her body regardless, his hand moved gently over the soft contours and down to her vagina even though he wasn't particularly excited himself.

'I could be in a lot of trouble, Zell,' he said. The words surprised him as much as her. 'S'why I brought the gun.'

'How do you mean? From some nut?'

'They're all fucking crazy. I'm into something a lot heavier, I tell you it's scaring shit outta me.'

'Jimmy?' There was anxiety in her voice. He hadn't sought that, but he was human.

'I guess I shouldn't be here. I shoulda checked into a hotel. I gotta stay clear of you for a while, honey. I'll leave you the gun.'

'Jesus, Jimmy, what the fuck will I do with that?' Fear was on the surface, but she resisted tears. 'Can't you call the police? Or have the Bureau help?'

Her reaction was understandable, though she ought to have known better, Vanesco thought.

'What about the kid? Can you find him a home?'

'He needs professional help. I guess that's up to his mother.'

'She ain't coming back, Zell. Either she's dead, or she's running.' He told her about Coley's not dying in Canada. 'I figure they're both dead.'

The woman didn't respond until she reached out to him and clung to him like a child afraid of the dark. She said, 'I couldn't use the gun, Jimmy. You might need it more. Just don't be too far away.'

Later they made love. Their tension eased, but none of the problems went away.

Twenty-six

On leaving the apartment late the next morning, Vanesco identified his tail by walking two blocks and ducking into a subway; he passed through the gate, then climbed back over it. A bald, bearded fat man with eyeglasses, side hair and unwashed Levis did the same. He was younger than Vanesco but had more problems. His partner was coming down into the subway as Vanesco was going up, he was dressed in a velvet suit, scarf and felt cap. He started up after Vanesco too soon and looked awkward when Vanesco turned to confront him. If he wasn't part of the tail, he probably wondered what the hell was happening as Vanesco kneed him in the chest and sent him sprawling down the steps. In New York such behavior could be blamed on a full moon.

Vanesco jumped into a cab that was traveling downtown on Seventh Avenue.

'Hey, whadda fuck?' the driver began. He couldn't stop, the street was full of moving traffic. 'I'm onna call, pal.'

'You're going my way. Ten bucks.'

The protest stopped when Vanesco thrust a ten dollar bill through the aperture in the heavy perspex grille. He jumped out at West Houston and took the Seventh Avenue subway uptown. At Times Square he transferred and took the Fourth Avenue and Broadway train to Lexington. He checked that he was clean before stepping into a phone booth.

There was no delay in getting to Cunningham. It was as if the lawyer had been awaiting his call.

'Where are you, Mr Vanesco?' That edge of fear was there in his voice again.

'That's not important. What I want is for you to call Walle-chinsky and set up a meeting.'

The lawyer hesitated. 'I don't know that gentleman. I have no point of contact. You're mistaken in your impression that I have.'

'You're full of shit, Cunningham.' He knew this man couldn't set up such a meeting, that was why he was on Lexington in the mid-50s, not downtown.

'I've been authorized to settle your account. If you'd give me the exact figure...'

'S'eleven grand. You got the expenses covered in the five grand I already took,' Vanesco said. 'That isn't much for six lives, even if they did kill the President.'

A quake emerged in Cunningham's voice when he spoke. 'If you stop by the office, I'll have cash ready for you.'

The money would almost certainly be waiting, but Vanesco knew there was no possibility of his collecting it and simply walking. Instead he would suddenly be accident prone.

The basement garage in the glass tower on Third was like a car catacomb where decay had been momentarily arrested by nocturnal-like attendants who placed vehicles in neat rows, and rubbed bodywork until it shone. This was neither a labor of love nor gainful employment but a ritual of envious aspiration: one day they figured someone would be parking their limos.

An hour and forty minutes was how long Vanesco waited, watching, breathing the carbon monoxide which these subterranean workers seemed to thrive on. He didn't know which car he was watching or he'd have waited in comfort.

Harry Kohn emerged briskly from the elevator like he was running late for lunch. Right then his driver was more concerned about not delaying his boss than protecting him. He made Vanesco's move much easier.

'Hello, Harry.' Vanesco stepped in behind him, the Browning in his hand.

'Oh shit!' Kohn said when he turned. He didn't enjoy this.

From the car door the driver saw there was a problem, and was reaching for his piece.

'Why don't you tell him to forget it, and take a walk, where we can see him.'

Kohn told the driver, who looked like he knew he had fucked up. Vanesco suspected he might try something stupid to retrieve himself, but hoped he wouldn't.

After collecting the driver's gun, he had Kohn climb in the front of the car, and got in the back himself.

'You been giving Cunningham a hard time.'

'He's a worried man. He knows almost as much as I do – maybe he hasn't made the connexions yet. Those guys get out of touch.' He suspected the lawyer would have an accident.

'Vanesco, you weren't such a hot recommendation after all. You musta really fooled them other guys. You gotta big mouth. You got lucky, is what I figure.' He smiled as if doing so was painful. 'You know where your bread is – you want it.'

'I want to go on living.'

'Change your profession, pal. Don't cross any streets. What the fuck do you want me to do – hold your hand?'

'Call your friend in Washington. Set up a meeting.'

'You crazy. You are fucking crazy. You're about the last guy he'd wanna see.' He was angry.

Vanesco waited, watching him; also his chauffeur.

'He's busy packing,' Kohn explained. 'He's addressing the UN on Thursday, then he's off to China. Haven't you heard?'

'Tell him I have some questions for him.'

Kohn smiled. 'Ask me instead.'

'What would a hood know about John Kennedy's body in an unmarked grave in Skorpios?'

The color drained from Kohn's face. He was a while recovering. 'I got forty grand in my office. That's a piece more than your fee. Get smart, cop the dough, collect the girlfriend and take a long trip. I recommend it for your health.'

Vanesco resisted. 'Call Wallechinsky,' he said. 'I don't plan on going anyplace, until either we've had a meeting or I've talked to some people on the Senate Foreign Relations Committee.'

Twenty-seven

Stopping the rented car on Oriental Boulevard in Brooklyn, Vanesco set the brake. He sat behind the wheel, looking over the beach. He was reluctant to get out of the car for he had a strange heaviness in his limbs; fear was raising its head again but that alone wasn't the problem, rather the recurring malaise: resistance to truth.

The meeting was set and, despite himself, probably because of himself, Vanesco knew he couldn't not make it. Ambassador Wallechinsky was waiting, had broken into his heavy New York schedule to discuss the problem the skip-trace had. Vanesco was supposed to be grateful to this busy man for finding the time. And was a little amazed at how easily it had come about. Maybe Wallechinsky had been keeping an opening in his busy schedule.

Vanesco reached into his coat for his Browning. He'd have felt a lot better taking it along, but knew that might cause problems, even get him shot – they'd say he had come to kill the ambassador. Maybe they shoot him and say that anyway.

He locked the gun in the glove box. Climbing out of the car, he stepped across the boardwalk onto Manhattan Beach where a black Lincoln was waiting on the sand. A light drizzle was falling and no one else was around apart from a solitary jogger way along the beach and a man with a dog. The summer season wasn't here, and what pleasure-seekers the Brooklyn beaches hadn't lost to Fire Island, they had in the rain today. Doubtless Wallechinsky hadn't planned the weather, but Vanesco would have felt easier with more people around, more than the ambassador's security men that was. However, people were no guarantee of safety, Kennedy being shot in Dallas was proof. Anything could happen if a person was either determined or desperate enough.

As he approached the car, Wallechinsky climbed out with two secret service men. Vanesco recognized them by their fixed, determined looks, which suggested they were trying not to smile.

'Mr Vanesco, I'm Lawrence Wallechinsky,' he said extending his hand like a politician soliciting a vote. He wore a dark overcoat, scarf, hat and black leather gloves.

Vanesco didn't offer his hand as he looked at him. There was something unexpected about his face, the youthfulness he guessed it was. It took him a moment before he realized that Wallechinsky had had a facelift. Vanesco thought how frail and insecure a person was who had cosmetic surgery to remove the pulp and bags, how dishonest; it meant they were scared of what they were. Vanesco believed then that he could best this man. He glanced at the secret service agents flanking Wallechinsky, a third man stayed behind the wheel of the car. 'What are these? Witnesses?'

'You're not behaving predictably. I'm an important representative of the US government. I rate security.' There was mockery in his tidy face. He nodded and his security people moved in on Vanesco. 'I apologize for the necessity.'

'You figure I'm dumb enough to bring a gun?'

The ambassador held his look as the two men made a thorough body search. 'If I thought that, Mr Vanesco, I wouldn't bother being here. You might have been stupid enough to wear a wire.'

The secret servicemen and Wallechinsky were satisfied.

'So, you've got your meeting – I'm a busy man. What's the problem'

'You want them to know?' Vanesco said.

Wallechinsky considered this. There would be danger in having them hear what Vanesco knew. 'Let's walk.'

The secret servicemen kept a discreet distance.

'Surviving's my problem,' Vanesco said. ''Sall I'm trying to do.'

'That's what we're all trying to do. It's the eternal problem. That is why I'm going to China. Maybe mankind will survive longer as a result.'

Vanesco almost smiled at the bullshit. Political appointees often got into that same rhetoric as those people elected to office, they got so puffed up with selfimportance that they figured they were no longer doing a job but had a mission to fulfill.

'The way I see it, Wallechinsky, I'm a danger to you. You're not a man who's prepared to live under a threat. Especially not my kind.'

'What kind of threat is that, Mr Vanesco? Here we are walking along the beach in the rain. I don't feel threatened.'

'Reach into those dark recesses of your mind and consider that I know you set up the Kennedy shooting in Dallas. After that there was no turning back. Everyone who has access to that information has been killed. Five to my certain knowledge. It was no coincidence that the people you hired me to find should have died as they did, after I had either contacted them or contacted someone who knew their whereabouts.'

'What makes you think I had you hired?'

'Why else would you have made this meeting?'

Wallechinsky conceded the point, but also confirmed, he believed, something vital to his own safety: it was evident that the only proof Vanesco had lay in whatever admissions he made. There would be nothing left to survive him, there could be nothing left to survive him.

'I'm interested in Skorpios. That's why I'm on this fucking beach in the rain talking to a madman. Get to it.'

'You're an accommodating guy. You accommodated people in LA back in '63, a rightwing political powerbase owned by Onassis, you set up the President for them, only your men with the guns didn't manage to kill him, so you accommodated Lyndon Johnson and had Kennedy shipped to vegetate on Skorpios. While this was happening you were systematically having killed any witness that connected you with either of the conspiracies, including the medical staff in the trauma room at the Parkland hospital that night.'

Piece by piece Vanesco laid it all out, information he had gotten from Erhart, things he had worked out himself, and what he didn't know he surmised. He was beyond the point of no return, having passed it when he had started across the beach toward Wallechinsky's car; down in Mexico, on realizing he was involved in something more than simply tracing six guys, that had been the time to pull out. It was as if his entire existence had been a preparation for this confrontation, to deal with a truth, which until now he had been merely avoiding. There was no longer any way to escape it, no way not to go forward, no way back. He was one on one with the man who had taken a satanic leap and made the unthinkable a dismissable reality.

When Vanesco finished talking the ambassador stopped and looked at him. There was both amazement and amusement on his face. His round eyes that showed yellowing whites flicked in the direction of the secret servicemen, either to make sure they were too far to overhear him or close enough to save him should Vanesco make a move.

'That's interesting, Mr Vanesco. I'm amazed at your enterprise. When I reach the office I one day mean to occupy, I guess the smart thing would be to make you head of the FBI. We need someone sharp in there to keep up all those balls Hoover had in the air. Jesus. Do you realize what kind of government we'd have had if those assholes out in California had gotten the reins? Onassis wouldn't have been able to control them.'

'You changed horses mid-race,' Vanesco said.

Wallechinsky smiled. 'I change as often as the wind. The trick is not being seen changing. This is America, for Chrissake. No one cares what you do so long as you don't get caught.' He considered this, then nodded to himself. 'Let us accept this amazing hypothesis. That I set up Kennedy, then switched sides and helped Johnson, thus avoiding a constitutional crisis by covering the fact that the President was still alive when he left Parkland hospital. Even that Onassis had all he wanted in the US. What do you figure you can do about it, Vanesco?' He shook his head. 'Zero. Absolutely nothing. You could take it to the press, assuming you had some kind of proof.'

'You're assuming I haven't.'

A smile lit Wallechinsky's face like a triumphal torch. 'I know you haven't, friend. That's why you're here instead of taking it to the Washington Post, or whoever you could get to listen.'

Vanesco saw clearly that this man had misread the situation. He hadn't come to this meeting expecting to get a single piece of evidence with which he could convince anyone else, all he needed to do was finally convince himself.

'I could write it all down and leave it in the event of my death.'

'You couldn't hide it where my people wouldn't find it. Assuming you walk away.'

Vanesco glanced over at the secret servicemen. 'I figure you won't involve those guys. It'd mean you have to take care of them, then of whoever took care of them.' It was Vanesco's turn to smile.

The ambassador didn't like this idea. It entered his brain like a cutworm.

As he walked away Vanesco felt their eyes. Survival now would be determined by one thing, destroying Wallechinsky. He knew that the chances of doing that either politically or through due process of law were nonexistent, which left him one alternative. But his imminent departure for China, with all his secret servicemen, Vanesco thought, made that impossible. Then probably the same response was offered when the shooting of John F. Kennedy was first mooted. Vanesco figured he had more reason for killing Wallechinsky, the best reason of all.

Twenty-eight

Was he safe?

The question plagued Lawrence Wallechinsky. He wasn't considering his physical safety in New York, but whether he had dealt with those loose ends which might connect him to what had taken place back in '63. He knew every single connection hadn't been taken care of simply because he wasn't taking care of things himself. That wasn't possible, he wasn't physically skilful, couldn't go into the field and do the kind of things he had been having his people do. But having had those original six guys put on ice made him feel a lot easier. Along with Colonel Alan Parker, they had been the last direct link between the Kennedy assassin and himself. Neither Onassis nor the people in Los Angeles were a threat, their vested interest in the veil of secrecy was too vast for them ever to seek to remove it.

But was he safe? Still the question remained. Faces swam in at him as he sat in his suite at the Waldorf Astoria. There were a lot of people who had been in Dallas on that day and had foolishly stepped forward to give evidence, which subsequently would have conflicted with the official version, but he felt no stab of conscience over their fate. The Warren Commission concluded that they were mistaken in their impression, the shots could not have come from any direction other than the book-depository where Lee Oswald had been waiting. Then the Warren Commission had shared Lyndon Johnson's vested interest in concealing the truth: conspiracy to murder the President of the freest democracy in the world was unthinkable, Chief Justice Earl Warren had known that if that conspiracy emerged, so too would the one he was brought in to help conceal. Had it gotten out that Kennedy was still alive then a constitutional crisis unprecedented in the history of the United States would have developed. All bills signed into being by both Lyndon Johnson, and afterwards Richard Nixon, would have been illegal; the result of such a disruption to the administration would have been disastrous. Not everyone appreciated that, however; even the Warren Commission later found two dissenting voices in Richard Russell and Hale Boggs.

Wallechinsky thought about the man who had been briefed to take care of such people. Brad Coley had gratefully returned to the fold, and had proved as efficient as ever. He had seen three benefits to himself: making money; restoring his status; removing threats to himself. Wallechinsky wondered if any of the witnesses had recognized him. Coley was expert at making people appear to die accidentally, fire and auto smashes had been a specialty. But Wallechinsky knew he wasn't as good as Michael Chu. He was a master, the one person he knew he could rely on.

Why didn't he feel safe? Wallechinsky questioned. Despite the witnesses who had died he didn't feel as easy as he should. Maybe there were holes, people whom he had missed. He thought not. Time and again he had been through the lists of witnesses, their affidavits, and every other piece of collated evidence. The final direct danger resulting from Erhart's actions had been in Erhart himself, Radulovic, Paley, Torbert, Niles, Coley and Colonel Parker; now they didn't exist, and still he didn't feel entirely safe.

There was Vanesco, who had found these men; Cunningham, who had hired Vanesco; Harry Kohn, who had recommended him. These links between the President's death and himself were tenuous, Wallechinsky decided, but they nevertheless existed. He would discuss what to do about them with Michael Chu. Kohn had been useful in the past and he had a lot of respect for him, but such considerations weren't pertinent. Wallechinsky planned to survive, and make his position impregnable as he made his bid for high office.

Then he thought about Michael Chu, his most trusted emissary. Would he ever be safe all the while Chu knew what he did? Recognizing that worm of doubt now in his conscious thoughts, he knew why the question of his safety had been plaguing him. But who would take care of Chu?

Twenty-nine

Jimmy Vanesco was a practical man, and although he knew survival meant his dealing with Wallechinsky, he knew it depended on money also. So despite the risk involved he was

on his way to Wall Street to the offices of Dean, Englewood
and Cunningham, unannounced, to collect his eleven grand.
With the money he had made in the past four years Vanesco
wasn't poor, but he needed all he could get for after what he
had planned he would have to leave New York, how long for
he wasn't sure. He had a notion about going to Mexico,
maybe keeping bees like Peter Radulovic; however, unlike
him Vanesco knew he couldn't sustain a solitary existence.
His plan included Zell and Sam, only Zell was emotionally
attached to the city and he wasn't sure she would go; he tried
not to think about that, and when doubt edged in he forced it
out.

There was a lot of activity on the seventh floor of the office
building, more than Vanesco expected for the kind of
business these lawyers handled. People walked around with
the jerky, disconnected movements of shock victims. When a
uniform of the NYPD loomed before him, Vanesco broke his
step, thinking this represented danger.

'You have business here, sir?' The cop's politeness was due
to his surroundings.

'To see Mr Cunningham.'

'You'd better see the young lady there.'

He pointed him to Cunningham's receptionist, a woman
with a blotchy face and puffy red eyes. When Vanesco said
who he wanted to see, she couldn't hold the tears back. Cunningham was dead, he had committed suicide shortly after
having a luncheon appointment in his office. The information surprised Vanesco, but he knew it shouldn't have.

'He was holding eleven thousand dollars for me.'

She didn't know anything about that. Nor did Cunningham's partner when she checked with him.

'What was the money for, Mr Vanesco?'

Vanesco shook his head. There was no point pursuing it.

That feeling he had had that things were out of his control
recurred, something in his wake was gathering momentum
and gaining on him. He was scared, but despite an urge he
had to increase his speed, he resisted running. He stopped in
at the post office on United Nations Plaza uncertain whether
he had a tail, but figuring illogically that he was safe in a US
post office. He stepped into a phone booth and called Harry

Kohn.

'You hear the news, man?'

'What news for Chrissake?' Kohn sounded agitated, and Vanesco concluded that he had heard something.

'You need a new lawyer. Your friend iced your legal eagle.'

'You're paranoid, Vanesco. Cunningham had business worries, couldn't take the strain.'

'You got the same pressure, Harry, you won't make it either. Unless you take care of your friend from Washington. You know more than Cunningham, Harry.'

'I know jack's shit, is all. You got yourself a big problem, buddy.'

'I figure I can keep moving.'

'Where are you? We should meet.'

'Go fuck yourself, Harry.' Vanesco rang off. His eyes slowly swept the post office, trying to identify a possible tail. If he had one inside the building, then whoever was real good. He thought about what he had told Kohn, maybe he should keep moving, forget about trying for Wallechinsky. But he didn't know if that was practical. The ambassador to China had a long memory. How long could he go on running? Those other guys had run for eleven years and still hadn't run either fast or far enough. The problem had to be resolved right here on the United Nations Plaza when Wallechinsky made his appearance before the UN. After that he would take his chances.

Vanesco pushed another dime into the slot and called Zell. He was surprised to find her in the office, and she was surprised at his calling.

'Are you okay?' she inquired.

'Fine,' he said. Her concern made him feel less anxious about what he was going to ask.

'The problems are stacking up, Zell. I've gotta get out fast.'

'Out, Jimmy?' She was resisting the meaning. 'Out of your job? Out of town? What are you saying?'

'Both. Out of the country maybe. The thing is, Zell, I want you and Sam to come.'

'You mean quit my job? Leave everything I'm into here?'

'Drop everything. Pack what you need, and take off. What d'you say, Zell?'

There was a long pause. Vanesco knew she was thinking about her roots, her life in New York, her work. He felt his stomach knotting, and he feared a yawning emptiness in his life. Before he had never cared about anything as he did about having Zell around.

'What if I say no?'

Vanesco assumed that was her answer. 'I have to go away, and fast.'

'Can't we talk about this, Jimmy?'

'That's what we're doing, for Chrissake.' Anger was covering his disappointment.

'Not on the phone. I don't want to talk on the phone.'

'I'll check with you later.' He didn't hear her say she loved him as he rang off.

Across the street from the UN building between 45th and 46th was an empty building taking up almost the entire block. Security dog patrol warnings posted on the building didn't deter Vanesco. He went in through the basement. Access was surprisingly easy. A chain that ran between two heavy hasps on the door had been broken and wired together; whether potential anarchists had been there planning to bomb the UN, or rummies to sleep, hippies to squat, or the building was being set up for burning, Vanesco didn't speculate. He climbed the debris-littered stairs and checked the rooms overlooking the United Nations Plaza. There was no electricity so the elevators weren't functioning. The building had a damp, uncomfortable atmosphere about it; empty places tended to make him feel uneasy. The position he was looking for was on the third floor, which had been an open plan office, and he decided he could get it done here. He'd be able to move from window to window, depending on the position of Wallechinsky's car. He moved along the windows, opening each of them to their full extent. He hoped the security company didn't show up and close them.

Moving on, Vanesco explored the rest of the building, looking for the best route out. He would need to leave in a hurry, and unimpeded. Nine flights of stairs led to an access door to the roof, where there was both a fire escape to the service alley at the side and a walkway to the next building, but in full view of the UN building. Finally he decided that he'd do better going downward, as he'd get clear faster and with less exposure. But he left the roof door jammed open as an alternative escape route.

In the basement he found a service tunnel carrying utilities, it led to the basement of the building on East 45th. There he could pick up a cab headed west and be gone before the cops reached the building. He felt elated.

The gundealer on West 14th had a large moist, onion-like nose that could sniff out anything explosive; he didn't have a store, that would have been too dangerous in Manhattan. All his business was by appointment. Vanesco used the man whenever he needed a gun, and the man wasn't fazed when the skiptrace told him he wanted a clean, untraceable Remington 806 with a Starflight sight. The gundealer persuaded him that a Mauser 621 would do anything the Remington was needed for, and better. Also he had one there.

'Is it clean?' Vanesco asked.

'So clean, my friend, you could shoot Nixon with this and drop and no one would trace it here.'

'That's what I might be doing.'

'In that case the rifle's a gift. Anyone else don't tell me about. It costs a grand.'

'Jesus Christ,' Vanesco protested. The price was high but he was paying for the gundealer's discretion. 'I can drop it, it's safe? Right.'

'You don't leave your fingerprints on it, my friend.' He wiped his moist nose on the blue polka dot handkerchief.

They made the deal. Vanesco knew he'd have no problems with the gundealer, whatever the rifle got used for.

Things were coming together and he was feeling confident. Overconfidence didn't make him careless, the problem was that the opposition was good. When he reached the street with the dismantled rifle in a brown paper package he carefully checked around, before flagging a cab that was setting a fare down. As he was about to step into the cab he felt the muzzle of a gun behind his ear, a handgun's appearance on West 14th Street causing no alarm. He was told to get into the cab, the tail followed and the cab started away like a regular pickup.

'What the fuck?' he said as the man with the gun settled beside him. It was a pointless protest, and the man didn't respond.

Heroics were something got into through thoughtlessness, impulsive reactions to dangerous situations; the more thought and calculation taken the less likely they were to happen. Caught like this he was probably going to his death, he thought, as the cab made a right turn on 11th Avenue and headed along by the deserted piers. It was a good place to take care of someone, he could lie in one of those empty warehouses until rats or time made him unrecognizable. He remained aware of the gun pressed into his side. The point at which he imagined himself capable of heroics was that fraction of a second before death, when survival instinct took over.

They went to an hotel on 11th Avenue. It was home from home for itinerants, sailors, those who liked the juice but hadn't reached the level at which they'd take a night in a doorway with a bottle.

'You want a room, brother?' the clerk said without looking up from his racing sheet.

'Just visiting.' The man with the gun motioned Vanesco ahead of him.

Maybe this was time to make a move, Vanesco thought, but guessed he'd get no help from the clerk, who was looking for something at Belmont.

'Not exactly the Royal Danieli,' was how Vanesco was greeted when he reached the room. It was everything he expected, with faded, flyblown decor. A faint smell of urine and vomit lingered from earlier guests. Erhart was the surprise, and Vanesco wasn't sure whether he felt relieved or angry when he realized that he wasn't going to die after all.

'You figure this'd get it done?' Erhart took the package.

'You're a pretty good second guesser.'

'Maybe. We've been tailing you.'

'Were they your guys?'

'The ones you lost weren't.' He inspected the rifle components and nodded. 'It's ironical it should come to this.'

'Things have a way of coming round.'

'Sure.' He smiled. 'Could you make that shot across the

Plaza? I tell you, friend, it won't be easy. Maybe with a little help.'

'From you? Killing Wallechinsky won't halt Sino-American relations. They'll bury him, appoint someone else.'

'It'll stop Wallechinsky stirring up a mess of trouble. A lot depends on how he dies, or to be more precise, who appears to have killed him. There are other interested parties who'd happily stop this appointment. A faction of the CIA doesn't want it. Nor does the money that supported Wallechinsky over the Kennedy business, that hasn't changed its views on America opening her arms to communism. They prefer Chiang Kai Shek's ideology to that of mainland China. Any number of Nationalist Chinese right here in New York would shoot Wallechinsky if they believed it would wreck détente. What we need is some with the right connections to do this job.'

'It so happens you got them ready and waiting. Right?'

'We have Chinese Nationalists who are readily traceable to the CIA. Peking will quickly make the connection.'

'Yellow Lee Oswalds,' Vanesco observed. 'What's my role?'

'You tip off the FBI. Call someone you know there. If those guys get it wrong they're going to go on being wrong. They're not going to climb down publicly.'

A feeling of relief slid through Vanesco. This was like a reprieve: the killing which his continued existence depended upon was being done by someone else. He wasn't sure it should be that easy, so thought that maybe he should hang in there make sure of Wallechinsky himself, but didn't press the point. He questioned the morality of this; people being set up for fall guys; murder being premeditated. However, once he reasoned out such things, he realized these men were political, and questions of morality didn't go down on the table.

'When does this happen?'

'Like you were planning, we'll do it when he arrives at the UN.'

Vanesco imagined John F. Kennedy's assassination being discussed in a similar unemotional atmosphere, his death being considered expedient as Wallechinsky's seemed to be.

Possibly those participants went through the same rationale.

New York on a damp, cold day was New York at its worst. Traffic squelched, tires throwing up soot and exhaust laden water that had collected on pavements. On such a day the appeal of Mexico grew stronger, even if it meant going alone, as he believed it would. If he hadn't been so close to the wet beneath the phone canopy by the park next to the UN headquarters he wouldn't have considered the weather. He watched the traffic on 1st come through United Nations Plaza. Soon Wallechinsky's car would be there, Wallechinsky would die; he'd be safe; China wouldn't get an ambassador; the world would be no nearer but possibly no further from unity. Zell wouldn't go away with him. He tried resisting that thought. He looked at his watch. It was 3.15. Wallechinsky was due at 3.20 to address the assembly at 3.30. It was time to call his ex-boss, who would crap himself at being handed such information. Vanesco pushed in ten cents. If necessary he would keep the Bureau chief waiting, but wouldn't give him time to alert either Wallechinsky or the UN security. Zell entered his thoughts as he dialed. He took her rejection hard, especially as she had turned him down for this city, which was like being rejected for a whore. He couldn't avoid the real reason; she didn't love or need him enough. Then maybe he hadn't given her enough. She had been badly hurt by Sam's father. Perhaps he had merely reinforced that hurt while answering her physical needs, instead of helping to repair the damage. It hadn't been her problem alone, it had been his problem. He hadn't cared enough, he concluded.

'FBI,' a woman's voice said. 'May I help you?'

Vanesco saw Wallechinsky's car signal for the forecourt of the UN. Even his car was working against him, his regular armor plated limosine being en route to China. The danger was at home, schmuck!

'Give me Jack Lang. It's important. Tell him it's Jimmy Vanesco calling.' The name meant nothing to her, but did to the special agent in charge of the field office. He was put through. Lang was a jerk, Vanesco thought, like most of the guys working for the Bureau. Under a system other than the one Hoover had devised they might have been okay, but conditioning had gone so deep all these guys could do was suck. Vanesco had kept those thoughts private and had gotten along with Lang, and his colleagues. But he had sucked too, he realized.

'Jimmy. Good to hear from you. You got a problem'

'I'm not sure. It looked pretty big, but it could be crank stuff.'

He watched the car draw to a halt outside the entrance of the UN.

'You were usually reliable. What did you get?'

'An assassination attempt. Like I told you, Jack, could be it's crazy. Let me start at the beginning.' He knew the FBI man had switched the phone to record.

Vanesco's eyes traversed the building opposite the UN, there was no sign of life; the light favored the gunmen, the sun being well up over New Jersey at that time of the afternoon. The east-facing windows were in total darkness.

'What's the story, Jimmy? Who's going to get it?'

'I had this Chinese guy come up to my office wanting me to trace his son, who's been mixed up in Tong wars. It was real old terror stuff. The kid belonged to the Red Hand gang and had been involved in skirmishes for the Chinese Nationalists in their takeover of China Town.'

He watched a secret serviceman climb from the limousine, followed by Wallechinsky, then another secret servicemen, whose eyes swept round, missing the building opposite. Here it occurred to Vanesco that perhaps Erhart had been turned, that he was back working for Wallechinsky and it was himself being set up. He resisted the thought.

'The old guy figured his kid was in big trouble with the Tong. About three months ago he changed sides. Some Shanghai radicals got into town, and the kid went overboard for them. Those guys make Mao seem like a psalm-singing liberal. Their brand of communism doesn't tolerate any contact with the West. The local Tong ordered the kid's execution, so he went on the run. But not before spilling the plan the Shanghai bunch had for this assassination.' That was the story Erhart had worked out.

Vanesco barely heard the shots above the traffic roar, but

saw Wallechinsky grab his head like he was trying to hold it together as hair, bone and brain exploded. The sight alarmed the skiptrace.

'Lawrence Wallechinsky, the ambassador to China is the target. When he addresses the UN.'

'Jesus H. Christ!' Lang said. 'I'll get back to you, Jimmy.'

'I guess you will,' Vanesco said after the agent had gone. He watched the activity outside the UN, as security people ran forward, pointing to the windows of the building opposite. Secret servicemen dove through the traffic, guns drawn. Vanesco knew it was time to go. If he was picked up in the vicinity having made that call he'd certainly be drawn into the conspiracy. Again those paranoid thoughts started up: maybe this was what Erhart had planned, to get him so involved that he'd reveal everything of the earlier conspiracies. But the East German's objective had been to prevent Wallechinsky going to China, and now he was dead.

Vanesco resisted running. He walked calmly away uptown, people this far away hadn't realized what had happened so he wasn't at all conspicuous. He crossed 1st on a green walk light at 48th, and walked two blocks before picking up a cab to West 42nd and 8th. The driver had the news about the shooting, but didn't know who. Just some dude at the UN.

A surprised reaction was expected. They talked about the assassinations in America since Jack Kennedy, and the conspiracy theories surrounding them. America was obsessed with conspiracy, Vanesco reflected. That and cancer were two prime obsessions; maybe one fed the other. People everywhere felt instinctively that the truth was being hidden from them; while people from all classes were dying of cancer. Both had a lot to do with the way people lived, he thought, but most people weren't prepared to do anything about that.

From 42nd Street Vanesco took the 8th Avenue subway to 23rd. He was headed for his apartment to collect the few things he'd need; he would call Zell again, and if necessary beg her to go with him. But with her or without her he knew he had to go, while he was still alive.

Thirty

The phone was ringing when Vanesco reached his apartment but there was no one he was in a hurry to speak to. It stopped before he got the door open, and wasn't one of those calls that came again immediately. He thought briefly about Clark E. Cunningham's urgent calls that had gotten all this started, but let that one go.

The apartment was still a mess, Vanesco hadn't attempted to straighten it out, not even to push some of the stuffing back into the bed. He had been sleeping in an hotel, where he had a valise. Fetching another bag from the bedroom he picked through the debris for articles of clothing he'd need. There wasn't too much. Sometime he'd come back, when or how he wasn't sure, right then it didn't matter. He saw the telephone among the debris and thought about calling Zell to ask her to go with him.

The buzzer startled him; it was followed by a sharp rapping at the door. Vanesco drew his gun and cracked the door open to find Zell there with Sam. She was shaking and unable to speak. He pulled them inside and checked the hallway before shutting the door.

'Zell? What's the problem, honey? Take it easy.'

Sam clung to his mother like he believed this was his last chance.

'I didn't think you were here. He's got Sam, took him out of school . . . He just took him hostage.' The words tumbled out, not making much sense. 'He came and got him'

'Who did? Sam's right here, for Chrissake.'

The woman shook her head. 'Darren. He took Darren.'

''Kay, 'sokay. We'll get him back. Just slow down, Zell.

227

Tell me who took him, why he was taken.'

'He wants you, Jimmy. You gotta go get him.'

Vanesco's thoughts started jumping as he made the connexion. Brad Coley came to the fore. Vanesco assumed he was still alive and had grabbed his kid. But why would Coley figure that meant anything to him? Obviously he hadn't heard that the man who had been in back of him was dead.

'He thought he had Sam,' Zell said, clasping the boy hard. 'He got him out of school. Left a note with the teacher's aide, for Chrissake – they're not supposed to allow that . . .'

'What did the note say?' She offered it him. It said he would keep Zell's kid until Vanesco came to get him. He would call later. It was unsigned.

That ruled out Coley. He wouldn't have made such a mistake.

'Did he call yet?' Vanesco asked. The guy hadn't. He thought about the phone call he'd missed on getting back here. He considered why Zell was worrying about a kid who was probably psycho, and wasn't her responsibility anyway; however, if Darren was her responsibility then he was his also. He wondered what difference it would have made were it Sam: Zell had turned him down, refused to make the commitment he wanted, so he guessed he wasn't obliged to do anything, it wasn't his problem, it was best left to the cops; kidnapping was a federal offence, the FBI would run the guy down. But those thoughts didn't lay. He had made his commitment, which included her son, and by that reckoning the kid she was taking care of also. He realized he couldn't have a relationship for as long as he had with Zell without accepting those responsibilities. He couldn't walk away, ignore the problem. Maybe that was what he had been doing, continuing the relationship without the responsibility, which was why Zell wouldn't commit fully. She needed him, and by coming here like this she was unconsciously testing him. He was the first person she turned to for help. But whatever the value of those concepts, on the base line was the fact that he had gotten Zell involved with this problem.

The telephone bell made Zell jump.

The voice down the phone seemed familiar, but the skip-trace couldn't match a face.

'I have the kid. I'd sooner have you, Vanesco. You want the boy back you must collect him.'

There was no point telling the man about the mistake. 'You Coley?'

'He's dead. This little fella goes the same way if you don't show.'

'Where's the meeting going to be?'

'Vanesco, you show up with the cops, he gets it.'

'There's no problem, not anymore. Didn't you hear the news. I ain't a threat to the guy who hired you, not anymore, pal. He's dead. Wallechinsky bought it outside the UN an hour ago. All the news bulletins are carrying it. Turn on the radio. Your boss is dead.'

There was a long silence, as if the caller was uncertain how to deal with this. Finally he said, 'That means nothing, Vanesco. Absolutely nothing.'

Doubt swamped Vanesco. Had he made a mistake about Wallechinsky? Was there someone directly above him? Maybe this guy was doing this for his own reasons.

'Meet me in an hour on the corner of East 137th and Willis. There's a boarded up tenement, sheet steel over the windows, you can't miss it. The door'll be fixed, you'll get in okay. The kid walks the minute you get up to the fourth floor.' He hesitated. 'Vanesco, you come alone.' The phone went dead.

South Bronx.

Vanesco felt depressed thinking about the place. Like many New Yorkers he vaguely believed that if he didn't think about its problems they'd disappear. He had been born there, or rather abandoned there, so assumed it was where he had been born, and thought it ironical that in his forty-second year, the period of most change in his life, he should be going back possibly to die there.

The place had changed since his childhood, was constantly changing, always for the worse. This was apparent as the cab crossed Willis Avenue Bridge from Manhattan. Before him lay a battlefield where people patched together remnants of lives in which they tried to live; whole blocks that had been red-zoned by the banks and were too costly to repair had been burned for insurance. Scumlords did that all over the city, but nowhere more than in South Bronx; there they had black and

Hispanic kids – the overspill from the Harlem ghettos – the unemployed and often unemployable, fire the buildings, paying them only peanuts. When the cops and fire companies got there, the same youths who had set the torch would stone the cops and firemen. No one was on top of the problem, no one cared enough, apart from insurance companies, who worked trying to prove arson, and more often couldn't; but they cared for the wrong reasons.

A plan for springing the kid and getting himself clear was shaping in Vanesco's head. He reached over and took Zell's hand. 'Stop right here,' he told the driver as they passed the intersection of East 135th. 'I want you to wait. Okay?'

'Jeez', man. You know this neighborhood? They'll steal the goddamn wheels I sit here.'

If the cab set them down it would mean his taking Zell and Sam with him, or leaving them on the street. He wanted them to wait while he got Darren out, then leave with the kid. That shouldn't take long, but he had other plans that would take a while longer, assuming he could set them up and make his meeting on time.

'Tell you what you do. Take a ride out of the neighbor-hood with the lady. Meet me right back here in fifteen minutes. Right. Don't get caught in no traffic jam.'

'Jimmy.' Zell sounded anxious.

He smiled. 'Everything'll be fine.'

He stood on the broken sidewalk and watched the cab draw away.

The guy whose help he needed was a doper who lived in a city project on Lincoln Avenue. There was a chance he had moved, but Vanesco started to walk the two blocks.

The looks from blacks who watched him from stoops, where they huddled out of the damp, and on faces of people on the street, weren't friendly. There were no other white faces, South Bronx had become a white no-go area, unless you were a cop or a get-well man. From their expressions people believed he was one or the other; anyone else would get mugged, even though it wasn't night on the streets. Some resented his being there, figuring the reason was to bust a brother; some saw hope in his heading for Billy Russell's apartment. Billy was a dealer who didn't do much dealing on

230

account of his not being reliable. He gobbled up the supply himself.

Vanesco avoided those eyes that sought his; he had no particular fear, figuring he could take care of most situations with his Browning, but if he got into some hassle he wouldn't get done what he had to do. Passing some bucks he heard one say, 'Hey, look at the colored fella!' It made Vanesco smile.

The communal parts of the housing project were in need of repair, and littered with garbage, like nobody cared; when their environment was crumbling around them and there was nothing practical to be done about it, people got locked in a vicious circle and ceased caring. A project in South Bronx was about as vicious as you could get. The only escape was crime, either by getting lucky or taking a jail sentence.

'He ain't here,' was how the woman who opened the door greeted him. She figured it was a bust.

'Tell him Jimmy Vanesco wants to see him.'

'He ain't here. I swear he ain't, mister.'

Vanesco had made enough house calls to know when his party was at home. The woman was scared, and not because she believed he was a cop. 'Tell him,' he insisted. 'This ain't a bust, sweetheart. He gets to make a piece of dough. Jimmy Vanesco.' He motioned her into the apartment, without attempting to cross the threshold.

There couldn't have been too many places to hide in the small apartment, maybe Billy Russell had gone down the fire-escape. After a moment eyes peered cautiously around the door jamb; the whole head emerged, then the body. Billy Russell smiled.

'Hey, man, how are you?' he said from the dingy hall.

He was a thirty-five-year-old emaciated New York black who looked fifty-five; his hair was gray, his eyes popped, his bones were so prominent they looked as if they would burst through his skin.

'You ain't been doing too good, Billy,' the skiptrace told him.

'Shit, man. Welfare forgot what I look like.'

'You wanna make some money?'

'How much is some?' He wasn't interested in what he had

231

to do. He looked no further than his next fix, and never that far with certainty.

'Two hundred bucks'll take care of it.'

The man's eyes lit up. 'Good news. When do I get it? I got me this bad ache.'

'Sure. Soon. I can't take long, s'no time.'

'What is it?' He watched Vanesco, afraid of being unable to fulfill his needs.

'I want a building on Willis Avenue burned. I want someone reliable to do it.'

'Shit, man. When you need it done?'

'Now.'

Russell whooped with relief at not being asked something impossible, or something that would be a long time coming together. Right then he led Vanesco to see a street gang, who he said had fired more buildings. They knew the property in question, figured there were no problems, apart from his wanting it done in daylight with someone waiting inside the building. Vanesco said he would bring the guy out. They wanted fifteen hundred dollars. Vanesco got them down to a grand, which they wanted up front.

'Go fuck a duck,' Vanesco told the black kid, who did just that, strutting in a small circle, thrusting his hips forward, mocking the detective while the other kids laughed.

'Like this man? What you want? You wanna collect insurance, then pay us? You go fuck the duck.'

'I'll have Billy hold the thousand bucks. You a hundred for exes for your gasoline.'

They hooted at that.

'Gasoline, man. Where you been? Gasoline. Shit. Fire you building with that you don' get no insurance. You need diesel oil, man. Dem fucking insurance dicks don't know for nothing then.'

'I don't give a jack's shit about insurance. It ain't my building. What I want is a fast fire.'

'Gimme your gas money,' the gang leader said.

Vanesco peeled off a hundred dollars, then went through the details of just how it was to happen and when. They saw no problems, not even at the speed he wanted. They could do it as quickly as it took to pick up the gas and reach the building.

'You make sure the kid and me get clear before you set the fire. One of you guys catch hold of him and take him down the block. There'll be a cab waiting for him. You got that?'

'No problem, man,' the leader said. He looked at Billy Russell, who was sweating. 'Jes' make sure you don't shoot up none of our long green.'

The black kids left.

Vanesco returned with Billy Russell to Willis Avenue. As they waited for the cab to arrive back. Vanesco said in a subdued tone, 'You figure they're gonna get it done, Billy?'

The dealer smiled. 'I's the only problem, man. Dem motherfuckers'll cut me in pieces I ain't here with their bread. I's got me a real need on.'

'Hang in there, Billy. You're doing fine.'

Vanesco looked at his watch. It was five-forty-five. They had fifteen minutes to the deadline set by the kidnapper. He guessed the cab had gotten caught up in traffic as commuters headed home to the suburbs of Westchester. Automobiles streamed along the elevated Major Deegan Expressway, which cut through South Bronx.

Vanesco felt anxious as time crept away. It didn't matter that Zell wasn't there, he could still go in for the kid, but there was no sign of any action from the arsonists. Then he figured that was how it should be if they were as good as Russell claimed; he expected them to be swarming around with gasoline cans, and hadn't spotted them each time he stepped outside the black barroom two blocks away.

The cab with Zell and Sam got there as Vanesco was about to head down to the building.

Zell was unhappy about his going into the building, also about being left with Billy Russell, whose condition was deteriorating. 'Can't you get the cops?' she said.

'Not now.' He paused and looked at her, feeling there was so much to say, to ask, but knowing this wasn't the time or the place, even though there might not be another time or place. 'When Darren comes down, get out of here. Understand? Just get the hell outta here.'

'What's going to happen, Jimmy?'

'Nothing. I'm going to get the kid.' He kissed her, glanced

at Sam, then climbed out of the cab. 'Take it easy, Billy. You're doing fine.'

Vanesco slammed the car door and went along the street without looking back. Covering those two blocks seemed to take a long time, his feet didn't want to get him there as he picked his way along the litter strewn sidewalk. He could feel tension in his legs, like something was trying to prevent him moving forward, his gait was awkward. Tension crept through his chest, causing him difficulty breathing. He was thinking too much about this instead of just doing it. That process was fatal.

Any doubts about the street gang getting done what they were being paid for receded as he reached the building and smelt the gasoline. The vapors in the entrance hall were quite powerful. He wondered how far up they had gone with it, and if whoever was holding Darren had smelt it also. Vanesco was startled and reached for his gun as a black kid with a gas can stepped from a room on the first floor. Vanesco waved him on out and watched him go before starting up the broken stairs.

With the windows closed over with sheet steel the building was dark and before Vanesco's eyes became completely used to the dark he stumbled, giving the person waiting a warning.

The man who was in a room on the third floor smiled, bringing his top teeth over his bottom lip. 'Looks like you're going to be rescued, little fella,' he said kindly.

The boy heard but didn't respond. He had scarcely said two words since being picked up, but the man wasn't concerned. They probably had nothing to talk about anyway. He smiled at his joke, then again as he heard Vanesco go past the room, and head on up toward the fourth floor. He stepped from the doorway.

'Hold it,' the man said.

Vanesco stopped on the stairs and swung round. He could see the man's shape below him but he couldn't make out who it was. 'Where's the kid?'

'Right here.'

Vanesco saw the smaller shape alongside the man. 'You okay, Darren?'

'I want to go home. Can I go home?' The boy was subdued, close to tears.

'You get to go right now, lad,' Vanesco told him. 'Zell and Sam are outside. Get going. Can you make it down in the dark on your own?'

'I think not,' the man said. 'Go up stairs to him, kid. He'll take you out.' He smiled again, but Vanesco couldn't see this.

The man had reneged on their deal. Vanesco knew it was naive of him to believe that the kid would be let walk but he had hoped. Hope and prayer went for nothing in his business, for worse was to come; Vanesco knew if he didn't kill this guy, Zell would almost certainly be the next victim. Right then it looked like the man had bested him, Vanesco assumed he smelt the gas and figured out that the kid getting clear was the signal to fire the building. The smell of gasoline was strong, even this high up. What a dumb-fuck he had been.

'Who are you?' Vanesco asked in order to buy some time so that he could work out a couple of moves.

'It's not important. Move, kid.'

'Yes, sir.' The boy stumbled up to where Vanesco was. 'I want to go home, please.'

'In a while, Darren, I promise. We'll get to go home.'

'Back up the stairs. Move!'

'Give me your hand, lad.'

With his left hand Vanesco caught hold of the boy, then suddenly dragged him to himself, and threw both Darren and himself flat on the stairs, getting a shot off as he did so.

It wasn't a smart move. Either the man had seen it coming or Vanesco's movement caused the shot to go wide; and he drew fire as he scrambled up the stairs with Darren. They lay flat on the debris strewn landing, his arm across the kid, who had started sobbing.

'You crazy motherfucker!' Vanesco shouted. 'Where's the percentage in this. Your boss bought it at the UN today. He's dead.'

'So are you, friend. If Wallechinsky's dead, and he hired me to take care of you, then, my friend, logically you must die, as no one can rescind the order.' He laughed, amused by this thesis.

'You really are something. You're killing because you

enjoy it. Right?' Vanesco figured if he stalled, then those black kids'd get tired of waiting and fire the building, then he'd get the edge he needed. 'How many you take care of so far? Six? More than six?'

'More than six.'

'You get all the guys I was hired to find?'

'With some help. You're stalling, Vanesco. It won't do you a bit of good, my friend.'

'Maybe. I guess you'd call this a Mexican standoff.'

'I see here a clear advantage.'

'You won't go no place without I get you.'

'I guess that makes you feel good. Fine.'

Vanesco was reaching for a loose piece of bannister rail. Without warning he hurled it down the stairs. 'Run, Darren!' he shouted, but held the kid fast.

That drew fire, two blasts, the flashpoints of which Vanesco made in the darkness, and got off seven shots in less than five seconds. He suspected he'd hit the man, but was in no hurry to find out in case it was a trick.

The man's teeth clamped over his bottom lip, not in a smile, but trying to shut off the cry that was looking to escape. A bullet had torn through his side just above his hip. He was lucky, he guessed, the bullet could have smashed the hip instead of his bottom lift rib. Right then he was sure the pain was no less. It was time to go. Being wounded he couldn't afford to delay. Reaching for his cigarette lighter, he set fire to the rags in one of the gasoline filled jars. He hoped his wound wouldn't prevent him getting clear before the gas on the third floor exploded.

Vanesco's curiosity at the flickering light turned to alarm as the Molotov cocktail hurtled through the dark and exploded on the stairs. He realized why the smell of gasoline hadn't alerted the kidnapper. Others followed, engulfing the stairs in flames. The only way clear was upward, he didn't know whether there was a way out, but had no choice. He grabbed the kid and ran.

Pausing to watch the flames sweep through the stairs, satisfaction caused the man to forget his pain; he knew how to handle fire better than most. He had chosen this building carefully, Vanesco and the kid couldn't escape, unless he was

Batman. He started to laugh, but his side hurt him too much.

The heat was intense as he moved out of the room, but he knew he could get down the stairs before flames filled the entire stairwell.

His careful descent had got him no further than the fifth stair when the gas behind him exploded. It rocked the building, hurling him forward onto the next landing. He lay stunned, the pain in his side causing him more problems than the fall itself. Slowly he gained his senses, and imagined he could hear Vanesco and the kid screaming above the roar of the flames. He had never experienced that before and smiled; the pain merged with his newfound pleasure, it was almost orgasmic. He shut his eyes and recalled other occasions. He took pleasure in killing people, pride also, it was something he did well.

When he opened his eyes flames were closing on him down the stairs, the heat was intense, the air choking. If delayed any longer he'd die here. The pain in his side was vicious, but he got to his feet by concentrating instead on the searing heat around him. He was going to make it, he started down the last flight of stairs.

Micheal Chu knew nothing beyond the initial explosion as the fire descending through the building ignited rising fumes from the gas-soaked first floor. The resulting fireball ripped out walls and windows, and spread the fire throughout the lower part of the building. There was no way fire companies could put that one out.

Smoke and flames drove Vanesco and Darren to the top of the building, causing them to stumble on broken stairs and debris. The exit to the roof was locked and Vanesco threw himself against it, trying in vain to burst it open. Finally he emptied his Browning into the wood around the lock, five slugs split it sufficiently for him to break out. The evening air on the roof was a relief from the choking fumes rising through the stairwell, and they stopped for a moment sucking it in. Vanesco had never known New York to taste so good. It wasn't until flames spread from the door behind them that they moved. He dragged the boy on a complete circle of the roof looking for a way down. There was none, other than jumping, and from the seven-storeyed building that would be a pretty sure death. The fire-escape had long since rusted away, or been dismantled, and on either side of the building there were empty lots. The crowd that had gathered below to watch the blaze offered no hope of rescue, and if hope did arrive in the form of the fire service, the kids would probably hamper things.

After a moment Vanesco became aware that Darren was screaming, letting out a terrified wail. He yelled at him to shut up, but both were drowned by the roar as the building disintegrated. At once he realized how unreasonable his reaction was, in view of what the kid had been through and was going through right then. He pulled the kid close in his arms to comfort him, but wasn't able to offer him much. He felt the heat under his feet and knew the roof would soon burst into flame or fall in; either way they'd be in the heart of the fire.

He carried Darren to the parapet overlooking an empty lot. It wasn't the narrower of the two gaps, as he estimated, and although he believed neither were jumpable, he decided that this one offered marginally more hope, for the building that stood some twenty-five feet away was two storeys lower. With a fall of twenty feet or so he figured he might be able to boost the kid across the gap. If he misjudged it he might kill him, but his head could be smashed in, or his neck broken even if he made it. At least this would give him some slight chance, he argued, while jumping straight down wasn't worth contemplating, and they couldn't stay put. There was no sign of a firetruck.

'I'm gonna throw you across,' he shouted.

Whatever he understood of the words, the meaning they conveyed caused Darren to scream louder and cling harder to the man. Vanesco prised him off and began swinging him round by the arms, picking up speed. At the moment he figured he should let go, he wasn't able to; he knew the kid wouldn't make it. Maybe a firetruck would get here in time.

Flames started eating through the roof around the exit, and Vanesco changed his mind about the fire service getting there in time. He shouted at Darren, telling him to relax, but it was meaningless, the boy was rigid with tension. He swung him again, quickly increasing the arc; he couldn't go any faster without collapsing with giddiness. Either he let him fly or they would both burn. Vanesco shut off the thought and let go. Darren sailed over the parapet, plummeting through the gap at a sharp angle. He wasn't going to make it. A sickness welled in Vanesco as the child hit the parapet opposite, but then there were hands grappling for him. Black kids who were watching the fire from that building held him.

They were shouting at him and at first Vanesco thought they were saying the kid was okay. Then he realized they were telling him to jump. He considered the gap, and knew he couldn't make that jump. He turned back. Flames had gotten through the roof, the asphalt around him was melting. He was choking; there was no breathable air in the fire, and the heat was becoming unbearable. He reached for his gun, figuring how he'd eat that rather than burn to death. There were no bullets left. He found some in his pocket and loaded the clip. He raised the muzzle to his mouth.

The flames almost reached him as he crowded into the corner. He hesitated, knowing that what was needed to pull the trigger was a bigger quantity of what it would take to make that jump. With imagination anything could become possible. That thought got him onto the parapet wall, and as he did so the roof fell in. Now it would be a matter of minutes before the walls collapsed. He inched backward along the wall that fronted the street, away from the gap, below the people watched, but he was aware only of the intense heat that was trying to suck him in. Do it, a voice said. Adrenalin was running; he decided he wasn't going to die. He started to run along the parapet, his feet finding the wall each time, boosting what speed he could, challenging the unthinkable. He took that imaginative leap, attempting to spring the gap.

Epilog

The Beth Israel medical center situated at 16th and 1st on Manhattan's lower eastside had one of the most advanced neurosurgical departments in the United States. If a patient wanted and could afford the best that was where the patient got taken to have a brain tumor treated or when involved in an automobile accident that resulted in brain damage. Sometimes the patient was in no condition to make those decisions, and sometimes the case was so complicated that there was no choice if there was to be any chance of survival. Sometimes those decisions were made, though not often, when the patient's financial status couldn't be established as credit-worthy.

There was no such problem with two patients on the third floor who had been admitted only hours apart yesterday and had passed the critical twenty-four-hour post-operative stage. Both patients were in intensive care units, one door apart and constantly being monitored by the same crew. The best medical ingenuity was being provided. For one no expense was spared, the government was picking up the tab; the other carried Blue Shield, and his bankbook indicated an ability to defray any additional expense.

One of them hadn't been expected to live, but now twenty-four hours had passed his prognosis substantially improved; however, certain beyond doubt was the fact that this patient was likely to remain in coma, and not reaching a responsive state. The reason was extensive brain damage caused by a 9mm projectile penetrating the top of his cranium and exiting via the neck, destroying a large area of nerve cells and cortex. The life support system he was hooked to would continue holding him until somebody decided there was no point prolonging this unnatural existence. That decision wouldn't be taken by anyone in the State Department, who had ordered a vigorous investigation into the shooting of the US Ambassador to China outside the UN, despite two gunmen having been killed by the police. Their connexions with both Nationalist China and the CIA were causing President Nixon a lot of embarrassment at a time when he was looking for as many successes as he could find as an antidote to his escalating problems over Watergate.

Police, FBI, State Department officials and the news media provided constant traffic on the second floor at the Beth Israel, but neither Wallechinsky nor the patient two doors along were aware of it. More important for Jimmy Vanesco was the fact that no one was aware either of him or his tenuous connection with the ambassador. It was one of life's ironies that both men were brought to the hospital on the same day and ended up in neighboring intensive care units. Possibly it was natural justice that there the similarity ended.

The prognosis on Vanesco was good. The damage to his spine, hips, knees and feet, sustained in his fall, was severe but with time could be overcome. The extent of the paralysis resulting from damaged spinal nerves couldn't be fully determined; initially it was thought he might not walk again, but the neurologists were becoming more optimistic. The impact with that roof thirty feet below had burst his spleen and caused a rib to spring loose and perforate his left lung. Both had been satisfactorily operated for. Time was the important factor. Every passing minute that pulled him further out of the critical zone lengthened the odds in his favor. He had yet to fully regain consciousness so he hadn't determined a will to live, but it was expected that he would, with help from Zell, who had scarcely left his side since he had been brought out of the operating theater.